STAIRWAY TO MURDER

A Detective Joe Ezell Mystery

Book Two

Phoebe Conn

Cover and book design by eBook Prep
www.ebookprep.com

March, 2017
ISBN: 978-1-61417-927-6

ePublishing Works!
www.epublishingworks.com

CHAPTER 1

Los Angeles
Summer, 1947

Monday morning, Joe Ezell started up the stairs to his second floor office carrying a copy of *The Los Angeles Times*. Focused on the headlines, when he slipped, he fell hard, hit his chin on a step and actually did see stars the way cartoon characters do. He sat where he'd fallen to gather himself. Feeling like a clumsy fool, he wiped his chin on his handkerchief, but the blood on the stairs wasn't his.

Cleotis Cotton, the custodian of the building, entered right after Joe had fallen. "Oh my goodness, Mr. Ezell, let me help you up. Do we need to call an ambulance?" He picked up Joe as easily as he would a bag of groceries, and set him on his feet at the bottom of the stars.

Joe took a deep breath to clear his head. His chin hurt like hell, and he felt thoroughly rattled, but he'd not complain. "No, CC, I'm fine. But something is definitely wrong at the top of the stairs."

Cleotis followed Joe's glance and took a quick backward hop. "Oh my Lord, there's blood dripping halfway down the steps. Does a body hold much more than that?"

"No detective worthy of the name faints at the sight of blood, so I'll go up and investigate. You wait right here and if this is as awful as it looks, go into the drug store and call the police."

"Yes, sir, I'll wait right here."

Joe avoided the blood-spattered steps as he went up, this time with a firm grip on the brass railing bolted to the wall. He needed to go up only halfway to see the woman sprawled on the landing. Her throat had been cut from ear to ear, and he was terribly afraid she was his 9:00 o'clock appointment.

"Call the police, CC," he called, "a woman has been murdered."

CC bolted out the door without asking if she was anyone they knew. Joe stood frozen on the stairs. He had met Georgia Dixon only once, when he'd picked up his girlfriend, Mary Margaret McBride, at the VA hospital in West Los Angeles where both worked as nurses. He recognized her now from her curly brown hair. She'd kept it in a coiled bun for work, but going out the door at the end of the day she'd shaken out the tight curls and let them bounce upon her shoulders.

They had spoken briefly when Mary Margaret had introduced him, but he remembered her when she'd called to make an appointment. Unfortunately, she'd not revealed the cause of her concern, but clearly someone had not wanted her to see him that morning. She lay with her arms flung wide and her legs crumpled beneath her. Her black handbag had fallen open and the contents were spilled near her feet.

Rather than be accused of tampering with evidence, Joe left the purse untouched, and took great care to retrace his steps to the bottom of the stairs and sat down. He rested his head in his hands, and took in great gulps of air. He'd opened Discreet Investigations as soon as he'd passed the test for a private investigator's license. He'd studied the subject and felt fully qualified to follow men cheating on their wives, and vice versa, or perhaps catch an office thief or a clerk pilfering from the till, but murder, with one notable exception, was way beyond his realm of experience.

Max Broderick, a dentist with an office across the hall from Joe's, pushed through the heavy door at the entrance of the building and came to an abrupt halt. "What's wrong, Joe, are you ill?"

Joe looked up and nodded toward the gruesome evidence trickling down the stairs. "A young woman's been murdered. The police have been called, and you better stay right where you are. Believe me, you don't want to see her."

"My god! A murder in our building?" Max gasped. A man in his fifties with thinning hair and thick glasses, he hadn't served in World War II and had no experience with dead bodies. His knees felt weak, and he leaned against the wall. "My patients are all scheduled for the afternoon, do you think the police will have cleared the scene by then?"

As always, Max was meticulously dressed, the handkerchief in the breast pocket of his gray suit matched his tie. He wore handsomely-tailored suits to his office even though he'd slip off his jacket and wear a short white coat to see patients. He seemed to be a nice enough fellow, and they often exchanged hellos in the morning, but neither had been inclined to linger for a full conversation.

"You'll probably have to re-schedule today's appointments," Joe advised. "The police aim to be thorough rather than fast."

"I could go up the back stairs to reach my office," Max replied.

"Better wait. If the police find you upstairs, they might suspect you know more than you actually do."

"Oh right. I'll stay right here then. Maybe I'll go into the drugstore and get a cup of coffee at the counter."

Joe nodded. "Go right ahead."

CC held the door for Max as he went out. "The police said they'd be right here. I told them we'd come into work and found a gruesome murder. That's the word, isn't it?"

"It's gruesome, all right." Joe wondered if Mary Margaret knew why Georgia had wanted to see him. If so, he hoped it wouldn't put the woman he loved in grave danger.

Jacob Lynch had been a detective with the Los Angeles Police Department long enough to have seen all types of grisly murder scenes, but when death involved such an attractive young woman, he considered it doubly tragic. "Do you know her?" he asked Joe.

Joe stood beside him on the second floor landing, carefully avoiding the blood pooled beneath the victim's head. "I believe she's Georgia Dixon, my 9:00 o'clock appointment, but I didn't check her purse for identification."

"Thanks for having the sense not to disturb her things," Lynch replied. "It's a rare trait." He bent down to pick up a brown leather wallet by her handbag. "You're right. Georgia Dixon. Looks like she works at the VA Hospital, or at least she did. Are you the dentist listed on the building directory?"

"No, that's Max Broderick, he's in the drug store. I'm Joe Ezell, a private detective, and I own Discreet Investigations."

Lynch rolled his eyes. "Wonderful, just what we need. Were you late getting into work?"

"No, I open the office at 9:00 o'clock and arrived a few minutes early. I didn't meet anyone as I came into the building, but there is a back entrance. It's meant more for use as a fire escape route than for general foot traffic."

The police photographer came up the stairs carrying his 4x5 Speed Graphic camera and a satchel of flashbulbs. He took a half-dozen photos of the crime scene and left after a nod to Detective Lynch.

"I'd hate to have his job," Joe murmured. "Do you suppose he can shake the nightmares his day brings?"

"I doubt it," Lynch responded. He walked down the hallway to check the restroom and went down the stairs to the backdoor. When he came back up, he spoke to CC who stood waiting at the bottom of the front stairs. "Do you always keep the building this clean, or were you expecting trouble?"

"No, sir, we never have any trouble here," CC replied. "I keep everything neat as a pin every day. Today was nothing special."

"What time did you get here?" Lynch asked. He had a small notebook in his hand and jotted a few brief notes.

"I leave everything ready to go for the next day before I leave at 6:00 o'clock in the evening. I come in around nine, just like Mr. Ezell."

"Who locks and unlocks the building?"

"That would be Dr. Raymond," CC responded. "He's the pharmacist in the drugstore downstairs, and he owns the building. He's here early to open the drugstore around 8:00 o'clock and closes up at 8:00 o'clock at night. I only have the master key to the offices."

"What happens if a tenant wants to stay late? Do you have a building key, Mr. Ezell?"

"No, none of us do, but we can exit the building after the door is locked for the night, we just can't come back in."

Detective Lynch pursed his lips. "There's an accountant listed on the directory, where is he? Have you seen him this morning?"

"That would be Mr. Bennett," CC answered. "He works long hours at tax time, and vacations most of the summer. He'll be back around the time school starts again in the fall."

"All right, so Miss Dixon enters the building early for her nine o'clock appointment and someone either follows her in or was here lying in wait," Lynch summarized aloud. "If the building had been open since 8:00 o'clock this morning, he would have had plenty of time to arrive before her."

"It's more likely he followed her," Joe interjected. "She mentioned needing to speak with me concerning a private matter. I doubt she would have told anyone she was coming here."

"Clearly someone knew," Lynch countered, "or she could have been a victim of a random killing and just been in the wrong place at the wrong time."

"How likely is that?" Joe asked. He couldn't bear to look at Georgia's body as they talked, and he dreaded having to tell Mary Margaret what had happened to her friend. "Wouldn't the killer have been drenched in her blood? How could he have left the building wearing bloody clothes and not been noticed?"

"Not if he came from behind, grabbed her hair, and slashed her neck in a single stroke," Lynch replied. "There's a blood spray across the wall. It would have missed him. He could have run down the back stairs and been gone before she took her last breath. Go downstairs, and wait in the drug store," the detective directed. "A forensic team will come in to gather evidence, and you shouldn't be in their way."

"Right," Joe replied. He went down the stairs with a careful hold on the rail and avoided stepping in the gore. "Come on, CC, let's get a cup of coffee."

"I could sure use one, Mr. Ezell, maybe two."

"It's on me," Joe added and they left the scene to the police. It bothered him that Lynch had opened the restroom door and smeared whatever fingerprints the killer might have left on the brass doorknob. It struck him as sloppy police work, but he'd keep his opinion to himself.

Joe had work planned for the day, but after such a ghastly morning, he was in no mood to follow errant husbands and went to his favorite driving range to hit a bucket of balls. There was something enormously satisfying in swinging his driver and watching the small white ball fly into the sky. He'd been working on distance, and had gained a couple of yards in the last month.

When he could no longer put it off, he drove to the VA hospital to wait for Mary Margaret. She was little and cute with curly bright red hair that made her easy to spot when she exited the building along with the others on her shift. He waved so she'd be sure to see him, and she greeted him with a delighted smile.

She reached up to kiss him. "I didn't expect to see you today. Did we have something planned?"

He took her hand as they walked to his car. "I felt like driving you home. I'm afraid I have some awful news, but I'd rather wait until we reach your place to share it."

She climbed into his Chevrolet sedan and smoothed her white uniform skirt to get more comfortable. "That sounds ominous. Won't you give me a hint?"

He shook his head. She rented a place close to work and they were there within minutes. The Spanish style building had a sparkling white exterior and a red tile roof. Bougainvillea in a vivid magenta gave the façade a shot of color. He parked at the curb and went around the car to open her door. She had one of the front apartments on the second floor and stopped to open her compartment in the brass mailbox with a tiny key she kept on her key ring.

There hadn't been any keys among the items that had spilled from Georgia's purse, and Joe was disgusted with himself for not noticing. If whomever had killed her had taken her keys, he would have had time to search her home long before the police arrived. He had Detective Lynch's card, but from what he'd seen, the man wouldn't welcome questions from the public.

The stairs to the second floor apartments were located in the courtyard of the U shaped building. Joe and Mary Margaret often teased each other as they ran up the steps, but that afternoon, he could barely find a smile and his steps were slow.

Mary Margaret unlocked her door, went inside and tossed her purse and keys on the table in the entryway. She went on into the kitchen. "Do you want something to drink?" she called.

"No, thanks," Joe replied. He walked into the living room and gazed out the front windows. He'd practiced what he'd wanted to say, but going over it again in his mind, it sounded stilted and unfeeling.

Mary Margaret carried in a glass of water, sat down on the sofa and bent over to untie her thick-soled white shoes. She kicked them off, wiggled her toes and looked up at him. "Well, we're here, now what is it you wanted to say?"

He turned toward her and jammed his hands into his pants pockets. "Georgia Dixon made an appointment with me for this morning. Did she tell you why she needed a private investigator?"

"No, but didn't she tell you when you saw her?"

"I found her dead in the hallway outside my office."

"What?" Her green eyes widened and then flooded with tears. "She just dropped dead in the hallway?"

He shook his head. "Someone cut her throat."

Mary Margaret made a dash for the bathroom, and he could hear her vomiting into the toilet. He took a long drink of her water and went back to the windows. He feared he'd done that poorly, but there was no way to soften the blow or undo it now.

She came back to the sofa with a box of tissues in her hand. "She was one of my dearest friends."

"I'm so sorry." He came and sat beside her and pulled her into his arms. He let her cry until her sobs turned into hiccups. "Do you know of anyone who might have wanted her dead? A jealous boyfriend, someone at the hospital, anyone?"

She cuddled against his shoulder. "Georgia thought Dr. Felberg was an ass, but he wouldn't have killed her. At least I don't think he would."

"What was it about him that Georgia disliked?"

"She thought, no, we all thought, that he discharged his patients too soon. He'd send them home with a prescription for painkillers and sign off on their charts. He appears to be totally lacking in the compassion a physician should possess."

"Anyone else come to mind?"

Mary Margaret sniffed loudly. "Georgia didn't get along with Gertrude Howland, the head nurse on our floor. Gertrude has been with the VA forever, maybe since the Civil War, and she criticized Georgia for flirting with her patients."

"Did she?"

"Yes, but they loved it. A young man who's lost an arm or a leg needs to believe he's still attractive to women. Georgia regarded flirting as a type of therapy to help her patients regain their confidence and heal faster."

Joe rested his chin atop her curls, and a burst of pain made him quickly pull back. Mary Margaret didn't notice. "Could any of the soldiers discharged early have believed Georgia was offering more than she meant to?"

"It's possible I suppose. She's been working Saturdays at Curtis Mooney's home in Hancock Park. He's a sweet guy, but had a head injury and has trouble coping on his own."

"Who looks after him during the week?"

"It's his brother's home, and there's a staff that sees to whatever he needs. The family was grateful to Georgia for her kindness to Curtis. Someone will have to tell him Georgia is dead, and it will break his heart."

Joe drew in a deep breath. He wondered if Detective Lynch would speak to the Mooney family, and thought probably not. "Was Georgia seeing anyone?"

"Not that I know of. She told me how lucky I was to have met you, by the way."

"I'm the lucky one," he countered.

"True, but Georgia still envied me. She never mentioned any living relatives, but her friends will have to be told. No one from the police came to the hospital. Do you suppose they will tomorrow?"

"Maybe."

She sat back and finally noticed the bruise on his chin. "What happened to you? Were you in a fight?"

"Only with myself." He told her how he'd fallen rather than make-up a story she might believe. He made it a point to always tell her the truth even when he'd sound like a fool, and she seemed to like him anyway. He leaned over to give her a comforting kiss, rather than a passionate one. "I've felt sick about Georgia all day, and I'm sure you do as well. I'll take you to dinner if you think you could eat."

"Thank you, but no. Maybe I'll open a can of soup later. You needn't stay. I should call our friends with the awful news, and it's not going to be an entertaining evening."

"Before I go, please give me a list of their names."

"You think one of her friends might have killed her?" She shuddered, appalled by the thought.

"No, but someone they know might know something. I just want to get a feel for the case. The police are still consumed with the hunt for the Black Dahlia's killer, and Georgia's death might go unsolved if I don't pursue it."

"Her friends could take up a collection to pay you."

"Georgia would have been a client, and I won't charge anyone for looking into her death. Maybe if I'd come in a few minutes earlier…"

"You might have ended up dead too. Did you think of that?" she asked. "If a man would kill once, why wouldn't he kill again to hide his identity?"

"Good point. I just wish I knew why Georgia wanted to see me. Did she have a roommate or live alone?"

"She had her own place not too far from here. After the chaos of the hospital, she liked having time alone."

"I didn't see any keys in the things that had fallen from her purse. Did she own a car?"

"No, she rode the bus to work. She had an apartment key and mailbox key on a ring with a rabbit's foot for luck."

She got up to get several sheets of stationery and a pen. She returned to the sofa and put a Saturday Evening Post magazine on her lap to serve as a desk. "Do you want her address?"

"Yes, if you know it." Joe thought the police should have searched Georgia's apartment for clues to her murder, but that didn't mean they had found any. When someone harbored a dangerous secret, they weren't likely to write it down and leave it out for anyone to see. "Put Dr. Felsnap and Gertrude at the top of the list."

"It's Felberg," she stressed. "Who's Felsnap?"

"My shop teacher in high school, sorry. Do you feel safe here, Mary Margaret? Maybe I should stay the night to make certain you are."

She concentrated on writing names. "That's the lamest excuse I ever heard."

"It is not. I'm worried that whatever got Georgia murdered, might be something the killer believes other nurses would also know."

"Georgia had a lot of friends. Maybe none of us is safe, and you can't stay with us all."

"I'll stay while you make the calls, then if anyone's reaction is off, you can tell me."

"Off how?"

"I don't know, too dramatic, or too unconcerned. Anything that strikes you as odd."

"I'm a nurse, not a detective."

"Humor me," Joe encouraged. "Your friend is dead, and this is important."

"All right. Give me a minute to think of what to say."

Joe remained by her side on the sofa, his voice low and reassuring, "There's no easy way to give such horrible news. Prepare them by saying you're calling to tell them something terribly sad."

"Thank you." She laced her fingers in his rather than reach for the telephone on the lamp table by the end of the sofa. "Georgia might have had relatives she never mentioned, but they wouldn't have been close, so her friends will probably have to plan the funeral. I don't even know where to begin."

"Did she attend church?"

"No, she wasn't religious, but there's a chapel at the hospital where we could hold a memorial service. Am I getting ahead of myself?"

"Probably, why don't you make the calls?"

She drew in a deep breath. "I'm afraid I'll just start crying again."

Joe reached over to tuck an errant curl behind her ear. He loved her red hair and every other thing about her. "The murder might be on the radio tonight. It's sure to be in the *Los Angeles Times* tomorrow. If you wait, you might not have to break the news after all."

"I'd hate for anyone to learn of Georgia's death that way." She kept her personal phone directory in her purse, and got up to fetch it. "I've never called Dr. Felsberg or Gertrude at home, but I do have numbers for most of the nurses Georgia knew."

She returned to the sofa and added numbers for the names on her list. She reached for the phone and cuddled against Joe before she dialed. No one answered at the first number, and she went on to the second. "Hello, Angie, I have some dreadful news."

Joe listened to Mary Margaret's side of the conversation and handed her a tissue from the box each time she was brought to tears. From what he could tell, her friends were not only heartbroken, several wondered if the lives of all the nurses at the VA might be at risk.

Mary Margaret covered the receiver and whispered, "What should I say when they ask if we're all in danger?"

"It's too soon to know," Joe offered. Some of Mary Margaret's friends took the sad news with surprising restraint, others sobbed so loudly he could hear them from where he sat. When she at last came to the end of her list, more than an hour had passed. He covered a wide yawn.

"I'm sorry," she said. "I didn't learn anything useful at all. Maybe tomorrow at work I'll hear something you can use."

He stood and gave her a hand to rise. He folded her list and slipped it into his pocket. "Don't pry, just keep your ears open. If someone knows why Georgia wanted to see me, give me a call."

She looked up at him. "Maybe you should stay with me, Joe, just in case there really is a murderer creeping about."

He laughed and pulled her into a comforting hug. "You're right, we shouldn't take the risk."

CHAPTER 2

W hen Joe came to his office on Tuesday, he'd rubbed his sore chin and been careful climbing the stairs. He'd known Georgia Dixon's body had to be gone, but he'd held his breath until he was certain of it.

He spent the morning gathering information about Curtis Mooney's family. He'd recognized the name, but hadn't recalled they were the type to build libraries in poor neighborhoods, or donate whole wings to hospitals. It made him wonder why Curtis had been treated in the VA hospital rather than a private one the family could well-afford. It was possible Curtis had been proud of his service during WWII and had wanted to be treated with other veterans.

When he saw CC, he was quick to compliment him. "The building looks clean as a whistle this morning."

"Thank you, Mr. Ezell, but I don't deserve the credit. Dr. Raymond sent me home yesterday and called a firm that cleans up after a crime. Horrible job I sure wouldn't want. No, sir, not me."

"I wouldn't want it either, CC, but they did an excellent job."

"You going to find who killed that poor young woman?"

"If the police can't, I might give it a try. Right now, I'm working on another case and need to get going." He had his camera and extra rolls of film. Sometimes he discussed his cases with the custodian, but this one wasn't interesting enough to share.

He spent the early afternoon following a business supplies salesman who made a long stop at a duplex where the resident, who didn't look to be in need of any item necessary for a well-run office, gave him a lingering good-bye kiss before he left her doorstep. Joe got a couple of incriminating photos, and dropped the film off to be developed at Pete's Cameras down the block from his office. Pete gave him the fast service Discreet Investigations required, and he tipped him generously.

Just to amuse himself before he picked up Mary Margaret after work, he began a diagram with Georgia's name in a circle in the middle. He drew lines to smaller circles all around and began filling in names of people who might have wanted her dead.

Dr. Felberg could have been worried about more than Georgia's criticism of early release of patients. She might have known of a career ending medical error. Desperate not to lose his license for malpractice, a physician could have swiped a scalpel across a young woman's throat with a practiced ease.

Gertrude Howland's name went into another circle. She might also be covering for a medical error. Or she might worry about losing her job to a younger, prettier nurse. He'd make it a point to speak with her at the funeral. Not that he could sense guilt in a single meeting, but often an averted glance or nervous gesture provided clues.

Mary Margaret might have considered Georgia a dear friend, but from what she'd said last night, she couldn't name anyone she'd been dating. Georgia had been a pretty girl, and should have had boyfriends aplenty. One could have been furious if she hadn't returned his affections.

At least Georgia hadn't been sliced in half and dumped in a field the way the Black Dahlia had been. He rocked back in his swivel chair. A stranger might have killed Georgia.

Just as Lynch said, he could have seen her enter the building, followed her up the stairs, grabbed her from behind, and slit her throat before she'd even realized he posed a threat. When there was nothing to tie the murderer to the victim, the case would be nearly impossible to solve.

He planned to find the link and drew a half dozen more circles on his chart and left them empty for the time being. He planned to visit Georgia's apartment, and with Mary Margaret along, they might be able to get in. They could say they were looking for a nice dress for the funeral. That was believable.

"There, the Chrysanthemum Court on your right," Mary Margaret pointed out. "Georgia had the last cottage on the east. This is such a pretty place, if there had been an opening when I looked for an apartment, I would have rented here."

Joe parked at the curb. The cottages were painted a soft cocoa color with white shutters and trim and forest green doors. There were three on each side of a well-tended lawn with a gurgling fountain in the center. As could be expected, an abundance of colorful chrysanthemums had been planted along the walks.

"This is as perfect as a movie set," he offered.

"I've always thought of it as a quaint English village," Mary Margaret replied. "Georgia raved about the parties the neighbors had on holidays."

"What do you really know about her neighbors?" he asked.

"Not much, I'm afraid. As I recall, three of the cottages are rented to married couples. There was another single woman, a teacher, and a widower who owns some type of shop. He's an older gentlemen, and Georgia considered him a good friend."

"She wasn't fond of the others?"

"She never said a bad word about any of them, Joe. Besides, none of them would have had a reason to kill her."

"Some people aren't nearly as nice as they first appear." He got out of his sedan and walked around to open her door. "Who owns the cottages?"

"Mike something or other. He handled repairs himself, and Georgia thought he was nice."

"Well, someone sure as hell wasn't all that nice, were they?"

"Joe!" She grabbed his arm and gave him a squeeze. "Please, try not to swear in front of Georgia's neighbors."

"I promise." He crossed his hand over his heart. He'd served in the Coast Guard during WWII and had heard cussing carried to the level of an art form, but he used a minimum of foul language with her.

There was a small sign with a white chrysanthemum drawn in the lush art nouveau style placed near the fountain. He copied the owner's name and telephone number into his notebook. "If we see anyone, let's use the dress story, unless Georgia would have preferred being buried in her nurse's uniform."

"Wearing her white stockings and sensible shoes? No, I don't believe so. She had pretty dresses. This is all so sad, Joe. Every time I think of Georgia, I tear-up all over again."

He took her hand as they walked to Georgia's cottage. The front door was open, and for safety's sake, he stepped in front of her before looking in. "Hello?" he called.

A man in a white dress shirt and navy blue trousers responded. His dark hair was liberally laced with gray but he appeared to be in his late thirties or early forties. "Word of a vacancy must have traveled awfully fast," he greeted them. "The tenant died unexpectedly, but the police have asked me not to touch her things. If you want to give me your names, I'll add them to the waiting list. I'm Mike Torres, the owner."

Joe gave their names and extended his hand. "Georgia was a dear friend, and we hoped we'd be able to take one of her dresses for the funeral. The police wouldn't miss a dress, would they?"

"No, probably not," Mike replied. "You better hurry. They've been here once, and will probably come back to do a more thorough search. Georgia wasn't killed here, and I don't know what they expect to find."

Joe had hoped for a chance to do a thorough search on his own, but Mike followed them into the cottage's single bedroom and waited at the door. "I'm not sure what to do with Georgia's belongings," Mike continued. "She didn't list any next of kin when she moved in. Maybe her friends would like to have something of hers, and I'll donate the rest to charity."

"What a lovely thought," Mary Margaret replied. "What do you think of this red dress? It's one of her prettiest, but would it be appropriate for a funeral?"

Joe sat in the overstuffed chair in the corner. "Choose whatever you think is best, honey. I'll stay out of your way."

"I don't know about red," Mike mused. "Of course, no one knows for sure what happens in the afterlife, so maybe Georgia would love to be wearing her red dress. I don't suppose she'll need a hat or shoes."

"Probably not." Mary Margaret kept looking through the closet. "This is a pretty gray suit, but that seems a bit formal, doesn't it?"

"Is there a rule about when a woman should wear a suit?" Joe asked.

"I don't know." She pursed her lips thoughtfully. "My mother once told me not to wear a suit to a party we were hosting in our home. Does that count?"

Joe thought she was doing a great job of stalling and hoped Mike Torres would grow bored with them and wait outside, but Mike remained right where he stood. "Sure, that counts. It sounds as though what we need is a flattering dress, something Georgia loved."

"Will they be able to have an open casket?" Mike asked. "From what the police told me…."

Mary Margaret was quick to interrupt. "I'm sure it was an awful scene, but the mortician will be able to make her appear life-like. If she's posed holding a bouquet of flowers close, some would cover her throat."

"She was such a pretty girl," Mike responded. "I can't believe someone could have wanted her dead. Take your time, I'll wait out front."

As soon as he'd left the room, Joe got up and looked into the nightstand drawers. The cottage had maple furnishings, good solid pieces that would survive many a tenant. "She might have had a diary the police missed. Check the hatboxes on the shelf."

He searched through the dresser drawers and yanked out lace lingerie. "Won't she need underclothes?"

"I suppose," Mary Margaret answered. She took down the round boxes, removed the hats, found nothing beneath them but tissue paper, and replaced the boxes on the shelf. She got down on the floor and searched through the shoeboxes with an equal lack of success. "I'm really leaning toward the red dress."

"You knew Georgia," Joe called over his shoulder. He looked under the bed, but there weren't even any dust bunnies in residence. They hadn't found anything in the least bit useful, and he stood and rested his hands on his hips.

"Shouldn't she have had a jewelry box? Don't most women have one?"

"Yes, they do. Georgia had a small blue leather one on her dresser. She wore only her watch for work. When we went out to a movie or to eat, she'd wear gold earrings and often bracelets and a pearl ring. I doubt she would have worn them to see you though, so they should be here. Do you suppose the murderer broke in and stole her jewelry?"

"I didn't see any keys with her purse, so he could have taken them and come here to pick up a few trophies from the crime. It's difficult to believe anyone could be that sick, but some clearly are. Let's take the dress and lingerie and go before Mike comes back to shoo us out."

They were at the front door when Detective Lynch walked up. A dark Ford sedan was parked at the curb and a uniformed officer stood beside it. "Ah, the detective," Lynch greeted Joe with a noticeable lack of enthusiasm. He nodded to Mary Margaret and gave her his card. "Mr. Torres, you were supposed to keep the cottage locked. How could you have misunderstood?"

"They came for a dress for the funeral, and Miss Dixon shouldn't be buried nude."

Lynch shook his head. "It's not uncommon for relatives to purchase new clothing for the deceased. Did that not occur to any of you?"

"Something new?" Mary Margaret mused aloud. "No, I think Georgia will be more comfortable in something she chose herself."

"The woman is dead," Lynch whispered. "It won't matter what she wears."

"It matters to her friends," Mary Margaret posed. "We want to remember how pretty she was." She wiped away a tear and Joe handed her his handkerchief.

"Do you want us to sign for the dress?" Joe asked.

Lynch turned away to look out toward the street. There was an elderly couple standing on the porch of the first cottage watching them. He waved. "No, take the dress, although red is an odd choice."

"Do you really think so?" Mary Margaret asked. "We could go back and take another look through at her closet."

"Leave now," Lynch ordered through clenched teeth.

"Thank you, Mr. Torres," Joe called to him. He took Mary Margaret's arm as they walked to his car. She laid the clothes on the backseat.

As soon as they'd pulled away from the curb, Joe patted her thigh. "You were amazing! Have you thought of taking up detective work? You sounded so sincere, both Torres and Lynch were fooled."

"I was sincere," she argued. "Or at least, mostly sincere, and no, I love nursing too much to change professions."

"Good, I don't need the competition."

"What do you suppose that couple watching from their porch knows?"

He pulled her hand to his lips. "Exactly what I was thinking. They ought to be invited to the funeral, don't you think?"

"Yes, all her neighbors should be, and that's a wonderful excuse to go back and dig a bit more. If Detective Lynch had told Mike Torres to keep Georgia's cottage locked, what do you suppose he was doing inside when we arrived?"

Joe winked at her. "That's another excellent question. I swear you have a gift for investigation."

"You promised, no swearing," she reminded him with a teasing giggle. She had the address of the mortuary where Georgia's body would be taken after the coroner's examination, and kept still as they rode there.

Wednesday morning, a man knocked on Joe's office door. He pushed it open and came in without waiting for a welcome. "Good morning, Mr. Ezell. I'm Marty Streech from the *LA Examiner*. I need some good quotes for an article on Georgia Dixon's murder. I've heard all the jokes about 'streeching the truth', and that's why I'm here, to get the real story from you."

Marty's light brown hair was flecked with gray and in need of a trim. His sport coat and shirt were disheveled and his dark trousers had lost their crease. He looked as though he'd been up all night chasing news stories he couldn't quite catch. Joe straightened up in his chair.

"Well, Mr. Streech, I read the *Los Angeles Times,* and they covered the story from the police report."

"Fine paper, and of course they did," Marty agreed. He slid into one of the chairs facing Joe's desk. "I want more. Give me your take on the murder. It's odd for a young woman to be murdered outside a detective's office, wouldn't you say?"

"Every murder is a tragedy no matter where it takes place."

Marty pulled a small notebook and pen from his pocket. "I like that." He mouthed the words as he wrote them down. "Did you know Miss Dixon well?" He leaned into the question as though he could already taste the juicy tidbits Joe might dish out.

Joe took an immediate dislike to him. "No, I did not."

"Why was she coming to see you?" Marty asked.

"I've no idea, and I wouldn't tell you even if I did. My firm is named Discreet Investigations for a reason."

"I can see you're the discreet sort," Marty replied with a dejected sigh. He tucked the notebook and pen back into his pocket. "Let's forget the story. I believe Georgia Dixon's murder is linked to the death of the Black Dahlia. She wasn't sliced in half, but maybe the killer didn't have enough time."

Joe turned away to glance out the window. After he'd come upon such a bloody scene, he didn't want to even imagine it might have been worse. "You should discuss your theory with the police. They may have more details than were in the *LA Times,* but I don't."

"Has to be a surgeon who cut the Dahlia in half. No one else would have the skill, or the raw nerve to butcher a woman like that. Working at the VA hospital, Ms. Dixon was surrounded by surgeons. She might have had a strong suspicion about who the murderer might be, and he killed her before she could identify him. You were lucky he didn't get you too."

"I am a lucky man indeed," Joe agreed, anxious to send the reporter on his way.

Marty stood and yanked on his cuffs, but his jacket remained ill-fitting. He pulled a business card from his breast pocket and handed it to Joe. "Keep my card, and if you think of something the public might need to know, to stay safe, you understand, give me a call at the paper."

The corners of the tan card were slightly curled, as though it had been carried around for weeks. Joe laid it on his desk. "The police don't consult with me, so you're better off attending a press conference with them."

"One never knows," Marty offered as he opened the office door. "If a valuable tip comes your way, give me a call." He closed the door quietly behind him.

Marty's Black Dahlia theory was wild enough to be true, and Joe quickly made notes of their conversation. He'd not share a word of it with Mary Margaret and scare her half to death for no reason, but he'd make certain he wasn't being followed wherever he went.

That afternoon, Joe had an appointment with the stationery salesman's wife, Paulette Dupré. She was a large woman who arrived wearing an unflattering floral dress. She had small feet and walked with mincing steps as she entered the office and took a chair.

"Would you care for coffee?" Joe offered. "I have a fresh pot."

Paulette placed her purse on her ample lap and clutched it tightly. "I'm not here for a chat. Just give me the bad news, Mr. Ezell. That's all I came to hear."

Joe opened a folder and handed her a photo of her husband and his lady friend. "Do you recognize this woman?"

She appeared disgusted rather than shocked. "No, she's probably some floozy he picked up in bar. Thank you for catching him so quickly." She laid the photo on his desk, opened her purse and handed him a check to cover his fee. "The photo is mine now, isn't it?"

"If you'd care to have it," Joe agreed. "Do you plan to show it to your husband?" He'd learned the hard way that the evidence he turned over to a client could lead to the worst sort of results. He'd provide a stern warning if Mrs. Dupré gave him any hint violence might ensue.

"Of course I'll show it to him. It won't be the first time he's stepped out on me. I'll threaten to take our sons and move to Omaha to live with my parents. He won't want to lose his boys, and that will put a real kink in his philandering for a good long while."

Joe nodded thoughtfully. She wouldn't be the first woman to use her children to get her own way. It wasn't the kind of family he'd care to have, but she'd not come to him for marital advice. He slipped her check into his top drawer, gave her a receipt, and handed her the manila folder for the photo. He stood when she did.

"I'm glad I could be of service, Mrs. Dupré."

She shrugged rather than offer a gracious reply and slipped out the door before he could open it for her. He was still thinking about the case when CC came in later to empty the wastebasket. "Are you married, CC?"

CC had a rich rolling laugh. "I sure am, Mr. Ezell. This is wife number three, and the best of the lot. I'm keeping her."

"I doubt I'd have the courage to marry more than once," Joe responded.

"Courage isn't the question," CC answered. "It's about an irresistible pull. Even if you try to leave, you'll snap right back to the woman you love. But it's a lucky man who gets marriage right the first time. You have yourself a nice afternoon now."

"Thanks, CC." Joe got up to look out the window at the busy street below. Mary Margaret was the only woman who'd made marriage an attractive possibility. He ought to propose, and soon, but certainly not during funeral preparations for one of her closest friends.

When Joe picked up Mary Margaret later that afternoon, they headed to Hancock Park to visit Curtis Mooney's family. Their home was an immense Tudor Revival style built of brick with a timbered stucco second story, and leaded glass windows. The lush landscaping was as beautifully kept as a royal garden. They stood at the curb for a moment and simply stared.

"No place like home," she murmured. "All Georgia said was that the house was big."

"Somewhat of an understatement," Joe offered.

"I'll say. I just wish we didn't have to be here, but she was too important to Curtis not to come."

He took her hand as they walked up the long flagstone path to the front door. A tall woman dressed in black with a crisply pressed white apron answered the door. "Good afternoon," Mary Margaret began. She'd remained in her nurse's uniform rather than change into street clothes in hopes the visit would appear more official. "May we please see Curtis?"

The woman nodded and slowly opened the door onto a tile entryway that held an impressive grandfather clock. "He's swimming in the pool, come with me."

Joe and Mary Margaret exchanged a worried glance, and followed the woman past an impressive staircase, through a formal dining room and out French doors to the terrace. The pool was near Olympic size and a single swimmer made his way toward them with a lazy overhand stroke.

"He shouldn't swim alone," Mary Margaret whispered.

"He isn't," a man left a bar on their right carrying a drink. "I'm Edwin, Curtis's brother. I keep an eye on him whenever I can, or someone else does. May I assume by your charming outfit that you've come from the VA hospital?"

Mary Margaret watched Curtis climb out of the pool. He was the better looking of the two brothers, plus taller, with a more impressive build, but his smile was sweetly childlike. She gave their names. "We've come with awful news," she whispered to Edwin.

"He knows about Miss Dixon, I told him when I read her name in the paper. He cried for an hour, but he's over it now. Would you care to apply for Miss Dixon's weekend shift?"

Joe thought the man decidedly cool. Georgia had been a lovely young woman, who had undoubtedly given Curtis extraordinary care, and she should not be reduced to someone who merely filled a shift. Curtis reached them before he could take exception to Edwin's remark.

Curtis dropped his damp towel and hugged Mary Margaret as though she were his best friend. "Have you come to be my new nurse? She's very pretty, isn't she, Ed?"

Mary Margaret patted his back and stepped out of his arms as quickly as she could. He'd left damp splotches on the front of her uniform. "No, I came to let you know Georgia's funeral will be Sunday afternoon at the VA chapel. She was so fond of you, Curtis, and I hope you'll be able to come."

Curtis appeared confused. "Should we go, Ed? Do we have to?"

"No, of course not," Edwin assured him. "Although it would be a nice gesture."

"We'll be there then," Curtis promised. "Do you want a soda?"

"Or something stronger if you'd like," Edwin responded. "I make a mean Tom Collins."

"I'd love one," Mary Margaret replied. "How about you, Joe?"

She seldom drank, but he understood she wasn't ready to leave. "I'd like one too, thank you." They all walked over to the bar where Edwin first handed his brother a cold Coca-Cola in a glass bottle.

"Did you serve in the war, Curtis?" Joe asked.

"He was at the VA hospital," Edwin pointed out. "Doesn't that tell you something?"

"Yes, but I thought he might have something to say," Joe added. "I served in the Coast Guard off Greenland. Fascinating world up there."

"I was a Marine," Curtis offered. "An officer wasn't I, Ed?"

"Yes, you were a Captain, and served honorably until you were wounded at the Battle of Iwo Jima in 1945."

"I can never remember that," Curtis complained. "I should write it down and read it every morning. Then maybe it would stick."

"There are so much more wonderful things to consider," Mary Margaret offered. Edwin handed her a Tom Collins complete with a lemon circle, and she took a sip. "Yes, this is very good."

"Come sit with me," Curtis reached for her hand, and she went with him to a glass-topped table surrounded by thick-cushioned chairs. He waited for her to take a chair and moved his chair so close their knees touched. "Do you like going to the movies? Georgia loved the movies, and we went as often as there was something good to see."

"Yes, I do love movies." There was a tennis court beyond the pool. "I can't recall if Georgia played tennis. Do you play?"

"I used to," Curtis answered. "Was I any good, Ed?"

"You were on the tennis team at USC. Your trophies fill a shelf in the library."

"Oh yeah, I remember." Curtis took a long drink of his Coke. "I can't concentrate well enough to play tennis yet, maybe someday I will. Georgia used to swim with me. Do you want to go swimming? We have bathing suits for guests to borrow."

"Thank you, but not today," Mary Margaret replied. "This is such a beautiful home and yard."

"Thank you," Edwin called from the bar. He sat on a stool rather than join them at the table, and Joe remained with him.

"Georgia spent her Saturdays here," Joe remarked softly to Edwin. "Did she ever mention having trouble with anyone?"

Edwin shook his head. "Her job was to keep Curtis entertained. They'd swim, play simple card games, and go to movies as he said. I'm usually working in my office and saw her only briefly when she was here. If she confided any problems in my brother, he's forgotten them. Do the police have any leads?"

"None that they've shared." Joe finished his drink, and went to join Mary Margaret and Curtis at the table. "We can't stay long, we have to invite Georgia's neighbors to the funeral."

Curtis frowned with concentration. "Is it Sunday?" he asked.

"Yes, it is," Mary Margaret responded. She turned toward Edwin. "Would you like me to ask Georgia's friends if they might be available to work here on Saturdays?"

"It would be a great help," he replied. "We've had nurses from a service, but they were all business and what Curtis enjoys is fun. Nurses from the VA ought to have more experience with working with young vets."

Mary Margaret finished her drink and stood. "If I can't find a friend, I'll come and stay with you this Saturday."

"Would you?" Curtis sprang from his chair like a jack-in-the-box and leaned down to kiss her cheek.

"Yes, I will." She thanked Edwin for the delicious refreshments, and both brothers walked them to the front door. Curtis stood in the door and waved until Joe's Chevrolet pulled away from the curb.

Joe regarded Mary Margaret with a skeptical glance. "Do you really want to work here on Saturdays?" he asked.

"Not really, but Curtis needs someone to look after him, and Edwin doesn't seem like much fun."

"No, he doesn't. I don't believe he smiled the whole time we were there."

Mary Margaret rolled down her window and shook her hair in the breeze. "He struck me as the serious sort, who'd be absorbed in his work and feel no need to relax. Do you suppose he has a family?"

"There weren't any kids' toys laying about, so I doubt it. He must have been too old to serve in the war, and stayed home to concentrate on business. From what I read, the Mooney's wealth comes from oil. They probably pay very well."

"We'll see. I don't plan to work a second job more than a week or two until we find another nurse who'd enjoy being with Curtis. Maybe Angie would like him."

Joe pulled over to the curb and stopped the car. "Do you suppose Georgia and Curtis could have had a romance going? He's as affectionate as a big puppy. Maybe she thought he'd make a fine husband."

Mary Margaret closed her eyes a moment to consider it and came to a quick conclusion. "No, absolutely not. Georgia never would have taken advantage of the Mooneys like that."

"Are you sure? They're worth an awful lot of money."

"Stop right there. Let's concentrate on her neighbors. We'll just knock on their doors and give them the details for the funeral and see what we can discover from them."

Joe started the car. "It was just a thought."

"Yeah, and one you ought to forget."

"Will do." He turned on the radio and found the Nat King Cole Trio singing, "I Love You for Sentimental Reasons," with a beautiful deep harmony. He winked at Mary Margaret, and she gave his thigh a gentle love pat. All was forgiven.

CHAPTER 3

Mary Margaret kept a small comb in her purse and ran it through her hair. "How do I look?"

"Exquisite, as always," Joe assured her.

"That's a little much," she scolded softly.

"Is not." Joe parked in front of the Chrysanthemum Court and cut the engine. They'd written the details for Sunday's memorial service for Georgia on three by five cards, and he thumbed through them one last time. "Let's stick to the facts, and if we're invited in, or the couple or person is friendly, let's let them talk."

She rolled up her window. "I'm all cried out, so I won't burst into tears, but I'm still awfully sad. I'll try and fake a better mood."

"You'll do fine." He opened her car door and held her hand as they walked up to the cottages. It was after six o'clock, and he thought someone should be home at each place. They checked the mailboxes for names, and he made a few quick notations in his notebook before knocking at the door of the first cottage.

John Cameron opened the door, took note of Mary Margaret's white nurse's uniform, and smiled. "Are you one of Georgia's friends?"

"I was," she replied. She told him about the memorial and handed him a card. "We hope you and your wife will be able to attend."

Phyllis came to her husband's side and saw the card. "I've just baked some lemon scones. Won't you come in and have tea with us?"

Joe responded with a wide smile. "We'd love to."

Their cottage was furnished with the Cameron's own furniture gathered during their long years of marriage. It was a jumble of styles, but each piece was attractive in its own right. Joe and Mary Margaret took seats side by side on the sofa. It was covered with plush wine-hued velvet and quite elegant.

John sat in his easy chair. "My wife's a wonderful cook. I was a postman and for many years walked off all the calories, but now I'm retired and have to be more careful."

Phyllis carried in a tea tray with a blue teapot and matching cups. The scones were on an orange plate and smelled luscious. She handed them each a linen napkin. "Would you rather have a plate?" she asked.

"This is fine," Mary Margaret assured her. "Like you, Mr. Cameron, as a nurse I'm on my feet all day and don't have to worry about my weight."

Phyllis poured tea for them all and sat in her favorite chair beside her husband's to enjoy her scone. "I could not believe my eyes when I read about the murder in the *Times*. It's just horrifying to think someone who lived so close to us could have suffered such an awful fate. I shudder each time I think of it, well, to be truthful, I try not to think of it at all."

"Of course," Joe agreed between bites. "This scone is perfection, Mrs. Cameron. Did you know Georgia well?"

Phyllis and John exchanged puzzled glances. "We thought we did," he replied, "but if someone wanted her dead, maybe we didn't know her nearly as well as we thought."

"She mentioned wonderful holiday parties here at Chrysanthemum Court," Mary Margaret offered.

"Oh yes," Phyllis answered with a charming smile. "We put tables on the grass and everyone shares their treats with everyone else. We'll have to wait and see who moves into Georgia's apartment before we plan another party."

"Halloween we all stay in our own cottages for the kids," John reminded her.

Joe and Mary Margaret made several attempts to turn the discussion to Georgia, but neither John nor Phyllis responded with anything useful for their investigation. "This has been a marvelous surprise," Mary Margaret exclaimed as soon as they'd finished their scones and tea. "We'd love to stay and talk with you longer, but we need to invite everyone who lives here to the memorial."

"Don't expect much from Amy Hudson in cottage five," Phyllis confided. "She was always a little jealous of Georgia. Georgia was younger and prettier, so there was really no comparison between them."

"You shouldn't gossip," John scolded.

"It isn't gossip if it's the truth," Phyllis insisted proudly.

"Thank you again," Joe said. "Before we go, I want to give you my card. If you think of anything more about Georgia, please give me a call."

John studied the business card for Discreet Investigations. "You're a private detective?"

"Yes, and Georgia had planned to come and see me when she was murdered. I want to do all I can to catch the brute who killed her."

Once on the walk, Mary Margaret refreshed her lipstick and brushed a stray crumb from her skirt. "Amy is the teacher. She'd have had to be a lot more than merely jealous to kill Georgia."

"Right. She'd have had to be in a murderous rage. She'll be on her summer vacation, so I suppose she'd have the opportunity, but it's doubtful a woman could have resorted to that level of violence."

The door of the second cottage opened before Joe could raise his hand to knock. A very pregnant young woman greeted them. "Saw you on the walk and figured you must be Georgia's friends. I'm Polly Hill."

Joe gave their names, handed her a card, and issued an invitation to the memorial. "It will be a gathering of her friends, rather than anything formal."

"Well, if I'm still waddling around here rather than in the hospital with a new baby, we'll be there." She looked over her shoulder. "Dan, come here a minute, please."

He was tall and blond with more freckles than could be counted in a single glance. He wore dress pants and a white shirt and had loosened his tie. "Did I hear you mention Georgia? I used to see her leaving for work in the morning. I can't believe she's dead."

"Neither can we," Joe added.

"She was such a nice person," Polly added. "She used to answer medical questions for me, nothing that needed to be too detailed, of course. This is our first baby, and I appreciated her advice."

"She was a very caring person," Mary Margaret agreed.

Polly licked her lips. "Maybe I shouldn't say this, but I don't sleep well with this dear little dumpling jumping around inside me half the night. One night last week, I got up for a drink of water and saw a man going into Georgia's cottage. It struck me as strange that she'd be entertaining callers at that hour."

"How late was this?" Joe asked.

"It was after 1:00 a.m., and I just wondered is all."

"Why didn't you tell me about it?" her husband asked.

"You have enough on your mind," Polly replied. "Besides, what Georgia did was none of our business, but if that man had anything to do with her murder, I should tell someone about it, shouldn't I?"

"The police haven't spoken to you?" Joe asked.

"No, they were here, but seemed interested only in her cottage. I didn't want to lumber over, volunteer information, and just look like a balloon-shaped busy-body."

"I understand," Mary Margaret offered. "I hope you'll be able to come on Sunday."

Dan read the card. "We'll try."

Joe gave them his business card, and encouraged them to call him if they thought of anything to help catch the murderer.

"Shouldn't we call the police?" Dan asked.

"Of course," Joe encouraged, "but they have many cases to solve, and I'm concentrating my time on Georgia's death."

They waited a moment in front of the third cottage while Joe hurriedly made notes on Polly's comments. "Could Georgia have been seeing a doctor from the hospital, perhaps one who worked late or had a very early shift?" he wondered.

"She doted on her patients, that's all I saw. If there was a doctor in her life, she didn't let any of us know. But if they were on different shifts, we would never have seen them together."

Joe knocked on the door of the third cottage and the widower, Patrick Wood, answered with a wide friendly smile. "You must be friends of Georgia's," he exclaimed. "I miss her terribly. Please come in and stay a while."

"We've come to invite you to the memorial service." Joe offered their names along with the card. He gestured for Mary Margaret to enter the cottage ahead of him. In contrast to the Cameron's eclectically furnished home, Mr. Wood had the same maple furniture they'd seen in Georgia's cottage. The living room was as neatly kept as a furniture showroom, with an imposing grandfather clock taking up a great deal of space.

Patrick followed their glances. "I'm a watchmaker by trade, and this is my baby. There's nothing better than the deep chime of a grandfather clock to mark time." He pulled a business card from his breast pocket. "My shop is not far from here. Come by any day, and I'll give you a deal on a new watch, or clock, or the repairs on a favorite. I do an especially fine job with pocket watches if your grandfather left you one."

"Thank you," Mary Margaret responded. She took the card and dropped it into her purse. "Georgia mentioned more than once that you were a special friend."

He gestured for them to take a seat on the sofa and sat across from them. "Yes, she was very dear to me. You know how it is when you meet someone and feel as though you've known them forever? I lost my wife years ago, and we hadn't had children. Georgia was like a daughter to me. We often had dinner together and those were wonderful evenings. I can't believe anyone would want her dead. It's such a tragedy for everyone who knew her, or now never will."

"Yes, it is." Mary Margaret agreed. "We seldom had time to discuss our personal lives at work, do you know if she was seeing anyone?"

Patrick pursed his lips. "Yes, I believe she was, but she never told me his name. Not that she was secretive about him, or it didn't seem that way at the time, but now I wonder. I wish I had a name to give to the police."

"Have they spoken with you?" Joe asked.

"No, they came after I'd gone to my shop, and I heard about the murder when I came home Monday night."

"Who told you?" Joe asked.

"Amy Hudson. She lives in cottage five. She and Georgia weren't close, but she cried the whole time she told me about her death."

"Did that strike you as odd?" Mary Margaret inquired.

"Well, not to be uncharitable, but yes. Her comments are usually rather dry, fleeting actually, if we should pass on the walk. She makes deviled eggs whenever we have parties. It doesn't matter what the occasion might be, the Fourth of July, or Christmas, she'll put out one of those plates with the little egg shaped hallows made especially for deviled eggs. It may be the only recipe she does well."

Believing they'd learn nothing more, Joe stood and offered his card. "Thank you so much for your time. If you think of anything that might help solve the crime, please call me."

Patrick noted the information on the card and appeared surprised. "Shouldn't we trust the police to catch him rather than a private investigator?"

"I'm sure they'd also appreciate your help," Joe assured him. He took Mary Margaret's arm and ushered her out.

Lights made the other cottages glow with an inner warmth, but Georgia's was dark. "Even her cottage looks sad," Mary Margaret mused. "Shall we go on to Amy Hudson, or have you had enough for the day?"

"I've definitely had enough, but I want to finish up here. Are you game for the last two?"

"Sure. I'd like to get it over with." She rapped lightly on the teacher's door and a long moment passed before it opened. Amy was tall and thin, a pale blonde dressed in an unflattering gray shirt and slacks. She seemed to droop all over as though exhausted, and she covered a wide yawn before greeting them.

Joe and Mary Margaret quickly introduced themselves and offered a card with the memorial details. When Amy didn't appear interested, neither was surprised. Joe offered his business card. "Georgia had planned to see me on the morning she died. If you think of anything at all that might lead to an arrest, please call me."

"You're not with the police?" she asked.

"No, I'm looking into the case on my own. Living next door to Georgia, perhaps you had a better chance to know her than your neighbors did."

"I knew enough," she nearly snorted.

"It sounds as though you did know something," Mary Margaret encouraged. "Won't you please tell us?"

Amy leaned against the doorframe rather than invite them into her home. "Let's just say she had visitors who didn't appear to like the light of day."

"Vampires aren't real," Mary Margaret replied.

"Not vampires, silly," Amy responded. "Just men who came calling at odd hours. I never saw her go out on a date in the evenings." She handed back the memorial card. "I doubt I'll be able to make it. Give it to someone else."

"Was it the same man you saw on multiple occasions, or several different fellows?" Mary Margaret asked.

Amy shrugged. "I didn't look that closely, so it could have been the same man."

"Other than her late night callers, did you have another reason to dislike Georgia?" Joe asked.

"I teach the advanced math classes at Hollywood High. By the time I get home in the afternoon, I'm ready for a nap rather than a chat with a neighbor." She began to close her door, and then almost as an after thought, added, "Good luck."

"Thank you." Joe called just as the door latched.

"Charming girl," Mary Margaret whispered. "Who rents the last cottage?"

"Number six." Joe checked his notes. "It's a Mr. and Mrs. Garcia."

Tim and Barbara Garcia proved to be a young couple, and they were so curious about their murdered neighbor they invited Joe and Mary Margaret right in. "We're having spaghetti for dinner and I always make too much. Would you care to join us?"

Joe and Mary Margaret exchanged a quick startled glance and replied in unison, "We'd love to."

The Garcia home was the most colorful one they'd seen. There was a lime green rug and two wing-backed chairs upholstered in a bright floral pattern on a white background that complimented the orange sofa.

"What a charming room," Mary Margaret exclaimed.

Tim Garcia laughed and hugged his wife. "We work in banks, different branches, of course, and after being surrounded by pale gray décor all day, we're in desperate need of color."

"It is cheerful," Joe observed. "Are you certain we won't be too much trouble?"

"No, of course not," Barbara assured them. "Please come and sit down. There is barely enough room for a dining table, but we prefer it to eating in the kitchen."

"Please let me help," Mary Margaret volunteered, and she followed Barbara into the kitchen.

Joe handed Tim his card before sitting on the sofa. "I'm doing my own investigation of Georgia's death. If you remember anything that might be helpful, please give me a call."

Tim slipped the card into his breast pocket. "Do you enjoy being a detective? Frankly, the bank pays well, and there's plenty of room for advancement, but the job bores me to death."

"Be grateful that it pays well," Joe offered. "Many months I don't know if I'll be able to make the rent."

Tim leaned over to glance into the kitchen, and whispered, "Before my wife comes back, one night I was up late, anxious to read to the end of an Agatha Christie mystery, when I heard someone walk by. I looked out the door, just to be safe you understand, and saw a man going into Georgia's cottage. I went to bed soon after and didn't hear him walk out. Maybe it was her nurse's uniform that always made her look so prim and proper, but I was surprised she'd entertain callers at that hour."

"Would you recognize the man if you saw him again?" Joe asked.

Tim shook his head. "No, all I could tell was that it was a man, an average sized guy, not anyone tall or particularly heavy. Maybe it was someone from the hospital dropping off something she'd forgotten. It could have been completely innocent, couldn't it?"

"Yes, of course," Joe agreed, but he wished they had some idea who Georgia's late night caller, or callers, had been.

With Mary Margaret's subtle suggestions, Barbara served the best spaghetti dinner she'd ever prepared. The Garcias were a charming couple, and for a brief while at least Mary Margaret was able to forget the sad nature of their errand. When they said good night, she took Joe's hand.

"Could we stop by Aunt Lucy's for ice cream on the way to my place? I want to talk over what we've learned."

"Aunt Lucy's it is."

The popular ice cream parlor had a black and white tile floor, marble topped tables, and red leather booths along the wall. It was always deliciously chilled inside and on a summer night, crowded. They had to wait a few minutes, but were then shown to one of booths. Joe ordered a banana split with two spoons.

Mary Margaret took a napkin from the dispenser on the table and reached into her purse for a pen. She drew a quick diagram of Chrysanthemum Court. "Phyllis Cameron in cottage one thought Amy was jealous of Georgia." She drew a dotted line from cottage one to cottage five. "Did we learn anything else from them?"

The waitress brought them glasses of water and Joe took a long drink. "No, they're a sweet couple, but even if Mrs. Cameron thought her husband was in love with Georgia, she wouldn't be strong enough to overpower her."

Mary Margaret tapped cottage two. "Right. Polly Hill saw a man entering Georgia's cottage, but she didn't mention what night. Should we have asked her to be more specific?"

"That she saw a man is enough for now. Tim Garcia also saw a man and was no more helpful."

"Really? Did you get the feeling Patrick Wood might know more than he was telling?"

The waitress served their banana split and Joe waited for Mary Margaret to take the first bite. "I wondered what they were talking about if they ate dinner together often. Georgia wouldn't have discussed her patients, would she?"

Mary Margaret started with a bite of chocolate ice cream and twisted it through the whipped cream. "No, we're all warned to be *discreet*, one of your favorite words. It isn't fair to the patients to share their injuries or treatments." She tapped cottage five on her drawing. "Everything about Amy Hudson was off. Why would someone so pale wear grey? And in the summer when most women choose more colorful clothes?"

"Beats me. Maybe she wears drab colors for work so she doesn't distract her students."

"She's on vacation. I wonder if she's dating anyone. No one mentioned seeing men calling on her at any hour."

Joe had eaten half the strawberry ice cream and concentrated on a slice of banana. "Maybe she prefers her own company and solves math problems for fun."

"I doubt she allows herself to have any fun," Mary Margaret teased. "That leaves Tim and Barbara Garcia. I wish he'd gotten a better look at Georgia's caller. In mystery novels, don't the suspects have some unusual characteristic, like a decided limp, or unusual height or girth?"

"They do, but that's not real life, and this is."

"True." She folded the napkin and slipped it into her purse. "Let's see if a tall guy with a limp shows up for the memorial service."

"We haven't had a chance to talk about your day. Were the police there asking questions?"

"Nope," she replied and took another spoonful of chocolate ice cream. "Maybe we'll see Detective Lynch tomorrow. He'd want to question Georgia's co-workers, wouldn't he?"

"Yes, and he should have been there yesterday," Joe said.

"Maybe he's overwhelmed with other cases."

"No, he's probably just running in circles with every one."

She took a sip of water and studied his expression for a long moment. "You don't like the man, do you?"

"To quote you, 'nope'. You've met Hal Marten. Lynch hounded him, although he was innocent of any crime. Lynch skims the surface rather than dig deep and chides me for being a P.I.; I earn my pay which is more than I can say for him."

She pulled the napkin out of her purse to make another note. "Then we should dig deeper. Georgia must have known something so terrible, someone would resort to murder to keep it a secret. Did anyone at the Chrysanthemum Court strike you as having much to lose?"

Joe smiled. "No, but the Mooney family might."

"Just what I was thinking," she agreed and they finished the banana split without needing to speak another word.

CHAPTER 4

Although Joe seriously doubted he'd ever find another dead body lying outside his office, he dreaded climbing the stairs. He wasn't the superstitious sort, but if Georgia's murder kept clients away, he would have to search for new office space when his lease ran out.

Thursday morning, he had an appointment scheduled with Harry Berg, a man worried about stock missing from his shoe store. Joe looked forward to a simple, ordinary case that could easily be solved.

Harry was painfully thin and sat on the edge of his chair. His suit looked new, as did his wing-tipped oxfords, but he was so nervous he couldn't keep still. "All my employees have been with me for a year or more, Mr. Ezell. It's not just the expense of the lost stock, you see, but the horrible sense of betrayal that goes with it."

"I understand." Joe asked questions about when the losses had occurred and how they'd been discovered. Harry had the answers and read them from a small notebook he pulled from his jacket pocket.

"It was last Saturday, at first I thought a pair of shoes or two could have simply been misplaced after they were shown to a customer. When the salesmen come in each morning, they check the inventory on the shelves and anything out of place is moved where the box belongs. I keep track of sales at the register, and reorder styles that are selling well."

"Have your most popular styles disappeared?"

"No, that's the strangest part of this," Harry replied. "What's missing are the shoes our older customers might wear, sturdy low-heeled pumps in neutral colors. They aren't the shoes any of the salesmen would take to impress a girlfriend or a wife. Rather than overlook this, I want the losses stopped before more occur."

Joe nodded thoughtfully. "Of course. Do any of your salesmen have elderly mothers who might reside in a retirement home?"

Harry bit his lip. "Just one. He's been with me a long while, and I'd have offered him an additional discount if his mother or her friends had needed new shoes. Do you think I should speak with him?"

"Yes, and if he admits to your losses, you can decide what to do then. You might want to let him keep his job and arrange for him to pay for the stock if he'll promise not to take from you in the future."

"Or I could just fire him," Harry added. "I'd hate to do that. Confrontation of any sort upsets me badly."

"Would you rather that I came and spoke with each of your salesmen?"

Harry nodded. "Yes, but would that be cowardly of me?"

"No, not at all. You can simply announce that I'm there to pursue the cause of recent inventory losses, and see what I discover. That way you won't inadvertently insult a salesman who might know nothing of the crime. Leave everything thing to me, Mr. Berg. I could come with you now if you like."

Berg leapt to his feet. "That would be ideal, Mr. Ezell. Let's get this awful mess over with quickly."

"I'll do my best," Joe promised and left with his client on what he hoped would be an easy case without a single dead body being found in the stockroom.

* * *

Mary Margaret ran up to meet Joe when he picked her up after work. She'd changed into street clothes and had her nurse's uniform carefully folded in a small travel bag. "Detective Lynch finally came to talk with us today." She waited until she was seated in Joe's car to elaborate. "He spoke with us one at a time and asked the usual questions: was Georgia having trouble with anyone at work, who was she dating, had she appeared to be worried about something, was she preoccupied? He was checking off a list in his notebook, as though Georgia's death were a matter of routine.

"I reminded him that Georgia had made an appointment with you, so something must have concerned her. He made the weirdest little sniff, as though the idea smelled bad. The other nurses and I have been talking about Georgia on our breaks, but if anyone knows more about her than I do, they haven't admitted it. We're all simply confounded by the whole matter. Patients have been affected as well. Georgia was a favorite of many, and they're taking her death really hard."

"Were any of the men who've been recently released overly fond of her?"

She pulled her lower lip through her teeth. "She was popular with patients, so such a man could exist, but why would she have wanted to talk to you about him?"

"Maybe she wanted me to meet with him and strongly suggest he find a more appropriate focus for his affections."

"That could have been it. It makes sense. Do you want to go to Clifton's Cafeteria for dinner? I feel like having their macaroni and cheese."

"Clifton's it is then." The restaurant was on Broadway, just north of 7th street and the façade featured a waterfall that sprayed those entering with a fine mist. Joe liked their meatloaf, while Mary Margaret had the macaroni and cheese and lime Jello. They found a comfortable booth and enjoyed their dinners for a long moment before she spoke.

"How was your day? I didn't mean to do all the talking tonight."

Joe drew his fork through the gravy pooling on his mashed potatoes to create a wavy pattern. "It was an amusing day for a change." He told her about the mystery at the shoe store. "The second clerk I spoke to broke down in tears and confessed to taking shoes he'd not paid for. It seems he'd borrowed them Friday night for his mother and four of her friends to wear to a Saturday funeral. They are all in wheelchairs, so the shoes wouldn't have had any wear, and he planned to return them first thing Monday morning before any were missed."

"But his plan went awry?"

"Yes, on Saturday morning, a woman asked to try on one of the shoes, and another salesman discovered the empty boxes. The poor clerk who had borrowed the shoes was so mortified he couldn't speak. He couldn't return the shoes as he'd planned, and the crime grew to enormous proportions in his mind."

"Poor soul. Was he fired?"

"No, the owner of the store is quite fond of him. He was also touched by the man's desire to provide his mother and her friends with new shoes. He'll take the wholesale cost out of the salesman's salary, so the women will be able to keep their new shoes."

"Isn't he worried his other salesmen may begin 'borrowing' shoes for their wives or girlfriends to wear for a fancy occasion?"

"No, he's thinking of having some shoes, party heels, that type of thing available for rental for special evenings, like a costume shop does."

"So you not only solved the crime, but your client also has an idea for a profitable new business opportunity. I'd call it a good day too. Did he give you a big tip?"

Joe laughed. "He paid my fee in cash and gave me generous discount coupons for new shoes which I'll gladly give to you."

"Macaroni and cheese and a discount on shoes! I am one lucky girl," she teased.

Joe loved her giggle, but he couldn't propose in Clifton's Cafeteria when she deserved something so much better. "You mentioned Georgia's patients, do you think any of them would know who could have wanted to date her once he was released? I don't want you to interrogate them, but just casually mention how popular she was and see what you hear in return."

"Sure, I could do that, but if one of the doctors killed her, it wouldn't bring us any closer to the truth."

Marty Streech had been certain a doctor had murdered Georgia, and Joe didn't want her angering a surgeon who might retaliate with a finely-sharpened scalpel. "Leave the physicians alone, but a lot can be learned in casual conversations with your patients. What about Saturday, are you going to work at the Mooney's with Curtis?"

"No, I won't have to. Angie said she'd love to have the job. She remembers Curtis, and doesn't believe she'll be in any danger."

He swirled his last bite of meatloaf in the remaining gravy. "If either Curtis, which seems highly unlikely, or Edwin killed Georgia, they won't be likely to kill another nurse who came to their home when it would focus the suspicion clearly on them."

"That's true. I wish Georgia had told you why she wanted to see you. It would make everything so much easier."

"It would, but unfortunately, not all cases are as easy to solve as the missing shoe caper."

Friday night they went to the movies and saw *The Romance of Rosy Ridge.* Van Johnson played a former Union soldier who traveled to Missouri and met Janet Leigh, a farmer's beautiful daughter. Her father still held the Confederacy dear and forbid her to see a Union man. Despite the father's fierce objection, the couple fell in love.

The plot had plenty of excitement with barnburners ravaging the countryside, and Van becomes a hero ending their spree. Eventually all conflict is resolved, and Van and Janet ride off into the sunset.

Mary Margaret loved romantic movies, and Joe was happy to take her and hold her hand. He was quick to offer a handkerchief if the story turned poignant and prompted tears. He pretended to love the sweet films too, but they always left him worried that he was sadly lacking in the romance department. He feared he would soon disappoint her and lose her to a man more like the film heroes she adored. Mary Margaret never complained, but he still feared she might one day soon.

Saturday morning, Joe played golf with Hal Marten, a man who'd hired him when his wife went missing. It had been Joe's most grueling case, and they'd become friends. Joe had once hoped to become a golf pro, but he'd given it up as an unrealistic dream after the war. Hal had wanted to work on what little he knew about the sport, but they often took more time talking about life and what was in the news than they did concentrating on improving Hal's golf skills.

They'd spent enough time at the driving range, and today were practicing at the putting green. "You've been married," Joe began as he plucked his ball from the hole. They were at the Griffith Park course near the Los Angeles Zoo, and the nearby hills were covered in scrub oak and a frenzy of native plants thriving without a gardener's attention. It was the perfect setting for a Western movie and more than one had been shot close by.

"I have," Hal replied.

Suddenly struck with how totally inappropriate his choice of conversation topic had been, Joe quickly apologized. "I'm sorry, that was stupid of me."

"Not at all. Are you thinking of proposing to Mary Margaret?"

Joe and Mary Margaret had gone to dinner with Hal and Gladys, who'd been Hal's attorney, so Hal knew how cute Joe's girlfriend was. "Yes, but I should have an engagement ring first, shouldn't I?"

Hal turned away to hide his smile. "Many men do."

"I'm afraid Mary Margaret would laugh at what I can afford. But if I can't afford a nice ring, I can't afford a wife either. Does that make sense?"

"It makes perfect sense, but our lives aren't easily predictable, and no matter how hard we try, sometimes two plus two just won't add up to four. If I were selling you an insurance policy with California West, I'd stress that point. Consider it this way, Joe, you'd be in worse shape if you had plenty of money and no one to love, wouldn't you?"

A red-tailed hawk flew in lazy circles overhead in a graceful search for a tasty mouse breakfast. Joe envied the simple focus of the bird's life. "I sure would be, but-"

"If you love the girl, then propose to her. I've seen the soft glow in her eyes when she looks at you. She won't say no. Or are you afraid she'll say yes, and then you'll have a whole new set of problems?"

The question hit Joe with the jolting force of a bucket of ice water. "Maybe we should concentrate on improving your putting," he countered. He was tempted to ask what Hal's plans were with Gladys, but Hal would see right through that ploy and tell him it was none of his business.

Hal sank a putt easily, and pleased his instruction was paying off, Joe brought up another of his problems. "You heard about the nurse who was murdered outside my office?"

"Yes, and I thought how often I'd climbed those stairs and was relieved I hadn't found her."

"I wouldn't wish it on anybody. I need to discover motives for the murdered to identify possible suspects, but everyone at the VA hospital seems to have liked her, and her neighbors don't know more than that she had a gentleman caller who dropped by at late hours."

"Mary Margaret doesn't know who he was?"

"No, Georgia failed to mention whom she was dating. Maybe someone will give themselves away during the memorial service tomorrow."

"Could he have been married?" Hal asked.

"That would be a reason to creep around late at night," Joe agreed. "Maybe the wife discovered he was cheating on her, and she killed Georgia, but I don't believe it was a woman when it was such a brutal murder."

Hal was ready to make his next putt, and focused on his grip and stance before giving his putter a gentle swing. The ball grazed the cup, but rolled away, and he had to take a second try. He made it easily, and bent down to retrieve his ball. "A doctor might not mind the mess."

"It was decidedly messy," Joe agreed. "A reporter from the *LA Examiner* came to see me. He believes Georgia's murder is related to the Black Dahlia's. There's already talk a skilled surgeon must have murdered the Dahlia, and Georgia worked with plenty of them at the VA Hospital."

"And he killed her before she could point the police in his direction?"

"Yes, and it's a reasonable theory. Detective Lynch, with whom you're well acquainted, doesn't appear to have much interest in solving the crime. The police may know more than they're telling. I wish there were a way to find out."

"Like having a snitch on the force?"

Joe sank a five-foot putt before speaking. "Snitch is too strong a word. Just someone who'd share the facts of the case."

"I know a Chinese bail bondsman who has a lot of resources. Do you want me to call him and see if he has any ideas?"

"I'd rather meet with him myself. Could you recommend me?"

"Sure, I'll give him a call. Let's play nine holes next week instead of just practicing. Do you ever play for money?"

"You can thank my excellent instruction for your swift progress, but you aren't nearly good enough to beat me. Besides, I play for the pure love of the game, and I'm saving my money to buy an engagement ring." He sank a long putt to prove his point, and wished proposing to Mary Margaret would be as smooth.

Joe walked into the Golden Bear Lounge that afternoon and had no trouble identifying Lou King; he was the only Chinese gentleman present. Joe took the stool beside him at the long mahogany bar. He introduced himself and Lou smiled and shook his hand with a firm, confident grip.

Mitch, the mustachioed bartender offered his own greeting. "This is my mom's place, so I warn everyone not to get rowdy."

"You have my word on it," Joe responded. He'd often driven by the bar, but this was the first time he'd stopped in. It was a classy place with lots of highly polished dark mahogany and forest green leather booths. He ordered a beer.

Lou King wore a handsomely tailored suit, a blinding white dress shirt and an expensive silk tie. Joe feared his slacks and sports shirt wouldn't impress anyone, but his clothes weren't really the issue that afternoon.

"I'm a private investigator, and last Monday, a young woman was murdered outside my office. The police detective, a man named Lynch, took an immediate dislike to me and won't share what he's learned, if anything. Hal Marten thought you might know someone on the force who'd be more informative. I'd expect to pay him, of course."

Lou nodded to Mitch, who brought him a fresh Scotch and soda. "I've met Lynch, and understand what you mean. He follows procedures to the letter, but lacks any real insight. There's a detective who recently retired who might be acquainted with someone who knows something, but then again, he might not. It will all depend on whether or not he likes you."

"I'm generally regarded as likable," Joe claimed, without anything in the way of actual proof. "I'm not expecting copies of police reports, nothing official, but just some inkling of where the police investigation is going. The murdered woman was one of my girl's best friends, and I'm doing this for her, as much as for myself. We want to see the murderer caught."

"I know the case," Lou responded. He slid one of his business cards to Joe with a name and telephone number written on the back. "Henry likes to chat, so be prepared to spend some time with him when you call. If he invites you over to his home, expect to stay for an hour or two."

"It will be worth it to clear my schedule if he can be of some help." He finished his beer, thanked Lou for the name of the retired detective and left with plenty of time to entertain Mary Margaret that night.

Mary Margaret was a terrific cook and served fried chicken with mashed potatoes, gravy and peas. Joe loved every bite. He wiped his mouth on his napkin. "This is absolutely the best fried chicken I've ever eaten."

She laughed. "You say that about everything I serve."

"Do I? It's the truth. I love your pork chops, but now your fried chicken has become my favorite."

"Thank you, I'll give you some to take home. I keep thinking about the memorial tomorrow and don't have much of an appetite. I've written down what I want to say, but I'm afraid it's not nearly enough."

"Read it to me later, and we'll see if there's anything we can add."

"Do you think the murderer will be there?" Her eyes widened at the terrible thought.

"He could be. I don't know the hospital staff, so you'll have to point out anyone you don't recognize." He rolled peas into a bite of mashed potatoes to keep them on his fork.

"Joe?"

He looked up. "Yes."

"If the murderer believes you know why Georgia wanted to see you, aren't you in danger too?"

He'd not expected her to make that leap. "If I'd had any ideas that pointed to his identify, I would have told the police last Monday. If he hasn't been questioned, then he must believe he's in the clear."

"Still, I'm worried about you."

"Please don't worry. After dinner, read your eulogy to me, and then let's continue our Cribbage tournament." He'd grown fond of the game while he'd served in the Coast Guard, and she'd played it on the beach with her friends as a child. He always had fun with her, and it led right where they both wanted to go.

CHAPTER 5

The chapel at the VA hospital overflowed with bouquets of white gladiolas and carnations surrounding the altar with a glorious snowy abundance. White roses tied with a white satin bow lay upon the open casket. The fragrant blooms perfumed the air with a lush garden's sweetness, but the mood of those gathered to bid Georgia Dixon farewell remained tearful. Nurses sat with the patients who had loved her, and both sniffed into their handkerchiefs with a muffled rhythm.

The organist, an ample-bottomed woman with silver curls, played familiar hymns while the last of the gatherers entered. The soft music hushed the scattered conversations, and most sat silently lost in their memories of the deceased.

Joe Ezell and Mary Margaret took seats toward the back of the chapel in order to observe the crowd while they paid their respects. He held her hand and smiled when she looked up at him. He raised a questioning brow, but no one looked out of place to her and she shook her head.

Curtis Mooney arrived with his brother Edwin. Both were handsomely dressed in navy blue suits. Curtis looked thoroughly miserable while Edwin simply appeared bored, as though he'd been forced to attend an extended board meeting. Curtis nodded to men he'd known while a patient and those remaining at the hospital greeted him with wide smiles.

"He must have been popular," Joe whispered.

"Of course, he was," Mary Margaret replied. "He's so good natured, he cheered up everyone he saw, including the doctors and nurses."

Joe still suspected that Georgia might have returned Curtis's affections much to Edwin's dismay. Edwin didn't strike him as a man who'd dirty his hands with something so crude as murder, however, but he had the money to pay someone to permanently remove a troublesome nurse.

A tall, rawboned woman in a starched nurse's uniform entered pushing a young man in a wheelchair. She had probably not been attractive even as a child, and a deep frown creased her pinched features. "Who is she?" Joe whispered.

"Gertrude Howland, the head nurse who often criticized Georgia's relationships with her patients. I'm surprised she's here. I thought she'd boycott the memorial on principle."

They were surprised to see Mike Torres, Georgia's landlord, enter with Patrick Wood. Joe had expected some of the other residents of the Chrysanthemum Court to attend. Maybe Polly Hill had gone to the hospital to have her baby, but he'd thought the retired postal worker and his wife would be there, as well as the young couple in banking.

People were still coming in as the hospital chaplain opened the service with a heartfelt tribute to Georgia's kindness and compassion that had touched her patients and members of the staff. He was a young man who had known her well, and his voice held the edge of tears.

Hearing the scrape of chair legs, Joe turned and saw Phyllis and John Cameron had arrived after all. They were seated in white folding chairs that had been added behind the last row of pews. A white-coated doctor stood alone in the corner behind them. He was a handsome, fair-haired young man, and clearly nearly overcome with sorrow.

Joe nudged Mary Margaret and nodded the man's direction. "That's Gabriel Webb, a surgeon," she murmured. "He hasn't been here long, but he looks heartbroken, doesn't he?"

"He does." Joe noted the other physicians seated nearby. They looked appropriately solemn, but none appeared to be nearly as distraught as Gabriel Webb. "I think we've found the man Georgia was seeing," he whispered. A woman seated in the pew in front of theirs turned to hush him, and he begged her forgiveness. He'd keep his thoughts to himself for the rest of the service, but he remained keenly on alert.

The nurses who had been closest to Georgia had chosen to speak in alphabetical order and Angie came forward to tell of a time she and Georgia had attempted to bake a cake to celebrate a patient's birthday. Unfortunately, their efforts were tasty, but too misshapen to share, and they'd bought him a cake from a bakery instead.

"Georgia had a talent for making each of her patients feel special in a meaningful way. We'll all miss her joy in life and gracious personality." Angie returned to the front pew and another of Georgia's friends followed her to the pulpit.

By the time Mary Margaret rose to give her remembrance of Georgia, most of those gathered were snuffling into their handkerchiefs. Except for Gertrude Howland, who was gazing out the pointed Gothic arched windows, perhaps lost in her own conflict with Georgia rather than sweet memories. She glanced at her watch, which Joe thought rude at such a gathering.

Mary Margaret had practiced her piece until she could have given it from memory. Joe thought she had done a splendid job despite Gertrude's inattention. He winked at her as she returned to her place beside him. She clasped his hand and focused on the last speaker. The chaplain then invited others who might wish to offer their thoughts and Gertrude had to push her patient's wheelchair to the front of the chapel. She moved off to the side as he spoke about how much he'd looked forward to seeing Georgia's friendly smile each day.

He was followed by other young men who had been grateful for Georgia's sincere interest in them. The memorial closed with the singing of *Amazing Grace.* Simple refreshments were offered in the adjoining hall and Joe looked for Gabriel Webb, but he had apparently already left. He simply couldn't help himself, approached Gertrude Howland, and introduced himself as a friend of Mary Margaret's.

"It must be especially difficult to lose such a fine nurse," he offered.

"Indeed," Gertrude uttered through clenched teeth. "You must excuse me, my patient mustn't become overtired."

Joe nodded and let her go, while the young man she'd been tending looked back over his shoulder, clearly wanting to remain a while longer. Joe stayed beside Mary Margaret and heard more stories about Georgia her friends had thought too personal to share.

"I'm sorry I didn't know her well," he remarked. "She must have been a wonderful friend as well as an excellent nurse."

His comment brought Angie to tears. "I managed to speak without weeping, but it was a challenge. I'll really miss her. After the graveside prayers, some of us are coming to my place for a drink. Do you want to come along?"

Mary Margaret gave her head a slight shake, and he understood she'd prefer to go alone. "I'm sorry, but I won't be able to go to the grave or your place. Can someone give Mary Margaret a ride?"

"I will," Angie assured him.

Joe waited a few more minutes and then kissed Mary Margaret on the cheek. "Find out what you can about Gabriel Webb," he whispered. "I'll pick you up after work tomorrow."

Rather than leave the hospital, Joe asked at the visitor reception desk where he might find Dr. Webb. The clerk gave him the directions to the physician's office, but doubted he'd be available. "That's all right if he isn't, I'll come back at another time."

Hospital corridors always struck him as a maze where even a bright rat would soon become lost. He succeeded in finding Dr. Webb's office, and the door stood open. He looked in.

"Dr. Webb, I'm Joe Ezell, a detective, and I'm looking into the death of Georgia Dixon. I'll make an appointment if this afternoon isn't convenient for you."

Gabriel stood by the window, his hands behind his back. "Today is as awful as it can possibly be, but tomorrow will be no better. Come on in." He took the chair behind his desk and gestured for Joe to take a padded visitor chair. "Are you with the police?"

Joe handed him his card. "I'm a private investigator, and Miss Dixon was killed right outside my office. I've no idea why she wished to speak with me, and I'm asking her friends if they might possibly know what troubled her." Up close, the doctor was even better looking than he'd been in the chapel. He had a movie star's chiseled jaw, vivid blue eyes, and his thick blond hair had a slight curl.

"What makes you think we were friends?" He studied Joe's card and set it aside.

"Miss Dixon was seeing someone, and I imagine hospital policy discourages dating among the staff. She didn't mention your name to her closest friends, but you're radiating a tangible sorrow, so she must have meant a great deal to you."

Gabriel opened his desk drawer, shuffled through a tray of pencils and found one newly sharpened. He reached for a scratchpad and wrote the date. "We'd dated briefly during the war when we both lived in San Diego, and lost track of each other until I came here to work. We'd both become more serious, and she was a woman any man would love."

The physician paused, apparently lost in his memories, and Joe spoke softly to lure him back to the present. "Did she mention someone or something she might have wanted me to investigate?"

He shook his head. "We both spent most of our time here, and we never talked about our patients, or what happens here. It was the very last thing we wished to do when we were together. We laughed a lot, and you can imagine the rest." He drew a line across the pad, as though crossing out whatever he might have written. "I'm sorry I can't help you. I wish I could."

Inspired by his wistful tone, Joe leaned forward. "Please contact me should you hear, or overhear something that strikes you as curious, wrong or in any way unsettling."

Gabriel frowned slightly. "I doubt I'd be any good at playing detective."

"Someone you work with may have killed Georgia. She could have discovered something that might have cost a doctor or nurse their career. A dangerous secret is a prime motive for murder."

The physician straightened up in his seat. "Unfortunate errors sometimes occur," he replied.

"Is there anyone who's particularly prone to them?" Joe inquired. "Is there someone on the staff you believe to be unqualified for the job he holds?"

Gabriel's laugh was closer to a dry cough. "There are several I'd like to see barred from practicing medicine anywhere, but that doesn't mean any of them would have killed Georgia to save themselves."

Joe shrugged slightly. "She was murdered for a reason. Give me a call if you think of something pertinent to my investigation." He stood and took a step toward the door. "It doesn't matter if it first strikes you as trivial. Call me rather than overlook it."

"Shouldn't I call the police?"

"Of course you should, but do so after you talk with me, please."

Joe left before he wore out his welcome, but he feared Dr. Webb hadn't taken him seriously. He found Detective Lynch standing outside the chapel by his Chevrolet and forced a smile. "Checking license plate numbers?" he asked.

The detective shoved his small notebook into his pocket. "Murderers often attend the funerals of their victims for the thrill. It sickens me, but it happens."

"I've heard that," Joe agreed. "What have you discovered so far?"

Lynch looked away. "Nothing I'd care to share with you. Watch your back, Mr. Ezell. You might have been the killer's original target."

"What makes you think so?" he asked.

"I stood outside the chapel door and listened to the near endless praise for Miss Dixon. With the obvious exception of one person, everyone seems to have loved her. If she wasn't the killer's first choice of target, then her death appears to have been a random killing, almost done for sport. Or, it could have been prompted by the Black Dahlia murder. It's received so much publicity, and a man who already possessed a hatred for women could have acted on it."

"Then he'll kill again, won't he?"

"I'm afraid so. If by some chance you stumble over anything interesting, give me a call. Don't attempt to solve the crime by yourself."

"That's excellent advice, I'm sure."

"Damn right it is." The detective crossed the street to an unmarked sedan and got in.

Joe waited for him to drive away before he unlocked his car door. A blond woman clad in gray hurried by and was gone before he'd gotten a good luck at her, but he thought she might have been the math teacher, Amy Hudson. She'd not kept the card with the memorial information, and he'd not expected to see her, but maybe she'd decided to come after all.

"Mr. Ezell!" Marty Streech hurried toward him. "I was hoping to catch you before you left. People are eager to give me charming anecdotes about Ms. Dixon, but no one has any idea who wanted her dead."

"Does that surprise you?"

"No, not at all, and it reinforces my theory that she's another victim of the Black Dahlia killer. Elizabeth Short liked to go out dancing and party, but she never did anyone any harm. Neither did Georgia Dixon."

"Detective Lynch mentioned the Black Dahlia, and you really ought to talk to him. He just left, and I'm sorry you missed him."

"I'll find him tomorrow," Marty promised. "You still have my card?"

"It's on my desk."

"Good." Marty turned away toward his car.

Joe watched him go and then checked his watch. He had the rest of the afternoon and evening free, and thought it a good time to call the retired detective and see what he could learn.

Henry Hilburn lived in the San Fernando Valley in a modest suburb popular with members of the LAPD. He was a tall, thin man with a round, bald head and a dark, piercing gaze. "I was surprised by your call, Mr. Ezell, although I'll admit to keeping in touch with the force for my own amusement."

They were seated out on the patio, and if there was a Mrs. Hilburn, she was nowhere about. Joe had accepted a bottle of icy cold beer and sipped it slowly. "Call me Joe. What can you tell me about Detective Jacob Lynch? We keep crossing paths in our investigations of Georgia Dixon's murder. He's ready to dismiss it as a random killing, but I'm sure there's a reason someone wanted her dead."

"Jacob Lynch," Hilburn mused thoughtfully. "I knew him. He dresses as well as the mayor, thanks to a rich wife from what I've heard. He could retire early, but maybe he'd rather not spend too much time at home, if you get my meaning."

"Interesting," Joe offered. Lou King had warned him Hilburn liked to talk, so he'd just sit and listen until something meaningful was said. "What's his reputation? Does he go after a suspect with real vigor, or is he more likely to sit back and gather clues?"

Hilburn gazed around his back yard. The grass was neatly trimmed, but there was little in the way of color. "He likes to be out and about, to be seen wherever he can be. I believe he's solved his share of crimes, and Los Angeles has plenty, but I don't recall him ever putting himself in harm's way to do so."

He remembered one case as being particularly involved, where Detective Lynch had received the credit for the combined work of several other men. "In other words, he isn't likely to share the spotlight. If it were a friend of mine who'd been killed, I wouldn't trust him to make an arrest. I'll see what I can learn about the case, if that's what you want."

"It would be a great help. Thank you." Joe left soon after he'd finished his beer, and promised to stay in touch. He could use a friend with an inside to the LAPD, and Henry had struck him as a man he could count on to tell him the truth.

CHAPTER 6

Douglas Wright scheduled an appointment with Joe Ezell for ten o'clock Monday morning. He arrived on time, and immediately plunged into his problem. "It's my wife, Betsy. She's the love of my life, and I'm afraid she's having an affair." He handed Joe a snapshot of her standing on their front porch.

Joe's new client was a dark-haired, heavy-set man with a booming voice. Fifty-pounds lighter, he might have been handsome, but today, he merely looked bloated and haggard. Joe studied the photo of the smiling woman. Rather than resemble a femme fatale, she looked remarkably sweet.

"What makes you suspect she's being unfaithful?"

At the question, Douglas began to weep. He pulled his handkerchief from his hip pocket and wiped his eyes before blowing his nose. "Forgive me, I'm not usually so, well, pathetic."

"There's nothing pathetic about loving your wife, Mr. Wright. When did you begin to suspect she might be seeing another man?"

"A couple of months ago. When I came home in the evening, she seemed, I don't know, brighter? She'd be dressed as though she'd been out, but she'd tell me she'd only been running errands and wanted to look her best. At first I thought she looked very nice, and appreciated it, but when it continued, I began to worry. I own a furniture store, and can't leave for hours at a time to follow her, and if she caught me, well, I don't even want to imagine how that might end."

"You'd like me to follow her and see what these 'errands' might be?" Joe asked.

"Yes. I need to know the truth, no matter how painful it might be. I'm not as handsome as I used to be, but who is? We can't all look like movie stars, can we?"

"No, sir. That's impossible, but if you're worried about your looks, you might want to add some exercise to your schedule and cut back on the size of your portions at mealtimes."

Douglas leaned back. "Is diet advice part of your service?"

Joe hadn't meant to insult his new client, but his recommendations had been sound. "All I mean is that women go to great lengths to be attractive to men, but unfortunately, many men aren't nearly as interested in keeping fit. I have your address, and I'll begin observing your wife this afternoon. It's possible she isn't going anywhere, but simply wants to be pretty when you come home in the evening."

Douglas blew his nose in a deep trumpet of barely suppressed grief. "Doubtful. We've not been blessed with children, so there's just the two of us. I took comfort in that until, well, until I began to worry she might want more than what I'm able to give."

"I hope my investigation will ease your mind," Joe offered sincerely. "You were right to come to me rather than give into worries that might prove to be far worse than the truth. I'll need fifty dollars as a retainer to begin." Douglas paid him without questioning the price.

"What happens when you find a woman's been cheating? Does she usually leave her husband for the other man?"

Joe had had more cases of women suspecting their husbands of stepping out on them than the opposite, and had no statistics to quote. "Each case is different, Mr. Wright. Give me a few days to observe your wife, and I'll call to schedule a time to present my report."

Douglas lurched to his feet. His handkerchief remained wadded in his right hand and Joe was grateful he didn't reach out to shake hands before he left. He walked him to the door, and shut it quietly behind him. He checked his watch and gave Douglas Wright time to leave the building before he grabbed his hat, and left to follow Betsy.

He parked down the street from their home in west Los Angeles. The houses in the neighborhood had been built in the 1920s, before the crash, and were small stucco structures their owners struggled to distinguish with colorful landscaping, and brightly painted front doors.

Betsy left home at 11:30 a.m. Joe followed her car through the traffic downtown to the Bullocks Department Store on the corner of Hill and 7th. The popular store connected to a second building on Broadway by the St. Vincent Court walkway. When Betsy entered the Bullocks' parking lot, he drove in after her and parked several spaces away to go unnoticed. He watched her walk through the employee entrance, and caught himself before he followed in right behind her. A guard was stationed at the door, and he greeted him warmly.

"Is this the entrance I use to apply for work?" Joe asked.

The man pointed to the sign. "Of course not. This is the entrance for employees. If you're not working here, you're not an employee, are you?"

Joe shrugged. "Guess not. Do you know where I should go to apply?"

The guard gave him the floor for personnel, and Joe thanked him. Douglas Wright hadn't said anything about his wife having a job, but clearly the guard was very particular about whom he admitted, so if Betsy hadn't worked there, he wouldn't have let her in. Joe entered the department store through the main doors and consulted the sign posted beside the bank of elevators. Douglas hadn't noticed his wife wearing a new perfume, so she probably wasn't a clerk at one of the fragrance or make-up counters. The fourth floor had women's clothing and lingerie, and he stepped into the next elevator going up.

He doubted there would be many men strolling the floor, and he'd tell anyone who asked that he was looking for a present for his girlfriend. He found a woman who resembled Betsy Wright working in Collegienne Sportswear. He edged close enough to read her nametag and sure enough, she was Mrs. Wright.

She was prettier up close than in a small photo, and he smiled and moved aside to wait for her to finish with a woman purchasing a blouse. When the shopper walked away, Betsy turned to him.

"May I help you?" she asked with a warm, welcoming smile.

"Yes. I want to buy a present for my girlfriend, and I'm not sure what to get."

Betsy came out from behind the counter to talk with him. "Tell me about her; is she tall, petite, how would you describe her?"

Joe noticed another clerk observing them with a stern, forbidding frown. He wondered if she thought men shouldn't be shopping in her section, or if she was annoyed Betsy had spoken to him before she could.

"She's five foot two, which I suppose is petite, with a cute figure. She has red hair and green eyes. She's a nurse and always eager to get out of her uniform by the end of the day. No, wait, that didn't sound right." Sincerely embarrassed, he didn't have to merely pretend to be.

She laughed with him. "I understand. She must prefer colorful clothes when she's not on duty. We have some beautiful sweaters in blues and greens that would compliment her coloring."

"A sweater would be a nice gift, wouldn't it?"

"Yes, it's a very thoughtful gift."

She walked with him to the display and the sweaters were so pretty, he decided to buy one for Mary Margaret. "I suppose she'd wear a small."

Betsy unfolded an emerald green sweater and held it up for him to judge. She was taller than Mary Margaret with a more rounded figure, but Joe got the idea. "Yes, that looks good. The green is pretty, but the blue is striking too."

"I understand, green is so green after all, isn't it?" She picked up the blue sweater. It was the vivid hue of a summer sky. "She could wear this all year."

"I'm sure she will. I'll take it."

"Would you like to have it gift wrapped?"

"No. It isn't for a special occasion; it's just because I love her."

"Aren't you sweet." She carried the sweater to the register. "I do have tissue paper and a box, will that do?"

"It will be perfect." Joe opened his wallet and was relieved he actually had the money, thanks to her husband's deposit, to pay for it. "You're a wonderful saleslady. Have you been working here long?"

"No, just a few weeks. I don't have children, and one can only spend so much time keeping house before the walls begin to close in on you."

"You needed some excitement," Joe offered.

She laughed. "A part-time job is as much excitement as I can stand, and I'm saving what I earn to put toward a vacation. My husband works much too hard, and I want to surprise him on our anniversary. I'm sorry, that's probably more than you wanted to know."

"Not at all, I could listen to stories of happy marriages all day. It gives me hope." He took the bag she offered, thanked her again, and left with what was one of the few uplifting cases he'd had. He looked over his shoulder and saw the frowning clerk still looked pained even if he had bought something rather than merely lurk.

Bullocks had a great soup bar below street level, and he looked forward to having his lunch there. He enjoyed getting out of the office; it was the best part of the job, and if he could work in lunch, so much the better.

When Joe drove to the VA hospital late that afternoon, Mary Margaret was waiting for him with her friend Angie, who was blonde, and taller than Mary Margaret, but then most women were. He got out of his car to speak with them. "If you've learned something, let's find a bench on the grounds and talk there."

"Right, we don't want anyone eavesdropping," Mary Margaret replied. "I want Angie to tell you how she got along with Curtis on Saturday. There was no time to talk yesterday at the memorial."

"Can't wait to hear it," Joe answered.

They walked past the first vacant bench and went on to one shaded by a pepper tree where they could be certain they'd not to be overheard. As soon as they were all seated, Angie began to speak with animated gestures. "I have a car, and drove to Curtis's home Saturday morning. He remembered me, or said he did, and we went out on the patio and played Gin Rummy for an hour or so. His brother, Edwin, came out to check on us, when he could have more easily just glanced out the window if he were curious about what we were doing. Quite frankly, he gave me the creeps."

"In what way?" Joe asked.

"It was just the way he looked at me, as though he were interested in spending time with me himself."

"I've met Edwin, and he didn't strike me as the type who'd like to flirt," Joe responded. He glanced toward Mary Margaret who nodded in agreement.

"He stood too close, looked over my shoulder to see what cards I held and pointed to which one I ought to discard. He completely spoiled the game, and I suggested we use the pool. I'd brought my swimsuit because Georgia told me

Curtis liked to swim. Rather than ask the housekeeper, Edwin showed me to a room where I could change my clothes. It was a bedroom with a lock on the door, and I used it. Then he came outside again and sat to watch us swim. Curtis likes to race, which was fun even if I couldn't catch him, but I could feel Edwin watching me the whole time.

"The three of us ate lunch together on the patio by the pool. Edwin didn't say much, but again, he watched me too closely and made me uncomfortable. I ate as quickly as I could and asked Curtis if he'd like to go to the movies. There was a Roy Rogers' film playing, *Bells of San Angelo*, I knew he'd enjoy. It's a story about smuggling silver from an American mine with chases across the Mexican border, and is in color. I was so glad to have my own car to drive us, rather than have to depend on Edwin, and we left as soon as we'd changed into our street clothes.

"Edwin had given Curtis money for the tickets and popcorn, but I had to remind him he'd be paying. He hummed along with the songs, but no one seated nearby seemed to care. When I took him home, Edwin wanted to know all about the movie. Curtis knew it was a Western with lots of horses and music, but Edwin shouldn't have put him on the spot by asking for details. I left the first minute I could, and I'd rather not go back, but Curtis is too sweet to abandon. I'll make plans to take him to the zoo next Saturday, or anywhere else we can be away from his house for the day, and avoid spending any time near Edwin."

"Did Georgia ever complain about Edwin being intrusive?" Joe asked.

Mary Margaret shook her head. "Not that I recall. She liked Curtis, and perhaps overlooked Edwin's subtle advances. I wish we knew more."

"Was I any help at all?" Angie asked.

"Yes," Joe assured her. "Edwin probably behaved the same way with you as he did with Georgia, and I doubt he'd take rejection well."

Angie shuddered and rubbed her arms as though chilled. "If Georgia had told him to keep his distance, could he have been so insulted he'd want her dead?"

"He's used to getting his way, so maybe. Let's just leave his name in the suspect column for now." He stood and walked Angie to her car before leaving with Mary Margaret.

"I'm relieved I didn't have to stay with Curtis on Saturday," she confided. "I'd have quickly made certain Edwin understood we'd be all right on our own, and he'd probably have sent me home."

"It's possible Edwin stuck close simply because he didn't want Curtis to become as attached to Angie as he had been with Georgia."

"Wouldn't he have just fired Georgia if he thought they were too close? Curtis might have been upset, but probably not for long when his memory is so poor."

"That's true, but our other theory involves Georgia discovering something Edwin didn't want known. From now on, I'll make it a point to ask anyone who calls my office why they are seeking my help. I won't need details over the phone, but enough to know whether it's a case of petty theft from a shop, or adultery. I wish I'd begun the practice before Georgia called."

They had dinner at a favorite Italian place, and Joe waited until he had taken Mary Margaret home to give her the sweater. "I was on an assignment in Bullocks, saw this and thought of you."

She opened the box and peeled away the tissue paper. "It's beautiful, and I love the color. I wish I had a present to give you." She leaned over to kiss him, and then stood and draped the sweater around her shoulders. She looked into the mirror in the entranceway. "What sort of job took you to Bullocks?"

"As easy one for a change." He came up behind her, wrapped his arms around her waist and gave her a warm hug. "Or at least it appears so for the time being."

She turned in his arms to kiss him. "Let's hope it stays that way."

Unfortunately, it didn't. Joe waited a day to call Douglas Wright and saw him late Wednesday afternoon. He greeted him with a hearty handshake. "I've good news, and you've no reason to worry."

As soon as Douglas was seated, Joe told him about Betsy's job at Bullocks. "She enjoys getting out and seeing people, and she's saving her earnings for a surprise for you."

Stricken, Douglas's face drained of color. "You mean she doubts I can provide for her?"

Joe swore he felt the room tilt. "No, Mr. Wright. Your wife is simply bored staying at home, and she enjoys working at Bullocks. It's a beautiful store, and it's a welcome change of routine. It has nothing whatsoever to do with your ability to provide."

His client sunk into a dejected slump. "Maybe she blames me that we haven't been blessed with children."

Joe drew in a deep breath and exhaled slowly. "Are you simply looking for trouble where none exists? Your wife found an enjoyable part-time job. Many women work outside the home, and it's no disgrace to their husbands. All you need do is pretend you don't know and act surprised when she tells you about the money she's saved."

His deep frown didn't lift. "I don't like her lying to me, and I'll not lie to her."

Greatly annoyed, Joe struggled to hold onto his temper. "You told me your wife seemed 'brighter'. You ought to appreciate her new sparkle rather than sulk. Were you hoping I'd discover she had a wealthy lover who owned a limo and a yacht?"

"No! Of course not, but I'm just shocked she'd get a job without telling me." He straightened up and brushed his hand over his hair.

"It's part of the surprise," Joe restated. "Be grateful Betsy loves you and wants to provide something special. What would you have said if she'd mentioned getting a part-time job?"

"I'd have forbidden it. Most married women don't work unless they have to, and she doesn't. It just wouldn't look right."

Joe nodded thoughtfully. "Now do you understand why she didn't ask? She's avoided an argument, and when you learn about the surprise, you'll be too happy to criticize her for making the decision on her own. Besides, how can you reveal you've learned she's working at Bullocks without admitting you hired me to follow her?"

Douglas stared at the floor. "So, I'm no better than she is, is that what you're saying?"

"No, I'm saying don't be a fool when you have such a devoted wife. Have you ever considered having her work with you at the furniture store? She's an excellent saleswomen, and would draw in new business."

Thoroughly uncomfortable, Douglas twisted in his seat. "I could use some help with sales, but I never thought of hiring Betsy."

"Well, think about it," Joe advised. "When is your anniversary?"

"It's next month."

"Why don't you wait until she offers the surprise, and be sure to look appropriately amazed when she tells you she has a part-time job. Give her an especially nice present too. Then a day or so later, ask if she'd consider coming to work with you. Tell her you've been thinking about it for a while."

"You think she'd leave Bullocks to work with me?"

"Sure she would. Just be patient, and everything should work out beautifully. I don't say that to many clients, so be grateful, Mr. Wright. Now I only worked one day on your case, so I owe you a partial refund."

Douglas considered his situation as he pulled himself to his feet. "Keep it all, Mr. Ezell. Your advice was well-worth it."

"Thank you for taking it," Joe responded. As with most of his cases, he'd solved a problem, but would never know where it led. In the Wright's case, he hoped they would have a wonderful anniversary vacation and that Betsy would be eager to go to work with her husband. He had Douglas' business card. Maybe in a few months, he could stop by the furniture store and see how everything had worked out.

As Joe left his office that afternoon, the accountant, Stephen Bennett, was also leaving his. "I haven't seen you in a while. How was your vacation?" Joe asked.

Bennett was a trim, gray-haired man and always more serious than the occasion required. "Too short. I had to come in to work on settling a client's estate."

"I hope he wasn't a close friend."

Stephen paused at the top of the stairway. "No, but a client is a client."

Believing he might not see the accountant again for a while, Joe had a question for him. "If you have a minute, could you tell me how someone heading up a large corporation could siphon off funds?"

Bennett frowned. "What's his reason? Is he hoping to cover the cost of a gambling debt, or perhaps eager to provide for the expense of a mistress or a collection of racing cars?"

"It's a hypothetical question, so it doesn't matter what the reason is."

"Of course it does," Bennett insisted. "If it's a small sum, he could pad his expense account. If he needs more, he might create an expense that didn't actually exist, a phony charity for example. In a large firm, accountants would handle the finances, and board members would expect yearly reports and audits. Few read them, however, and deductions for the phony charity could slip by unnoticed. That's asking for a whole lot of trouble from the IRS, however. It would be far easier to simply increase his salary. Is this for a case of yours?"

"No. I'm investigating motives for a murder."

The accountant rolled his eyes. "Well, my late client wasn't murdered, but his heirs are at each others' throats over who'll inherit his money. Do you have a will?"

"No, I've nothing to leave anyone," Joe replied.

"Draw up one anyway," Bennett advised, "then you can add details when you do have property to leave to your heirs." He hurried on down the stairs, and Joe returned to his office to make a few notes.

The Mooney family was known for their generous support of worthwhile charities. Edwin might have created one that paid into his own pocket, but why would he risk his family's fine reputation in the community? Maybe he wanted an extra deduction at tax time, but if so, would he have left evidence of the scheme on his desk where Georgia might have found it?

"That's a stretch," he murmured. It was far more likely Edwin's motives had been far more personal and concerned Georgia's relationship with Curtis. Joe leaned back in his chair and tapped his pencil on his desk. He trusted his instincts, and felt something was off about Edwin Mooney. From Angie's report, she also thought he was creepy. Being creepy wasn't a crime, however, or a lot more people would be serving time.

Joe kept an eye on his watch and drove to the VA hospital to meet Mary Margaret. When he found her standing in front speaking with Gabriel Webb, a fierce stab of jealousy shot through him, and he hated it. Facts were facts, however. Gabriel was a handsome physician, and a smart woman might choose to be a doctor's bride rather than a humble detective's.

Mary Margaret saw Joe coming toward them, and she rushed to meet him. She grabbed hold of his arm and reached up on her tiptoes to kiss his cheek. "Gabriel, Dr.

Webb, wants to set up a scholarship for nursing students in Georgia's memory. Do you want to help us plan over dinner?"

Joe pulled back. The last thing he wanted to do was to dine with Gabriel Webb, but he wasn't about to leave Mary Margaret alone with him either. "What a great idea. Of course I want to come."

"Do you like Lawry's?" Gabriel asked. "I haven't eaten all day and could use a thick slice of prime rib. It will be on me."

It was difficult to find a smile, but Joe struggled to look pleased rather than horribly embarrassed he couldn't afford the popular restaurant on his own. They agreed to meet there, and Joe found a parking place on La Cienega rather than pull into the valet parking lot. He helped Mary Margaret from the car, and gave her hand a fond squeeze.

"I can't remember the last time I ate here. It must have been before the war."

"I haven't been here in a long while either," she whispered, "but Gabriel, Dr. Webb, apparently has plenty of money and doesn't mind sharing it."

Joe halted on the sidewalk. "I don't want to take advantage."

"We won't be. Now be sweet and let's see how much we can decide tonight. It will probably take several meetings to settle all the details."

"Great."

The interior of Lawry's was as elegant as the items on the menu, with plenty of forest green leather and rich, dark woods. Joe sat across from Gabriel with Mary Margaret taking a chair between them facing the fireplace. The enticing aroma of roast beef filled the air and made his stomach rumble. "I don't recall eating lunch either," he admitted. Their waiter handed him a menu and he chose the prime rib with Yorkshire pudding as quickly as Gabriel had.

Mary Margaret took more time to peruse the choices and ordered salmon with the asparagus and creamed spinach. She returned her companions' incredulous glances with a sassy tilt of her chin. "Not everyone enjoys a huge slab of beef at the end of the day."

Gabriel laughed, and instantly looked five years younger. "I didn't say a thing, and I wanted you to order whatever you wished."

"I did," she assured him.

Joe wasn't about to allow them to flirt in front of him, and with Georgia dead little more than a week, he considered it in very poor taste. "The scholarship is a meaningful tribute. Did you intend for it to be for a student at a particular school, or could anyone studying nursing apply?"

"Georgia attended the UCLA School of Nursing, so it's my first choice," Gabriel responded. "Finding the time to handle the details will be the main problem."

"All her friends will want to help," Mary Margaret assured him. "Leave everything to us, and we'll see what must be done to set up a scholarship."

"Thank you. I'll make the first donation to get it started, and when the scholarship actually exists, we can encourage others to contribute," Gabriel offered.

"Sounds like a good plan," Joe agreed. He listened as Gabriel and Mary Margaret discussed whether the scholarship should be based on merit or financial need. They talked at length, each taking first one side and then the opposite while he waited for an opening to say something that wouldn't make it painfully obvious he knew absolutely nothing about the subject under discussion.

He was greatly relieved when a chef rolled a covered cart to their table and slid it open to show off four standing rib roasts. He swallowed hard to keep from drooling as the man carved thick slices for Gabriel and him. Their waiter returned with Mary Margaret's plate and once their sides were served, they were all too hungry to carry on much in the way of conversation.

Joe watched how deftly Gabriel handled his knife, which could certainly be expected, but it suddenly struck him that he had heard only the physician's account of his relationship with Georgia. No one else, not even her closest friends, knew anything about them as a couple. He wiped his mouth on his napkin, and schooled his features rather than look as worried as he'd suddenly become.

"A reporter with the *LA Examiner* came by the hospital today, asking questions about Georgia," Gabriel said.

"Marty Streech?" Mary Margaret asked. "He spoke to several of us after the memorial, but we didn't like him either."

"I didn't say I didn't like him," Gabriel corrected softly. "I refused to see him so we've never met."

"I've met him," Joe interjected, grateful to finally have something valuable to say. "He struck me as an earnest reporter, and he hopes to tie Georgia's death to the Black Dahlia's. Why was he interested in speaking with you?"

Gabriel looked up. "I believe he asked to speak with any physician who'd worked with Georgia. He didn't single me out."

"How could he when no one knew you were seeing her?" Mary Margaret asked.

Joe held his breath and when Gabriel shrugged and continued to enjoy his dinner, he spoke. "After you set up the scholarship, people will assume you two were close."

"Whatever they assume is fine," Gabriel replied, "but I want the focus to be on the scholarship in Georgia's memory, not on me."

If he didn't understand his generous offer of a scholarship would make him a suspect, Joe would not point it out.

When they entered Mary Margaret's apartment, she tossed her keys on the table and turned to face Joe. "You were awfully quiet on the ride home. Please don't be jealous of Gabriel Webb."

"I'm not," Joe lied, and he hoped smoothly.

"Good, because he's really not my type." She cuddled up close. "And you are."

"Why is that?" A slow smile tugged the corner of his mouth.

"He doesn't make me laugh. I realize this is an awful time for him, but humor doesn't appear to be part of his character."

"I'm good for a laugh. Is that it?" he teased.

"That's not the way I put it." She reached up to kiss him, and he kissed her back.

He took her hand and led her to the sofa. "Let's think about Dr. Webb for a minute. If Georgia didn't tell anyone she was dating him, then we only have his word that they were a couple."

She drew back. "Why would he lie about it?"

"Why indeed."

"Oh no, Joe, you don't think he killed her do you?"

"He could have, but I doubt her death had anything whatsoever to do with the Black Dahlia's. He told me he'd dated Georgia when they were both in San Diego. What if she moved to Los Angeles to avoid him, and he followed her here?"

She drew her lower lip through her teeth. "It's plausible, I suppose. But if he'd come to her apartment when she didn't want to see him, wouldn't the neighbors have heard the two of them arguing?"

He spoke softly, "It's possible to carry on a heated argument in hoarse whispers."

"What about the scholarship? Do you think it's simply a smokescreen?"

"Could be, but he hasn't realized how swiftly he'll be drawing attention to himself."

"Would you like coffee?" she asked.

"No, I'm fine. Fix some for yourself if you'd like." He followed her into her kitchen. It was barely big enough to turn around, and he stayed out of her way. "Did Georgia ever strike you as the secretive sort?"

"No, she was very open and friendly, but now that I think of it, she would listen more than she talked. I know you like to pursue one theory after another until you find the truth, but I just can't accept Gabriel Webb as a killer."

"You hardly know the man," Joe reminded her. "If you're going to work on the scholarship with him, make certain to do it at the hospital and with friends present. Don't ever be alone with him."

She turned away from the coffee pot to face him. "Tell me again that you're not jealous."

"I shouldn't have to. It's gotten late. Let's call it a night."

"Fine, I'll walk you to the door. See you tomorrow?"

He bent down to give her a quick kiss. "Maybe, I'm not sure yet." He left grateful she wasn't the type to fight over nonsense as some women were. As perhaps Georgia Dixon had been.

CHAPTER 7

Joe couldn't sleep, and he blamed a stomach too full of prime rib, which was his own damn fault. He quickly grew bored with staring at the ceiling, tossed back the covers, stretched, and went into the living room to check the bookcase for something to read.

As soon as he flipped on the light, he was struck by how small and uninteresting his apartment was compared to Mary Margaret's bright and attractive home. The walls were a pale tan and the upholstered sofa and easy chair were covered in brown tweed meant to hide stains and wear through several tenants before they would have to be reupholstered. The rug was new, but a muted brown pattern that added no sense of style to the room.

Mary Margaret's place was far roomier, her furniture more colorful and comfortable, and the artwork on the walls hadn't been included in the rent. Those sad impressions swiftly brought him to how far he was from being able to propose to the only girl he'd ever loved. He'd have to boost his income to improve his chances, which meant he needed to sharpen his skills as a detective to attract more complex cases and better paying clients.

That decided, he reached for his copy of the Complete Works of Sherlock Holmes. He had always enjoyed the complicated stories and the brilliant Scottish detective's remarkable solutions to puzzling crimes. Sherlock possessed an intensity of concentration and passion for detail any detective would admire.

Joe believed he did well in assessing his clients' emotions, but he missed the frayed cuff or callused fingertips Sherlock would quickly notice and relate to an occupation or a crime. That meant he ought to work at being more aware. He'd begin first thing tomorrow, and opened the book to *The Hound of the Baskerville's,* one of his favorites.

The first appointment at Discreet Investigations on Thursday morning was with Jeanne Roth, a young woman who was concerned with her boyfriend's sudden passion for tennis. Joe had gotten the initial information during her first telephone call, and hoped he'd not have to be knowledgeable about the intricacies of the sport.

He made notes to keep the interview fresh in his mind. Jeanne appeared to be in her early thirties. Her figure was more stocky than voluptuous, and her mouse brown hair failed to compliment her delicate features. Her large hazel eyes were bright, clearly she was an intelligent woman, and he listened closely as she explained her dilemma.

"Earl Seeley and I live in the same apartment building. That's how we met. We've been dating nearly a year, and I don't want to waste another minute on the man if he's not as seriously interested in a future together as he claims."

She was dressed in a tailored navy-blue suit and a broad-brimmed black straw hat. He tried to discern her occupation from her appearance, but too many possibilities from bookkeeper to librarian came to mind. "I understand completely, Miss Roth. Was it difficult for you to leave work to meet with me today?"

"No, I'm the principal of a private elementary school, and occasionally need to be off campus for an hour or two."

She looked exactly like a school principal now that she'd said it. He'd not thought of it, but his question had prompted the desired result, and it pleased him. "You're wise to question the merits of your relationship before you become too deeply involved with Mr. Seeley. Tell me why you've become suspicious."

"He's begun leaving early on Saturday mornings, dressed in white tennis shorts, white shirt, and shoes for the game. He says his instructor is helping him develop a more powerful serve. Earl describes his lessons in detail, but I've noticed he returns looking as fresh and neatly pressed as when he left. He claims he showers at the tennis club before coming home."

Joe nodded thoughtfully. "So you've a good reason to suspect Earl is playing more than tennis."

"Thank you for taking my concerns seriously." She gave him her apartment address, and a photo taken with Earl at a restaurant. He was a sandy-haired fellow with a bright smile. She had a card from the tennis club where he supposedly played.

"You don't play tennis?" Joe asked.

"No, I'm not the athletic sort or I'd have signed up for lessons myself to keep an eye on Earl."

"You're wise to trust me with the matter. I'll come by on Saturday morning and follow Earl. If he's playing tennis as he claims, it will put your mind at ease."

She rose. "Thank you, Mr. Ezell. I've always prided myself on having a natural appreciation for character, but unfortunately, romance has played havoc with my judgment and common sense."

Grateful she understood, Joe showed her to the door. He made a fresh pot of coffee and returned to his desk to again focus on Georgia Dixon's murder. He scanned his diagram. What had he overlooked? Were there clues aplenty Sherlock Holmes would have caught instantly that he'd missed? He kept thinking of how quickly Detective Lynch had grasped the bathroom doorknob. Clearly he'd been searching for the bloody aftermath of the murder rather than fingerprints.

Inspired to replay the tragic scene, he went out into the hall. He went down a few steps and pretended to follow Georgia up the stairway. Apparently she hadn't seen or heard the man coming so he must have been wearing soft-soled shoes. Or, he could have left his shoes at the back entrance. He could have tiptoed around to the front of the building in his socks, but surely someone would have noticed his lack of shoes before Georgia died. He dismissed that possibility as absurd.

He practiced sneaking up the stairs and if he moved slowly, the sound of his footsteps remained too soft to hear. When CC arrived, he involved him in the reenactment.

"Good morning, CC. I'm going to stand by my office door. Will you please come up the stairs again so I can see when whoever followed Georgia would have been visible?"

"Yes, sir, happy to help." The custodian went back to the entrance of the building and came up the steps slowly. "Is this right?"

"Yes, thank you. Stay close to the far wall." Joe's office door was a dozen feet past the stairwell. Georgia's purse had lain open when he'd first seen it. It could have fallen open when she dropped it, or she could have been looking through it for something she meant to show him. If her attention had been focused on her purse, she might not have noticed she was being followed.

Joe looked down, as though preoccupied, and CC remained out of his line of sight until he reached the landing. He turned toward CC. "At nine o'clock, a man wearing a hat and coat would have looked as though he were on his way to his office. Georgia might even have greeted him and turned away. But rather than walking by, the man must have grabbed her hair and slit her throat before she could regard him as a threat."

CC shivered. "I don't like thinking about that morning."

"Neither do it, but Georgia deserves to have her murder solved."

"Yes, sir, she does. I'll concentrate on that angle instead."

There was a bench outside Joe's office door, and Georgia could have been seated. "Would you please come up the stairs once more, CC?" Joe sat on the end of the bench, and CC quickly came into view. Even if Georgia had been searching through her purse, had she been seated, she would have noticed a man as he approached the landing.

"Thanks for your help, CC."

"Anytime." CC went on down the hallway to his janitor's closet by the restroom.

Joe quickly followed him. "Do you keep this closet locked?"

"Yes, sir, I do." He pulled the chain clipped to his belt and removed the key from his pocket to unlock the door. "I don't worry that the tenants would steal the mops and brooms, but it's my job to clean up any mess they make, and I like to keep everything in order."

The restroom door had frosted glass at the top half. The custodian's closet was solid wood like the office doors with the purpose printed in small gold lettering. Detective Lynch hadn't tried the door before he went down the backstairs, so he'd apparently thought it unlikely the murderer could be hiding there. But he hadn't even tried the door. That was another mark against Lynch in Joe's view.

Joe went back to his office, and quickly recalled Georgia didn't own a car, so she would have taken a bus to see him. There was a display of bus schedules near the entrance of the drug store downstairs, and he went down to look through them. William Raymond, the pharmacist who owned the building, saw him from his counter and waved.

Wanting to keep a good relationship with his landlord, whenever Joe was in the drug store he made a point of speaking with him. First, he turned away from the counter to look out the front window at the bus stop. The pharmacist had a clear view of people leaving and boarding the bus. He should have noticed it earlier.

"Did Detective Lynch ask if you'd seen Georgia Dixon get off the bus the morning she was murdered?"

Dr. Raymond was a man in his fifties. He kept his graying hair cut short and a neatly trimmed mustache accented his smile. He was a friendly man, or made a point of being so to encourage customers to return often. "No, Lynch looked around, asked a few questions about the tenants and left his card. The bus comes by every fifteen minutes or so, and I haven't noticed who's coming and going for years. You think she rode the bus here?"

"I do." He opened the schedule for her neighborhood. She rode a bus from a pick-up close to the Chrysanthemum Court to the VA hospital. She would have boarded a different bus line to reach his office. He traced the times with his fingertip. "She could have been on the eight forty-five bus, it's the closest one to our appointment time. I was here before nine o'clock and discovered her body."

"That's not a horror I'll soon forget," Dr. Raymond offered. "It hasn't harmed business though. People often seem drawn to the ghoulish, as you must have discovered."

"I have. Whenever I introduce myself as a detective, the first question asked is how many murders I might have solved. It's plain they're hoping for gory details."

A woman approached the counter with a prescription and Joe left Dr. Raymond to attend to business. He walked out front, and wondered if the murderer could have also ridden the eight forty-five bus with Georgia. People rode the same bus to work every day, and someone might have noticed Georgia and caught a glimpse of a man who got off at the same stop and followed her into the building.

Monday morning, he'd ride the bus and see if anyone remembered the morning of the murder. It had happened less than two weeks ago, so someone might recall a girl as pretty as Georgia had been.

* * *

That night, he told Mary Margaret how he'd extended his investigation, and his plan to be on the bus.

"Do you think Detective Lynch might have already questioned those riding the bus that morning?" she asked.

"From what I've heard, he's not the most thorough man on the force, so I doubt it. I'll drive over to the Chrysanthemum Court and take the bus to my office. I have Georgia's photo from the *Los Angeles Times* to show. In any group, there is usually someone who keeps an eye on everyone else. I'm hoping such a person regularly rides that particular bus."

Mary Margaret nodded thoughtfully. "Wouldn't they have gone to the police?"

"They might not be aware of the murder so they wouldn't have made the connection. What I'm hoping is that whoever killed Georgia followed her off the bus and that someone can describe him accurately enough to be recognized. If so, I'll give their name to Detective Lynch and let him deal with it."

"Good plan. If Georgia was focused on removing something from her purse as she waited outside your office, what do you suppose it could have been, a photo or a letter?"

"Those were my first thoughts, and it must have been alarming to inspire her to call me. I'm often at the office before nine o'clock. I wish I had been there that morning."

"It scares me just thinking about it, Joe. Losing Georgia has been so terribly sad, and I'm so glad you weren't murdered too."

"So am I." He leaned close to kiss her, and pushed any thought of death from his mind.

Joe got up early Saturday morning, and forced the requisite eagerness to trail Earl Seeley. He parked across the street from the pink stucco building where both Earl and Jeanne Roth lived. Stately palm trees grew high above the two-story structure, and a lacy display of white azaleas bloomed along the front walkway.

He didn't have long to wait before Earl Seeley came bounding out of the building dressed in white and carrying a tennis racquet in one hand and a can of tennis balls in the other. He got into a Dodge coupe and drove away with Joe maintaining a discreet distance as he followed. He had checked the location of the tennis club on an Auto Club map, and Earl was headed in the opposite direction.

"This doesn't look good," he murmured to himself. He'd hoped Earl had actually been playing tennis simply for a break in his routine, but no, the man appeared to be headed for trouble rather than a tennis lesson.

Earl turned into Herbert's Drive-In at Beverly Blvd. and Fairfax. Seconds after he'd killed the engine, a slim young woman with long black hair slid into the front seat beside him. Joe parked two spaces away where he had a good view of the pair. The drive-in was built in a streamlined style with parking circling the round building. At night, neon lights enhanced the modern structure with a garish glow. Their food was good, and when the carhop came to Joe's car, he ordered bacon and eggs without needing to see a menu.

Drive-In restaurants had become popular in Los Angeles before the war, and Joe frequently stopped by one when he had finished a surveillance. It gave him time to write a few notes while his thoughts were fresh, and he reached for his notebook now. To the casual observer, he'd appear to be a salesman planning his morning's stops.

Earl and his pretty companion ate breakfast from the trays the carhop attached outside their lowered windows. Joe ate his own breakfast while he kept them in view. They were laughing, clearly enjoying themselves. Joe had already finished eating and paid his bill before they were ready to pay for theirs. He drove out of the drive-in's lot and parked on the street. He held his camera steady, and when the young woman left Earl's car, he took a quick photo of her. She hurried to a Chevrolet she had parked on the street and drove away.

Joe was being paid to follow Earl, who now drove to the tennis club. He was there half an hour, and emerged looking as well-groomed as when he'd entered. Maybe he'd taken a brief lesson, or simply sat in the lobby reading magazines. He drove back to the pink apartment building and remained inside. Joe could report on the man's activities on a Saturday morning, and eating breakfast with a woman involved the mere hint of scandal, but he knew Jeanne Roth would see the whole episode differently.

Joe met Hal Marten at the driving range that afternoon to work on chip shots. "It takes practice to move a ball out of a sand trap onto the green for an easy putt." He dropped a ball into the sand, and showed how an effective chip shot was done.

Hal followed Joe's directions. He was a serious student of the game, and improving every week. He dug his feet into the sand and worked on an effective swing. "I get it, I need to keep my head down."

"Right, don't try to shovel the ball out of the sand, lift it with the force of your swing."

"Finesse is the key to a great many things," Hal responded.

Joe laughed. "Especially women."

They stepped aside to allow other men space to practice. "Speaking of women, how are things going with Mary Margaret?" Hal asked.

"Fine, love is wonderful, but if I solve Georgia Dixon's murder, I hope to be hired on more complex cases and be better able to provide for her. Frankly, I'm tired of following people simply to catch them cozying up to Mr. or Miss Wrong." He briefly described his morning. "The man did actually go to a tennis club, but he stopped to have breakfast with an attractive young woman on the way."

"Breakfast?" Hal asked. "That seems innocent enough, but I suppose it could mean more."

"Who knows? I report only on what I actually saw rather than analyze cases to justify behavior. I'm saving that energy to work on Georgia's murder."

"Granted it's a far more important case than who ate breakfast with whom."

"It sure it is, and I haven't forgotten Georgia was a real woman her friends loved, and not merely an intriguing puzzle."

Hal made three successful shots out of the sand trap before he spoke. "California West has its share of clients with questionable claims. If we have a particularly difficult case, would you consider handling it?"

"Sure, insurance fraud would be a welcome change of pace. The name Discreet Investigations invites infidelity cases, and I should have come up with a better name in the first place."

"Your office hasn't been open long, so a name change shouldn't hurt business. You can always emphasize discretion in your ads."

"I could. You've made a good start with chip shots, let's go over to the putting green to finish the lesson."

"Fine. After working in an office all week, spending an afternoon outdoors is paradise. You're an excellent instructor, Joe. Have you considered giving others lessons?"

Hal was sincere, but Joe wasn't interested. "Thank you, but scheduling would be a problem with detective work taking most of my time some days. I'm teaching you so I'll have someone to play with, and you'll be able to impress the bigwigs at California West. Now there's a powerful name. Investigations West just doesn't have the same ring to it. And people would ask if I took cases going south, east, or north."

They continued brainstorming new names for Discreet Investigations, but none of their ideas caught hold with Joe, and they focused instead on putting.

* * *

Saturday night, Mary Margaret greeted Joe with a kiss. "I'm hungry for onion rings. Could we go to the Jumpin' Plate? You like their burgers."

"Sounds good. Let's go."

The Jumpin' Plate's menu featured a dozen different burgers, onion rings, French fries, milk shakes and delicious homemade pies. The homey décor conjured up a loving grandmother's kitchen. The walls were painted a pale blue, and the wooden tables had chairs with thick cushions covered in blue and white gingham. The placemats showed a farm scene with every type of animal a farmer might raise.

Joe drew in a deep breath. "This place smells absolutely heavenly."

"Do you suppose they have fry cooks in heaven busy making bottomless baskets of fries?"

"They must." He studied the menu and decided on the Italian burger on sourdough bread. "I'll get fries."

Mary Margaret chose the old-fashioned burger with lettuce, tomato and a pickle on the side with her onion rings. "We should come here more often," she suggested.

"We could work our way through the choices of burgers, and then start with the pies."

"That might take us a whole year." The thought made her smile. "The committee working on the scholarship met this afternoon. Dr. Webb had a surgery scheduled and couldn't join us. I doubt we'll see much of him. He did open a bank account and deposit five thousand dollars, which is an enormous contribution to the effort right there."

"It certainly is," Joe could feel his face twisting into an uncomfortable grimace. "No one has anything negative to say about him?"

"Like what? That he chases nurses around the operating room?"

"Yeah, something like that. Few men are as perfect as he appears to be."

The table hid her gesture as she ran her toe along his pants leg. "You are."

Joe laughed at her extravagant praise. "Thank you. Just keep your ears open if someone mentions Georgia. She spent most of her time at the hospital, and it's still likely she learned something someone on the staff couldn't allow her to share."

Mary Margaret sat back as their waitress brought their plates. She reached for an onion ring, and her smile grew blissful. "Hmm, this is as good as I remembered. They must use corn meal in the coating." After eating several rings, she grew serious. "At this afternoon's meeting, it occurred to me that we could pay the Mooney brothers another visit. They might want to contribute to the scholarship. The residents of the Chrysanthemum Court might also want to donate to the fund."

Joe was embarrassed he hadn't thought of how useful the scholarship could be to his investigation. It wasn't an opening Sherlock Holmes would have missed. "Brilliant." He reached across the table to give her hand a quick squeeze, but Dr. Gabriel Webb didn't stray far from his mind. As they left, he dropped his business card in the round glass fishbowl on the counter and hoped they'd win a free dinner soon.

They went to see *On the Spanish Trail,* the Roy Roger's movie Angie had taken Curtis Mooney to see. Joe liked the action-packed Western much more than the romantic films Mary Margaret loved, and he was wise enough not to compare them aloud.

Sunday afternoon, they called upon the Mooneys. The stiff-backed housekeeper again escorted them out to the patio where both Edwin and Curtis were in the pool. As soon as Edwin saw them, he swam to the side and lifted himself out of the water. In swim trunks, his wiry, muscular build was more easily apparent than it had been in casual clothes. Cleary he had the strength to grab a woman from behind and slit her throat before she could break free.

Joe and Mary Margaret stood back. "I hope we're not troubling you," Joe began. "I don't have your telephone number or I would have called to make an appointment."

"We love company," Curtis called from the pool. He swam to the ladder in the deep end and climbed out. "Do you want something to eat or drink?"

"Thank you," Mary Margaret replied, "but we'll only be here for a minute or two."

"Why can't you stay?" Curtis asked. "We have plenty of swimsuits and you could swim with us."

Edwin grabbed a towel and tossed one to his brother. "We mustn't beg people for their company, Curtis. I'll plan a patio party someday soon."

"Well, if they're already here, they should be invited to stay," Curtis argued. He studied Mary Margaret closely as he approached. "Is your name Mary?"

"Yes, it's Mary Margaret. It's nice of you to remember me."

Curtis laughed. "You're welcome, but I can't promise to remember the next time you're here."

"You'll know they're coming," Edwin interjected. "That will help. Are you sure you don't have time for a Tom Collins?"

Their plan had worked so beautifully, Joe readily agreed. "That would be wonderful. Mary Margaret?"

"Yes, I remember yours as being especially good." She took a seat at the circular glass table, and Curtis scooted a chair close to hers.

Joe stayed with Edwin. "I know both of you were fond of Georgia Dixon, and we thought you might want to contribute to the scholarship for nursing students established in her memory."

"We can do that can't we, Edwin? I liked her a lot, or at least I think I did."

"Yes, she was a favorite friend and, of course, we'll make a donation. Where shall I send the check?"

Mary Margaret had anticipated such a question, and she got up briefly to give him a three by five card with the address of the bank handling the fund. "Georgia graduated from UCLA, so it will go to a student there," she explained. "We'll soon have brochures and cards printed. We hope to award a scholarship every year."

Edwin set the card aside and mixed their drinks at the patio bar. He gave Curtis a cold bottle of Coca-Cola, and Curtis raised it. "Should we have a toast to Georgia?"

Joe raised his glass. "To Georgia."

Mary Margaret raised hers as well. "To Georgia." She took a sip before she spoke to Curtis. "We went to see *On the Spanish Trail*, the Roy Rogers movie you saw last weekend with Angie. It certainly was exciting."

Curtis glanced toward the pool. "I'm sorry, but I don't remember it. Maybe Angie and I should go again. We could go to the same movie every weekend if she didn't mind, and I wouldn't know the difference."

Mary Margaret reached out to touch Curtis's arm. "I can't recall movies all that clearly either. I may remember the plot, but forget the actors and actresses involved. Or I'll recall an actress, and can't remember which movie she starred in. I love going to the movies though. They're meant to be fun for the moment, not something to be memorized for an exam."

Curtis nodded. "You're being kind. Thank you."

When Edwin and Joe joined them at the table, the detective remarked on the beauty of the yard. "Do you have a crew of gardeners?" he asked.

"We've had the same gardener for years," Edwin explained. "We've watched his sons grow up, and I suppose they constitute a crew. They work for others in the neighborhood as well."

The conversation flowed more smoothly than it had on their first visit, and when Joe and Mary Margaret excused themselves, the housekeeper immediately appeared to escort them to the front door. On a sudden hunch, Joe offered her his card. "If you remember something about Georgia Dixon, give me a call."

The housekeeper's eyebrows rose to a dramatic height, but she took the card and slipped it into her pocket. Her expression wasn't encouraging, however.

Once they'd reached Joe's car, Mary Margaret whispered, "Do you expect her to tattle on her employer?"

"No, not at all, but she might have seen one of the gardeners flirting with Georgia."

"True, but Georgia wasn't murdered with a pair of hedge clippers."

Joe couldn't help but chuckle. "I'm sorry, I shouldn't laugh. Why do you suppose Edwin was so cordial today?"

"To fool us into believing he had nothing whatsoever to hide where Georgia is concerned?"

"My thought exactly. What are the chances he'll actually host a swim party and invite us?"

"Zero. Curtis won't remember talk of a party, and Edwin won't remind him. It's a shame though," she added.

Monday morning, Joe parked near Chrysanthemum Court, and arrived first at the bus stop for the line going by his office. It was across the street and down a block from the bus line Georgia would have ridden to the VA hospital.

The day already possessed an inviting warmth, and he'd not needed a jacket. A few minutes before the bus was scheduled to appear, a dark-haired young man came bouncing into view, shadow boxing with a zigzag step as he approached.

"You ever box?" he called.

"Can't say that I have," Joe responded. He knew Joe Louis had been the heavy-weight champion since 1937, but he'd never had the enthusiasm for boxing many men possessed.

"It's the best sport ever. I depend only on myself, not a whole team of guys who'd be sure to let me down."

"That's one way of looking at it." Joe had become adept at carrying on a conversation without revealing a thing about himself. It encouraged people to believe he agreed with whatever they said, and become even more talkative.

"I'm Manny Muñoz." He showed off a few of his fancy steps punctuated with mock jabs. "I should get a shot at Ralph Lara soon. Lightweight matches are the best. Heavyweight fighters lumber around the ring rather than dance like we do."

"Clearly you know how to move." Joe had a vague memory of Ralph Lara's name, but wouldn't have placed him as a boxer had Manny not provided the context.

Joe showed him the newspaper photo of Georgia. "If you were on the bus two Mondays ago, did you happen to see this young woman?"

Manny froze where he stood. "She's dead, isn't she?"

"Yes, she is, and I'm looking into her murder. Did you see her on the bus?"

"I don't know. She looks familiar, but I could have seen her in the neighborhood."

Manny shifted from foot to foot. "I go to the Main Street Gym most mornings, and I'm thinking about working out, not who's on the bus."

Joe nodded thoughtfully and handed Manny his card. "If you remember anything helpful, give me a call."

"Discreet Investigations?" Manny appeared to be amused by the name. "Sure, I will."

A lady dressed in black with hair dyed darker than tar approached them. "She's here a lot," Manny whispered. "Ask her what she knows."

The woman moved with a ballerina's grace, but she had the forbidding dark eyes of a fairy tale gypsy. "Good morning." Joe introduced himself and showed her the newspaper photo. "I'm investigating her murder, and wonder if you saw her on the bus the morning she died. It would have been two Mondays ago."

The woman studied the photo with rapt attention and then spoke in heavily accented English. Her voice was low, forcing Joe to move close to hear. "I've seen her, but could not say when or where."

The bus arrived at their stop and Joe stood back to allow Manny and the woman, who could actually have been a gypsy, to board ahead of him. The bus was nearly full and he chose a seat beside a middle-aged woman holding a full grocery bag on her lap. She struck him as an average housewife, someone who took pride in minding her own business. Hoping she rode the same bus to the market every Monday morning, he handed her his card, and showed Georgia's photo.

"Someone riding this bus that morning may have seen something that will lead to the capture of the man who killed her," he said.

She pursed her lips thoughtfully, but soon handed him back the clipping. "Is there a reward?"

"No, but she was a nurse at the VA hospital and very well thought of," he replied.

The gypsy lady had taken the seat in front of theirs, and she turned to speak to Joe. "Doomed on the day she died, she would have been enveloped in a dark, forbidding cloud."

"Keep your morbid thoughts to yourself," the woman beside Joe snapped. "To hear you tell it, we're all riding a bus to hell."

At the bus's next stop, Joe changed seats, and continued to ask riders if they had seen Georgia, or anyone following her. He passed out his card, but no one had any useful information, and he discounted the gypsy woman's dark prediction. Los Angeles had no shortage of people with strange intensities, and she clearly numbered among them.

Sam Murphy drove the bus that morning. A large man, his stomach overlapped his belt to press against the bottom of the steering wheel. He'd watched Joe move from seat to seat and was ready with his own answers. "Plenty of pretty girls ride this bus," he confided with a sly grin, and then shrugged. "But I can't swear the one you're asking about rode with me two Mondays ago.

"Riders board at the front of the bus and exit from the rear, so I only get one look at them. Murder is a ghastly business, but at least she wasn't killed on my bus. I would never have lived that down."

Joe had no response for such an insensitive remark. When they reached the stop at his office building, he left the bus and waited at the light to cross the street and catch a bus for the return to Chrysanthemum Court. He needed to pick up his car before he forgot where he'd parked it. He'd handed out more than a dozen of his business cards, and it was possible someone might recall something later in the day and call him.

"Doubtful," he murmured under his breath.

CHAPTER 8

Joe rinsed out his coffee pot in the restroom, and as he stepped out into the hallway, he nearly collided with CC who was pushing his wide floor mop. Joe pulled back quickly. "Sorry. I'm preoccupied this morning."

"No need to apologize, Mr. Ezell. Solving a murder is serious business."

"It is, but right now, I'm searching for a new way to relay bad news." He checked his watch, and hurried to his office to be ready when Jeanne Roth arrived.

She wore a gray linen suit today with a pink blouse giving a surprising bit of color at the neckline. He picked up his file, but held it rather than slide it across the desk to her. He used the thoroughly business-like tone he'd perfected. "Saturday morning, Earl Seeley did go to the tennis club."

Jeanne's expression brightened. "He really did? Then I had no cause to worry so about him?"

"Give me a minute more, please. Earl made a stop along the way at Herbert's Drive-In for breakfast, and a young woman joined him in his car." He opened the folder to remove the photo and handed it to Jeanne. "Do you recognize her?"

Huge tears welled up in her eyes. "No, but she's very pretty, and quite young."

"I could follow Mr. Seeley again next Saturday morning, and gather more information about the young woman if she reappears."

Jeanne dropped the photo on Joe's desk and rubbed her hands on her skirt. "No, it doesn't matter who she is. If their breakfast were something innocent, he'd have mentioned her when we went out to dinner Saturday night. I don't need to know anything more."

"If you really care about the man...."

Her lips pinched into a downward curve. "Not anymore I don't. I'll see that he's evicted tomorrow."

Joe sat back. "Do you have that kind of influence with the landlord?"

Her laugh was a strangled bark. "I own the building, and I'll evict whomever I choose. Thank you, Mr. Ezell, you've saved me from becoming an even greater fool than I already was."

"I wouldn't have a business if everyone were who he seemed to be, Miss Roth. I'm sorry Earl Seeley disappointed you so badly."

"Not nearly as disappointed as I am."

They settled her bill, and Joe waited until after she'd left to make a final note in her file. He got up to stretch and leaned against his desk to answer when his telephone rang. "Discreet Investigations."

"Mr. Ezell? This is Madeline Price, the Mooneys' housekeeper. You gave me your card yesterday when you came to the house."

Elated, Joe shook his fist in the air. "Good morning, Mrs. Price. How may I help you?"

"I need to see you in person. Will you be free in half an hour?"

"I'll arrange it." He had nothing scheduled and hoped she had something valuable to share about Georgia, rather than merely needing him to follow a wayward husband. He began a new folder with a handful of blank paper for notes.

When Mrs. Price knocked lightly at the door, he leapt to his feet to meet her. With her hair in loose curls and in a flattering green dress rather than a prim uniform, he'd not have recognized her had she not made an appointment. "Good morning," he greeted her warmly. "Would you care for coffee? I can brew some fresh."

"No, thank you." She took a chair, gripped her purse on her lap, and waited for him to take his seat behind his desk. "I hope I can trust you to be as discreet as you claim."

"You can," he assured her. He might discuss his cases with Mary Margaret, CC, and Hal Marten, but he never offered names or any personal information to identify his clients.

"I do have some information about Georgia Dixon, but Edwin Mooney must never learn it came from me. He's never doubted my loyalty, and he mustn't now."

"Do you have a reason to be afraid of him?"

She opened her purse to remove a lace-trimmed handkerchief and twisted it in her hands. "My only fear is of losing my job and not being able to find another. My husband served in the Navy, and was killed on board the U.S.S. Arizona in the attack on Pearl Harbor."

"None of us will ever forget December 7th, Mrs. Price, and I'm so sorry you lost your husband."

"He played trumpet in the band, and they all died." She paused to breathe deeply. "Mondays are my days off, and I visit my mother and spend the night at her apartment. Our cook and the maids don't live-in, so they are gone by eight o'clock in the evening. On Monday night, a few weeks ago, I forgot my small suitcase and came back for it. I entered through the servants' entrance at the rear, and used the back stairs, so Edwin and Curtis weren't aware I was there. While I was in the house only briefly, I saw more than enough."

Joe opened the folder and made a notation of the date. "You saw something upsetting?"

"Yes, indeed I did. The living room is visible from the top of the stairs, and the sound of voices made me wonder who Edwin's guests might be. He hasn't entertained since Curtis came home from the hospital, but that night, there were two women there, attractive women I should say, the kind wealthy men invite to parties. Curtis shouldn't drink, but clearly he was. He'd been dancing with the redhead, and when Edwin urged him to take her upstairs to his bedroom, I left."

"So this was a Monday night, when Edwin expected they'd be alone in the house? Could he routinely provide his brother with liquor and women on Mondays?"

"I doubt that was the only time it occurred, and Georgia Dixon may have found out. She and Edwin exchanged words the last Saturday she spent with Curtis. While I heard only the angry tone of their voices, I couldn't swear to the gist."

"But it's enough to rightly make you suspicious. Georgia was killed shortly before an appointment she'd made with me. She could have objected to the company Edwin provided for Curtis, but I'm not certain what I could have done to stop it."

Madeline slid forward in her chair. "Edwin is well-known as a generous philanthropist, a pillar of the community. That he chooses to consort with whores would create a scandal that would badly tarnish his sterling reputation."

Taken aback by the bluntness of her language, Joe nodded thoughtfully to gain a moment. Mrs. Price had provided a motive for Georgia's murder, but an intriguing possibility wasn't fact. Wouldn't Georgia have said something to Gabriel Webb if the two were as close as he claimed?

"I'll look into this, Mrs. Price. If Edwin hosts intimate parties every Monday night, then his guests ought to be there tonight."

"What will you do, hide in the shrubbery?"

Joe bit his lip rather than laugh out loud. "There's no need to get that close. I'll park down the block and make a note of whomever arrives at the Mooney home."

"Don't stay too long, or one of the neighbors might call the police."

"Thank you, I'll take that into account."

After she'd gone, he opened his file on Georgia Dixon and added what he'd learned from Madeline Price to his notes on Edwin Mooney. He could arrive at the VA hospital a half an hour early that afternoon, tell Dr. Webb about Edwin's offer of a donation, and see if it prompted any pertinent recollections. Somehow he doubted it would.

Joe remembered where Gabriel Webb's office was located, and after entering the hospital he walked there with a confident stride, as though he had every right to be there. No one questioned him. Gabriel was seated at his desk, gazing out the window when Joe knocked at the doorjamb.

Gabriel swung around to face him. "Afternoon, Mr. Ezell. I have only a few minutes before I'm due in surgery." He stood and shoved his chair into place at his desk. "I always review the procedure in my mind to prepare."

"Call me Joe. I spend a good deal of time staring out the window and thinking myself, so I'll not criticize you. I wanted you to know Edwin Mooney has offered to send a check for the scholarship. He didn't mention an amount, so we'll have to wait and see how much enthusiasm he shows."

"Let's hope he's generous. Georgia enjoyed her Saturdays with Curtis Mooney, so they should have warm thoughts of her," the doctor replied. "I never met either of the brothers."

"Did Georgia ever comment on anything Edwin said or did that might have upset her?"

Gabriel came toward him. "No, why would she? She was hired to look after Curtis, not keep Edwin company."

The answer rang false on Joe's ears. Mary Margaret described whatever had bothered her at work with the minutest detail. If Georgia argued with Edwin about bringing whores into the house, why wouldn't she have confided in Gabriel? Didn't she trust him to be sympathetic? Or did she simply not trust him?

Mary Margaret began talking as soon as she was seated in Joe's car. "I called Detective Lynch this morning and asked for an update on the investigation into Georgia's murder. You'd have thought I'd asked to borrow his underwear!"

Joe couldn't help but chuckle. "He wasn't forthcoming, is that it?"

"Not 'forthcoming' is an understatement. He told me not to worry, and that the police would announce an arrest when they made one. He hung up before I could ask if that might occur anytime soon. I was tempted to call him right back and tell him what I thought of his lackluster investigation, if it even rises to that sorry level."

"But you restrained yourself?"

"Yes, but just barely. Let's go to Clifton's Cafeteria. I definitely need some macaroni and cheese tonight."

"Sounds good." Joe nodded as she continued to fume. When she paused for what appeared to be a long break, he asked softly, "Have you always confided in the men you've dated?"

"Sure, why not? I avoid men who don't let a woman get a word in edgewise. I'll bet Detective Lynch is like that. If he has a wife, which I doubt, he probably doesn't hear a word she says."

"He has a wife, and she's wealthy," Joe offered. "Maybe she has enough people straining to hear her every word and doesn't care whether or not he listens to her."

"Wealthy or not, she has to care. Poor woman," she murmured under her breath.

Joe waited until they were seated with their dinners at Clifton's before he mentioned what he'd learned from Madeline Price. "She's too afraid of losing her job to confront Edwin over the company he provides for Curtis, but if Georgia and Edwin had words, the entertainment he provided for Curtis might well have been the cause."

They were seated in a booth, but Mary Margaret took the precaution of checking the nearby tables to make certain they weren't being overheard before she whispered, "Could Edwin honestly believe he's doing the best for Curtis, or is he merely manipulating him?"

"I vote for manipulation."

She jabbed her fork into her macaroni and cheese. "I wish we knew why Georgia wanted to see you. It would make everything so much easier."

Joe had discovered nothing was ever as easy as he'd hoped it would be. He related his brief visit with Gabriel Webb. "If Georgia saw Gabriel that Saturday night, don't you think she would have told him what she'd discovered about Edwin and Curtis?"

"I sure would have," she responded. "It's possible she didn't see him that weekend, or even if she did, she chose not to ruin the time they'd have together with complaints about Edwin. Did you think of that?"

"No," he admitted. "I just assumed she'd have confided in him, unless she had a good reason not to."

She gave it a moment of serious thought. "Georgia was too fond of Curtis to have remained silent for long about the 'company' Edwin provided. She may have turned to you rather than tell Gabriel. Maybe she thought Gabriel would have been jealous of Curtis. That's possible, isn't it?"

"Yes, of course it is." He hadn't had macaroni and cheese in a while, and allowed himself to savor it for a few minutes before he told her he planned to observe the Mooneys' home after he'd taken her home.

"I want to go too!" she exclaimed.

"This will be work, Mary Margaret, not an hour of necking on a deserted lane."

She laughed between bites. "That's disappointing, but I still want to go along. If anyone asks why we're parked there, we can say we're arguing over directions to a friend's house. That would be a help, wouldn't it?"

Madeline Price had warned him the neighbors might call the police, so a pretty companion and a convincing story might work to his advantage. "All right, you can come, but all we'll do is watch to see if any women arrive around eight o'clock. We won't stay long whether they do or not."

"If we had a dog to walk, no one would notice us," she offered.

"Neither of us owns a dog," he reminded her.

"I'm well-aware of that. Mrs. Simmons who lives downstairs from me has a dog."

"I'm not walking a Chihuahua," he emphasized. "Besides, she probably wouldn't loan us her precious dog anyway."

"Maybe she would if she knew she'd be helping to solve a murder case."

Joe reached for a bite of her whipped cream topped lime Jello. "She always gives me the evil eye whenever I see her."

She squinted at him. "How does an evil eye look?"

He responded with a threatening frown. "Like that. She regards me about as warmly as she would gum stuck on the bottom of her shoe."

"All right, so maybe she isn't the one to ask. We've got to know someone else who owns a dog."

"I can't think of one."

"Fine, we'll reserve the dog walking for another night."

She ate her dinner with tiny bites, and he thought her absolutely adorable. "Thank you, Mary Margaret. I appreciate your offer of help."

She regarded him with a self-satisfied smirk. "About time. Do you have binoculars in your glove compartment?"

"Of course, what detective doesn't?"

The streetlights on the Mooneys' block were dim, and Mary Margaret had to lean across Joe to see. They had parked up the street in front of a house with a front yard the size of a football field. "It's a quarter to eight. Do you suppose Edwin's 'guests' will appear on time?" she asked.

"Yes, if they arrive, they'll follow their usual routine. Edwin might call them after the servants have all left for the day."

She adjusted the binoculars and swept the street with a slow glance. "This is such a quiet neighborhood. It's almost spooky."

"I'll protect you if any menacing ghosts arise from the shrubbery."

"Thank you, that's such a comforting thought. Look, here comes a taxi!"

A taxi with the Yellow Cab light on the roof turned into the street, slowed, and stopped in front of the Mooneys' home. Two women exited the back seat. Joe raised his fingertip to his lips to warn Mary Margaret to keep still. "Just watch," he whispered. When the pair reached the front door, the porch light revealed a slender redhead, and a buxom blonde. Edwin came to the door and ushered them inside. The taxicab drove away.

"Like clockwork," she murmured. "What if Georgia did complain about Edwin's paying women for their company, wouldn't he have denied it? He could call the women 'dear friends' who occasionally dropped in to see Curtis. If they were paid, it would probably be in cash, so how could Georgia have proved it?"

"Excellent question. Unless the women admitted it, which they wouldn't, she couldn't prove anything."

They were both startled as a slowly approaching police car rolled up behind them. The driver flashed his headlights before exiting the black and white Ford. "I've got this," Mary Margaret promised. She slid the binoculars under her seat and picked up the map in her lap. Joe had already rolled down the window, and she greeted the policeman before he could speak. He was a tall man who had to lean down to look in their car.

"Thank goodness you've come by, officer. We've been looking for Rocking Bird Lane for half an hour and can't find it."

"I'm sure it's Mockingbird Lane, sweetheart," Joe interjected.

"Well, whatever it is, it isn't around here." She smiled at the policeman. "Maybe we need a better map. I can't find anything on this." She waved a map of California.

The policeman laughed in spite of his best efforts not to. "You need a map of Los Angeles, miss, not one of the whole state. Mockingbird Lane isn't far from here."

Joe nodded as the officer provided concise directions. "I swear that's where we were headed until she insisted we turn down this street."

"Let's not argue," she replied sweetly. "Was there something you wanted, officer?"

The officer backed away. "No, not now, but people living nearby worry about parked cars they don't recognize. Have a nice evening, and get a new map tomorrow."

"Thank you, officer, we sure will," Joe responded. He turned the key in the ignition and pulled away from the curb. He planned to follow the policeman's directions in case they were being followed, but at the corner, the patrol car turned in the opposite direction.

"That was a stellar performance, Mary Margaret. Had you realized you had such impressive theatrical talent before tonight?"

She fluffed her hair with her fingertips. "Why yes I did. I starred in the senior play in high school."

"I'm sorry I missed it. Using the California map was a stroke of genius. We would have been sure to stay lost if we'd had to rely on it."

"But we weren't really lost, silly."

"Are you sure? You were so convincing he believed every word and didn't ask for our names. I don't believe he wrote down my license plate number. That's a cause for celebration right there. Let's get some ice cream." He headed the car toward Aunt Lucy's.

Mary Margaret felt like having a chocolate sundae and Joe ordered the strawberry. He toyed with the mountain of whipped cream and chopped almonds topping his dish. "My friend, Hal, gave me the name of a bail bondsman. He came to the memorial service Hal held for Faye. Chinese fellow, Lou King, do you remember him?"

"I do, very elegant dresser as I recall."

Joe knew no one would ever describe him as such, which was exactly as he wanted it. "He might know of a high-priced call girl who'd suit Edwin's tastes. I'll contact him in the morning."

"So you'll work the story from the girls' angle rather than badger Edwin Mooney for the truth? I like that approach."

"So do I." He lifted a spoonful of whipped cream. "Cheers."

"Cheers!" She laughed with him.

"I hope you weren't frightened," he said.

"Why would I be? You made it an adventure."

"You are a treasure, Mary Margaret."

"Thank you. You don't think we're too focused on Edwin Mooney, do you? You had a whole list of suspects in the beginning."

"I did, and we need to get back to the Chrysanthemum Court to tell them about the scholarship. Let's do it after work tomorrow."

Mary Margaret nodded. "Good plan, even if it can't be nearly as exciting as tonight."

"Let's wait and see." Joe's half-smile promised another type of adventure, and she laughed with him.

Tuesday morning, Joe called Hal Marten. "Before I ask Lou King for another favor, I wanted to check with you to be certain it would be all right."

"Sure, go ahead. Is this about Georgia's murder?"

"It is, and I need the names of a couple of call girls who might play into it."

Hal immediately had a name for him. "Crystal was a great help to me when we were searching for Pearl LaFosse. I'll call you back with her number. See you on Saturday?"

"I'll be there," Joe promised. A glance at his calendar showed the prospect for high earnings that week looked bleak. When the telephone rang, he counted to ten before answering in his usual effort to appear busy. "Discreet Investigations."

"This is Roberta Wren," she whispered.

Joe didn't recognize the name. "How may I help you, Mrs. Wren?"

"It's Miss Wren, but that's neither here nor there. I have a problem with a neighbor that I hope you'll be able to solve. I can come by your office now if that's convenient."

"It is." Joe offered directions Roberta insisted she didn't need. He hoped her problem was so severe it would take him a week or more to sort out all the details. She quickly abused him of the idea.

"I love animals as much as the next person," she claimed, "but my neighbor's dog barks ceaselessly. Animal Control is overwhelmed with complaints and told me they'd add mine to their list and try to come by next month. 'Try' was what they said, nothing definite. I've complained to the police, but they insisted they had better things to do with their time."

She was a fierce little woman with a straw hat plunked on her white curls. The tiny floral print of her dress only served to accentuate her diminutive size. Even seated on the edge of her chair, her patent leather pumps didn't graze the floor.

"There is nothing more annoying than a barking dog," Joe offered, and she smiled, clearly believing she'd come to the right place. "Have you spoken to your neighbor?"

"Of course I have, and so many times he won't open the door when he sees me on the porch. I'm at my wit's end, Mr. Ezell. That's why I've come to you."

Joe nodded as though he were deeply complimented by her enthusiasm for his abilities. "What is it you wish me to do?"

"Get rid of the dog! Isn't that obvious? I don't expect you to poison him. Just open the gate and encourage him to run off, or take him so far away he won't be able to find his way home."

"Kidnap the dog?" he asked.

"Dog-napping, maybe? Call it whatever you like. I'll pay double your usual fee."

"Mrs. Wren, forgive me, Miss Wren," he corrected. "You're asking me to do something illegal, and I won't jeopardize my private investigator's license for any case." Let alone a barking dog, he didn't add.

She fidgeted in her chair. "Do you have a colleague with noticeably lower standards?"

He tried not to laugh. "No, I don't. My advice is to stop at the pharmacy downstairs and purchase a pair of earplugs."

For a brief instant, her eyes narrowed menacingly, but once convinced his suggestion had been sincere, she slid forward and rose from her chair. "I suppose it's worth a try, but I don't have much hope they'll work."

He stood to walk her to the door. "Speak to Dr. Raymond, the pharmacist. He'll know which brand is best."

"We'll see," she declared, and left with a short, brisk stride.

Joe closed the door quietly behind her. She hadn't asked if there would be a charge for his advice, but he wouldn't have handed her a bill. The telephone rang again before he reached his chair, but this time he only counted to seven before answering.

CHAPTER 9

Hal Marten had the telephone number Joe had requested. "Gladys warned against this, by the way. Crystal is a favorite of Jack Dagna's, and you don't want to get mixed up with his crowd."

Joe knew Jack Dagna, the top mob boss in California, by reputation only. Dagna profited from every possible vice, but extortion was his specialty. "I understand, but I mean to ask her a question or two, nothing more."

"If she asks you to meet at the Bar of Music, suggest somewhere else. The police routinely conduct surveillance to keep tabs on the mob types who go there."

"I know the place, it has a funny bubble front."

"That's it. You have a fondness for redheads, but Crystal is beyond attractive. I'm sure you'll be tempted, but...."

Joe laughed. "Maybe, but she won't be, and that will save me. Thanks for the number and thank Gladys for the warning."

A redhead and a blonde had come to the Mooneys' door last night, but Los Angeles was filled with beautiful red-haired women, so Joe doubted Crystal could have been there. She probably didn't leave her satin-sheeted bed before noon, and he worked on what he wished to say while he waited for a better time to call. There were a dozen ways to approach her. He refined the one he thought best, and he wouldn't mention murder.

"Hello." Crystal answered his call in a sultry voice with a musical lilt.

Joe wondered who'd she'd been expecting and hated to disappoint her. He introduced himself as a friend of Hal Marten's. "Curtis Mooney was a patient at the VA hospital, and the nurses who cared for him there are concerned for his welfare. They've heard his brother, Edwin, is providing him with pretty female company. They want to make certain no one takes advantage of him.

"The Mooney family is prominent in Los Angeles, and I've no wish to embarrass them. I'd just like to reassure the nurses Curtis is doing fine. Do you have any idea who the young women in question might be?"

She responded with an impatient sigh. "Let me get this straight, you're curious about what's happening in the Mooney household? What makes you think I'd know anything about Edwin or Curtis?"

"Hal said you were acquainted with several important men in Los Angeles. I'd hoped Edwin Mooney might be among them." While she considered her response, Joe counted the seconds in his mind. His side of the conversation had looked good on paper, but now he wondered if he'd made a serious mistake and insulted her.

"Do you know the Bar of Music?" she asked.

"I do, but I'd rather not go there. What's your second choice?"

"Annette's Café is just up the street from it. Would that suit you better?"

Clearly her patience was growing thin. "Yes, it would. What's a good time for you?"

"I'll be there at one o'clock for lunch. If Hal told you anything about me, you'll recognize me easily enough."

"Yes, I'm sure I will." Joe hung up, checked the time, and got up to go. He'd have to refine his questions while he drove.

* * *

Joe entered Annette's Café with a few minutes to spare and immediately felt out of place. The small lunchroom was decorated in pink and white and filled with women, clerks in nearby shops or secretaries in the office buildings. It couldn't possibly be a mob hang-out, unless those present had disguised themselves to appear excruciatingly ordinary down to their clunky choice in shoes.

He was shown to a table near the kitchen and perused the menu for something worth eating, but he forgot all about food when Crystal joined him at the table. She had covered her hair with a long aqua scarf and tossed the trailing ends over her shoulders. Only a single gloriously red curl peeked out to brush her brow. Perhaps she'd arrived in a convertible. Her eyes were a golden brown, and her burnt-orange lipstick suited her. Her off-white slacks and matching sweater were much too pale for someone so colorful. He tried not to simply stare at one of the most beautiful women he'd ever seen.

She regarded him with a single glance, her expression more perplexed than curious before focusing on the menu. "The tuna salad is good," she said, her voice still soft, but now lacking the sultry edge. She greeted the waitress by name and ordered one. "With iced tea, please."

"Make it two," Joe added. "Thank you for meeting me."

She shrugged. "I'm fond of Curtis, and if this concerns him, I'm interested."

"Were you with him Monday night?"

"No. I met Curtis before the war, and visited him when he was in the VA hospital, but he didn't remember me. He may look well physically, but he's simply not the same man. Regrettably, he's not the only one the war has changed, but it's particularly tragic in his case. He used to be so much fun."

Joe could not imagine any man forgetting such a stunning young woman, but he'd met Curtis, and believed her. "I'm curious about the blonde and redhead who went to the

Mooneys' home Monday night. Do you have any idea who they might be?"

"I might. Hazel Craig has been a redhead the last few months. As for the blonde, there are too many to make a guess."

"She was pretty, but a bit plump."

"Voluptuous is a kinder word," she suggested. The waitress brought their salads, and tea. She waited until the girl had left them to respond. "Hazel has a friend who'd fit your description. Her name is June something. Neither of them has the brains to do anything more difficult than slap two pieces of bread together and call it a sandwich. Edwin must have his brother's best interests at heart, and a couple of pretty girls won't harm him."

Joe nodded and took a bite of his salad, which proved to be as good as promised. He hoped she wouldn't throw hers at him. "Maybe not, but an attractive nurse who worked with Curtis on Saturdays is dead. Someone had a reason to kill her, and I want to cross Edwin and Curtis off the list."

She blotted her mouth with her napkin. "Curtis is a sweetheart, or was. Edwin is another story all together. He's a mean drunk. Was the nurse partying with him?"

"No, she died at 9:00 o'clock in the morning outside my office."

"Are you a suspect?" It was a casual question, not an accusation.

"No, I'm not."

"Do you have other suspects?"

"I do," he admitted, "but something about Edwin is off, and I need to eliminate him first."

She arched a well-shaped brow. "Or prove he did it?"

He watched her turn her fork to spear a hunk of tuna and continue eating as though they were discussing something far less violent than murder. "The nurses would be relieved to have the case closed."

"Are they in danger too?"

"I hope not."

"Hope isn't much of a weapon, Mr. Ezell."

She spoke in a matter-of-fact tone, as though she were well-acquainted with all manner of weaponry. "I agree," he answered.

Her salad held her attention for several minutes. She stopped eating to take a sip of tea. "I could pay Curtis a visit. Edwin knows we were close once, and he wouldn't be surprised, or suspicious, if I paid them a call."

In good conscience, he couldn't send her to the Mooney home. "I'd rather you didn't."

"Really? Then why did you call me in the first place?" She pushed her plate aside and waved at the waitress. "I'm finished. I'll give you a call if I learn anything worth knowing."

Joe sprang to his feet as she left the table, but he had to remain and pay the bill rather than walk her to the car he imagined to be a bright red convertible.

Tuesday evening, Joe and Mary Margaret stopped by the Chrysanthemum Court to invite the residents to donate to the scholarship fund. She had remained in her nurse's uniform to work every advantage to gain sympathy for their cause.

"Maybe someone has remembered something important," she said.

"No one called," Joe replied. "If they went to Detective Lynch, we'd never hear of it though."

"We should have brought treats, cookies maybe," she said.

"I'll help you bake them for our next visit," he offered. "Tonight, we want everyone to believe our only concern is the scholarship."

She held the newly printed brochures. "Right." She took his hand as they walked up to the first cottage where the retired postal worker, John Cameron, and his wife, Phyllis, lived.

John came to the door and smiled widely. "Come in. Phyllis, look who's here."

His wife came out of the kitchen wiping her hands on a dishtowel. "How nice to see you two again. Have you solved the murder?" Hope brightened her gaze.

"I'm still working on it," Joe replied. He described the scholarship and Mary Margaret handed John a brochure. "We're not taking up a collection today," he assured the couple. "We're simply passing out information, and if you care to contribute, you have the bank's mailing address for a check."

"I think we should send something, John," Phyllis replied. "Georgia was such a sweet girl, and I miss her. If you're able to stay a while, I have some fresh scones, right out of the oven."

Mary Margaret smiled at Joe. "We didn't plan the timing of our visit, did we?"

"No, but I'd love another of your delicious scones, Mrs. Cameron."

John urged them to a comfortable place to sit and Phyllis returned within minutes with a plate of still steaming scones and tea. "These are blueberry, one of our favorites."

"Do you share your recipes?" Mary Margaret asked. "I'd love to have this one."

Phyllis laughed. "I have only a basic scone recipe you'll find in any cookbook, and I add whatever strikes my mood."

"These are wonderful," Joe mumbled through a mouth of crumbs. He waited until they were all finished before he again mentioned Georgia. "Do you still have my card? I'm grateful for any clue that might lead to the murderer's arrest."

Phyllis sighed. "I've not a bad thing to say about the poor girl."

"It doesn't have to be anything derogatory," Mary Margaret stressed.

Phyllis glanced toward her husband. "Georgia and Patrick Wood were awfully close. He's too old to have been her lover, but still, I thought it a bit odd she'd spend so much time with him."

"Phyllis," her husband scolded. "He's a sweet guy, and everyone needs friends."

"True, but he must know more about Georgia than all the rest of us here put together. Didn't he have any ideas for you?"

"He was in shock the first time we spoke, and he may have thought of something by now," Joe volunteered. "Thank you for the tea and scones. We have to be on our way to speak with everyone living here tonight."

Phyllis and John walked with them to the door. When his wife stood back, John leaned close to whisper. "All gossip is lies."

Joe and Mary Margaret left without replying. As they approached the next cottage she looked over her shoulder to make certain John had closed their front door. "Maybe Phyllis has a crush on Patrick, and she killed Georgia to have him for herself."

"Unlikely possibility, but I'll make a note of it," Joe promised, but he couldn't see Mrs. Cameron wielding a knife.

At the second cottage, Daniel Hill answered their knock. His shirt was pulled out of his pants, and he looked as though he hadn't slept in several days. "I'd invite you to come in, but we have baby things strewn all over."

"Your wife had the baby!" Mary Margaret exclaimed.

"Yes, a little girl, and we named her Catherine Elizabeth for our mothers. Polly is in the bedroom attempting to rock her to sleep. We knew babies were cute, but we'd no idea how much work one took. How does anyone survive having twins?"

"Let me go and help her," Mary Margaret offered, and Daniel stepped out of her way. He came out on the porch with Joe, sat down on the top step, and rested his head in his hands. "Our mothers are taking turns helping during the days when I'm at work, but the nights are killing me."

"I'm sure it gets better," Joe offered. He sat down beside Daniel and looked out at the prettily landscaped courtyard. "It must, or no one would have more than a single child."

"I swear this is it for us." Daniel sighed, and then looked up. "Have you found who killed Georgia?"

"Not yet, but we will." He told Daniel about the scholarship. "Mary Margaret will give you a brochure. You have plenty of other things to think about now."

"No, just one beautiful, tiny, demanding person."

Polly Hill peeked out the door. "Mary Margaret knew just how to hold little Catherine, and she fell asleep! I'm going to take a bath while I can. Hello, Mr. Ezell, I don't mean to be rude, but…."

"No apologizes are needed, Mrs. Hill."

"Polly," she offered, and disappeared into the house.

Mary Margaret appeared a moment later. She handed Daniel a copy of the scholarship brochure. "Put this away for a better day."

Daniel stood and took it. "Thank you for whatever you did."

"My pleasure. Catherine is an adorable little girl. Come on Joe, we need to let Daniel rest while he can."

Daniel mumbled a good-bye and went inside.

When they reached the walkway, Joe pulled Mary Margaret to a stop. "What did you do?"

"I showed Polly how to hold a baby so they'd both be more comfortable. It's a simple thing really. Something I learned from my mother, rather than nursing school."

"You're the eldest of how many?" he asked.

"Five. I have two sisters and two brothers. I practiced playing mother to them, and it was all fun."

"Are you hoping for a large family too?" Joe held his breath, dreading the cost of raising a brood of kids.

"No, two will be enough for me. Now let's see if Patrick Wood has thought of anything helpful."

Greatly relieved she didn't long to have a dozen tots, Joe followed her to the widower's door with a new spring in his step.

Patrick welcomed them right in, and then reached for a notebook in his shirt pocket. "I've been trying to recall things Georgia said. Important things," he stressed. "She wasn't happy in San Diego, and still grieved for the patients they'd lost. I assured her she must have done all she could for them, but she worried not everyone had. Is that helpful?"

Mary Margaret sent Joe a questioning glance, and he squeezed her hand. "Yes, she'd made similar comments about the staff at the VA hospital here. Did Georgia ever mention any doctors by name?"

"No, and now I wish I'd asked. I keep thinking of what her last few moments must have been, and it breaks my heart all over again. Can you stay a while?"

"Of course we can," Mary Margaret assured him. She waited until Joe had taken the seat beside her to describe the scholarship. "Georgia took great pride in being a nurse, and we believe she'd love having a nursing scholarship established in her name."

Patrick pulled his handkerchief from his back pocket and blew his nose. "Yes, she told me she'd wanted to become a nurse from her year in kindergarten. When she entered UCLA, she filled her diary with inspirational quotes to stay focused on her goal of becoming an RN."

Mary Margaret swallowed a surprised gasp. "Do you know if she still kept a diary?"

"Why yes, she did. Every once in awhile she'd remark on something she meant to include in it. Wasn't it found among her things?"

As stunned as Mary Margaret, Joe hauled in a deep breath. "No, it wasn't. Was it small enough to fit into her purse?"

"I don't know. I never saw it, but she mentioned it on more than one occasion. She urged me to keep one to help me write my memoir, but I prefer to enjoy the present rather than dwell on the past. It would only make me miss my wife even more than I already do."

"I understand," Mary Margaret replied. "You've been a great help, Mr. Wood. We'd wished Georgia had kept a diary, and now all we have to do is find it."

As they left his cottage, they saw Mike Torres locking the door on Georgia's home. He smiled and came toward them. "I meant to call you, Miss McBride. If you and your friends want to come by on Saturday morning, you can take whatever you like of Georgia's things to remember her. I'll bundle up whatever is left for the Salvation Army. A cleaning crew is scheduled for Saturday afternoon, and then the cottage will be ready to rent."

"Do you have a long waiting list?" Mary Margaret asked.

"For the other cottages yes, but when prospective renters discover the previous occupant was murdered, they aren't interested in number four."

"Would you consider me?" she asked. "I have a nice apartment, but a cottage would provide more of a home."

Joe couldn't believe she was serious. Her pretty apartment was larger than the cottages, and he'd always thought she was happy there. "Don't you have a lease?" he asked.

"No, I rent month to month. I'll be happy to fill out whatever application you have, Mr. Torres."

"Wait here, I'll get one from my car." He jogged down the walkway to the street.

"What are you doing?" Joe asked.

Mary Margaret looked up at him, her gaze innocently adoring. "Saturday morning will give us another chance to search for Georgia's diary. If we don't find it, I'll move in, and we can tear up the place if need be. Very quietly, of course."

"The man who killed Georgia took her keys, and he must have come straight here to search for the diary. He probably found it."

"Maybe not. Georgia didn't openly share her thoughts, so I'll bet the diary was hidden in a place where no one would look."

"We searched everywhere but the tank of the toilet, and it wouldn't have been in there."

"No, we only searched her bedroom. Why are you getting angry? Are you mad I thought of something before you?"

"No, of course, not. I'm grateful for your help, but do you really want to live here?"

"Yes, it's a lovely place."

"Filled with people who like to keep track of their neighbors' comings and goings."

She studied his expression with a slow, perceptive glance. "You're really mad, aren't you?"

Before Joe could answer, Mike Torres rejoined them with the application. "Fill it out at home and bring it with you on Saturday morning. Good to see you again." He shook hands with Joe, and after Mary Margaret had given him a brochure, left them on the walk.

Mary Margaret folded the application and added it to her handful of brochures. "Is there any point in ringing Amy Hudson's bell?"

"Probably not, but we're going to do it anyway." He marched ahead of her, but Amy didn't come to the door. "Somehow I'm not disappointed."

"Should we leave a brochure?"

"She'd just toss it. Let's talk to Tim and Barbara Garcia and see how things are going at the bank."

Barbara answered the door and blew a strand of hair out of her eyes. She was still dressed in her navy blue suit, but barefooted. "Have they caught the man?" she asked.

"Not yet, but we will," Joe assured her. He kept quiet as Mary Margaret told her about the scholarship. Barbara took the brochure and called over her shoulder to her husband.

Tim joined her at the door. "Won't you come in? We were about to make fried chicken, and I'll bet you know how to make it extra good."

"I do," Mary Margaret replied. "Would you really like my help, Barbara?"

"Of course I would. Tim hasn't stopped talking about the spaghetti you helped me prepare. Come on into the kitchen. Get Joe a drink, honey."

"Yes, dear." He rolled his eyes, but his wife had stepped away and didn't see it. "Does Mary Margaret ask you to do whatever it was you intended to do before you can do it?"

"No, but I've observed it often enough," Joe replied. "How do you like living here? Georgia's place will soon be ready to rent, would you recommend the Chrysanthemum Court?"

Tim fixed them both a Scotch and soda before he answered. "It's a pretty place, but we don't intend to stay much longer. Barbara wants a dog, and pets aren't allowed here. We'd also like to have children before too much longer, and a crib would barely fit in the bedroom. I know the Hills are crowded in their place with their baby girl."

The banker gestured for Joe to take one of the floral print wingback chairs, and he took its twin. "Did I answer your question? The Chrysanthemum Courts is a nice place to live, but we've outgrown it. Are you interested in Georgia's place?"

"No, but Mary Margaret is."

Time leaned forward to whisper. "I hope she takes it, and then she could give Barbara cooking lessons."

"Mary Margaret is a wonderful cook," Joe agreed. "Have you thought of anything more you could tell me about Georgia?"

"Other than her night-time visitor? No. We miss her. Whenever we come home, her dark cottage reminds us of how short life can be."

"Yes, it does." He hadn't heard anything negative about the cottages, other than their small size, but he still didn't want Mary Margaret to move there. The superb fried chicken dinner made him feel marginally better, and Tim and Barbara Garcia were good company, but he was unusually quiet as he drove Mary Margaret home.

"I'm surprised you have such a negative view of Georgia's cottage," she posed. "She didn't die there, so it can't be haunted."

He liked things the way they were, but that was too selfish a view to confess. "I'll help you move if you want to go there. I like your place better is all."

"I do have a nice apartment, but I could use a change. Maybe we'll find the diary Saturday morning, and you'll be able to solve the murder. That would cheer you up, wouldn't it?"

"Yes, but I'll bet the murderer already found it, so it was probably torn to bits and scattered to the wind before Georgia's body grew cold."

She turned toward him. "The murderer took her keys, so he could have come back a dozen times, and there would have been no sign of a break-in."

"Mike Torres probably had the locks changed, or at least he should have." Joe turned his car around and headed back to the Chrysanthemum Court. "I want to see if there's an alley behind the cottages so anyone could have come and gone without being seen."

"We didn't even open the back door when we were there," she recalled. "There must be room in the back for trashcans."

Joe turned at the corner past the Court and found an alley in the rear. He drove down it, stopped the car, and they got out. "It looks as though the residents bring their trash to the cans here for pick-up." A tall, ivy covered trellis hid the view of the alley from the courtyard. Narrow walkways behind both rows of cottages led to the alley. The back porches weren't large enough to hold more than a drying mop.

Georgia had a potted palm on her porch, Amy Hudson's porch was bare, and Tim and Barbara Garcia had dishtowels hanging out to dry on the railing. "Pretty uninteresting view compared to the front of the courtyard," Mary Margaret mused.

Tempted to check for a key, Joe moved the palm aside, and found one. He picked it up. "What are the odds this still works on the backdoor?"

"Try it," Mary Margaret urged.

He brushed off the bits of dirt clinging to the key, and inserted it in the lock. It turned easily, and the door swung open. He pulled it closed and relocked it. "I'd rather not risk an arrest for breaking and entering. Let's wait until Saturday to search further."

"Don't you have a flashlight in your car?"

"Of course, but we're not going in." He pocketed the key. "At least not tonight, we're not."

"You're not usually so cautious."

It was already dark, so they couldn't be seen, but he kept his voice low, "I hate to disappoint you, but this just doesn't feel right."

"Oh, well then, if your *instincts* are against it, I won't beg to go in."

Her sarcasm wasn't lost on him, but he ignored it, and took her hand. "Thank you. Let's go home." He liked the sound of that, even if they didn't share one.

Wednesday morning, Gilbert Werner called Discreet Investigations to make an appointment. An earnest young man, he held his hat in trembling hands. His gray suit was new, but clearly off the rack rather than custom tailored. His black oxfords were polished to a bright sheen, and his maroon tie neatly knotted. He was fair-haired and blue-eyed, and Joe thought he would have been a better looking man if he generated more, or anything, in the way of confidence. Clearly he held a desk job, and not a particularly important one.

Joe greeted him warmly, and opened with a question he'd found useful. "Was it difficult to get time off this morning?"

"No, I'm with an engineering firm, and came in early to make up for taking a long lunch. I didn't tell anyone I was coming here."

"I understand, co-workers can ask embarrassing questions, and there's no need to inform them of your private business."

"Yes, it's that exactly. As I said when I made the appointment, I'm concerned about my girlfriend."

"Would you please expand on that, Mr. Werner?" No matter what his problem, Joe already felt sorry for him.

"I'm dating a beautiful girl. She's a secretary with an insurance firm, and a mutual friend introduced us. She likes me, but I can't understand why. It feels too good to be true. Her name is Christine Hethe. I know you can't foretell the future, but could you look into her other friends and activities and tell me if she's seeing another man she might like better?"

"I could," Joe responded. "Do you see her on the same night each week?"

"We get together for a quick dinner after work on Wednesday night to talk about our week. On Saturday night, we usually have dinner at a nice place and take in a movie."

"Does Christine appear distracted when you're together?"

"No, not at all. She's very sweet and fun to be with. It's just that I'm not used to having such a pretty girl show any interest in me."

Joe chose to focus on the most obvious problem. "Why do you think you lack confidence in yourself, Mr. Werner?"

He shrugged as though he'd not known it was a problem. "I was only five feet four when I graduated from high school, and none of the girls were interested in a little kid like me. I grew eight inches while I was in college, but engineering students tend to be male, and it was difficult to meet young women. I have asthma, and couldn't serve in the military, and lots of men my age did and came home heroes."

"So you feel you can't compete?"

Gilbert studied his hat a long moment. "I suppose you could say that."

"It also sounds as though you lacked the opportunity to date before you met Christine?"

"I'd been out a few times with sisters of friends, but I didn't care if I ever saw any of them again, and I'm sure they felt the same way about me. Then I met Christine, and she kissed me goodnight on the first date."

"That's promising." Joe could easily imagine how exciting that must have been for him.

"Yes, I thought so, and we've been dating several months now. Everything is just too good, which worries me."

"I understand. Give me Christine's home and work address, and I'll see if she's seeing someone else. If she is, are you willing to fight for her?"

Gilbert's light tan faded to a pale pink, and Joe hadn't meant to frighten him. "What I mean is, would you confront the issue, perhaps tell her how deeply you care for her and ask if she cares for you? Wouldn't it be better to know where you stood?"

"I suppose, but I don't really know what I feel. That's the whole problem. I'm afraid to love a woman like Christine, who's just too good for someone like me."

"You strike me as an honest man, Mr. Werner. You're college educated and have a responsible job, and many women are looking for a solid young man with a bright future. You're neatly dressed, and if you thought of yourself as handsome, women would too."

Gilbert now blushed so deeply Joe feared he might faint, and he couldn't help but laugh. "I didn't mean to embarrass you. If you'll give me the addresses I need, I'll do some observation and with luck, I can assure you Christine's interest in you is sincere."

* * *

Saturday morning, Joe met Hal for another golf lesson. Hal was now practicing with his irons and getting nearly one hundred yards on the practice range. When they finished, they bought coffee at the shop at the course, and sat outside on the patio.

"How are you with questions on moral issues?" Joe asked.

"Is this personal, or about a new case?"

"A case." Joe described Gilbert Werner without naming him. "I followed the woman he's dating, and she isn't seeing another man. She met a woman for drinks on Friday night, and afterward they checked into a motel."

Hal had just taken a sip of coffee and choked as he swallowed. He quickly recovered. "What?"

"You heard me."

"I did." Hal took the time to appreciate the view of the lush green golf course before he spoke. "Maybe it isn't as shocking as it seems. Could the woman's friend have been from out-of-town? If so, they could have shared the room to catch up on news."

"Grown women don't have slumber parties," Joe chided. "And wouldn't an out-of-town guest have been invited to spend the night at my client's girlfriend's place?"

"Good point. Where does that leave your client?" Hal asked.

"That's the issue. I can address his question and reassure him that his girlfriend isn't seeing another man and let it go at that. Or, I can tell him she has a lady lover."

"Do you feel obligated to tell the truth?"

"I do, but both statements are true," Joe argued. "I didn't see the young woman in question with a man."

"That's only part of the truth," Hal replied. "Consider the reputation of your firm before you decide."

"I have, but I hate to break the guy's heart."

"Well, if his girlfriend prefers women to men, she'll break his heart eventually, won't she?"

"It seems likely." Joe sipped his coffee, and it was much better than what he brewed in his office. "I can understand women growing lonely when so many men were gone during the war, but I'm grateful most still prefer men."

"So am I. What does Mary Margaret think?"

"I haven't told her, and I'd rather not. It seems too personal somehow."

"If the man doesn't think much of himself…."

"Exactly. I doubt he'd go up on the roof and jump off the building, but there's still the possibility he might."

"Maybe you ought to speak to the girlfriend."

"And say what? Your boyfriend hired me to follow you? There's no way that could turn out well."

"Probably not, but how can you predict what any client will do after you give your report?"

Joe hadn't worried about the results of his investigations until his report to Hal's wife had sent all their lives rocketing downhill. "You already know that's impossible."

"You want to grow your business, and taking more complex cases will surely result in greater consequences to those involved. Problems like this man poses will come more often, and I understand your wish to protect your client."

Joe was grateful for Hal's advice, but his choice still wasn't clear. Maybe he could find a way to shade his report so Gilbert could draw his own conclusions. The man seemed like such a naïve soul, however, Joe wasn't sure he even could.

CHAPTER 10

M ary Margaret had ridden to the Chrysanthemum
Court Saturday morning with Angie. She met Joe at
the door with a light kiss. "Angie is here before she goes to
Curtis Mooney's, and there are several more of Georgia's
friends stopping by. They should be here soon. I brought
donuts and made coffee. Why don't you have some?"

"You know I can't pass up a donut. Hi, Angie, how are
things going with Edwin and Curtis?" He asked the
question in a genial tone, as though he were merely passing
the time of day, not pursuing a murderer.

"Edwin was away from home last Saturday, and I hope
he's gone again today. Curtis is easily entertained with the
pool, and card games. I almost hate to take Edwin's money
for being with him."

"Almost?" Mary Margaret asked.

Angie laughed. "Well, I'll admit it's nice to be so well-
paid for my time." She checked her watch. "I'll take the
dress I liked and get going. Nice to see you again, Joe. If I
learn anything about Edwin that will help with your
investigation, I'll contact you."

"Thank you, but don't let Edwin suspect we're watching
him."

"Absolutely not," she swore and crossed her heart.

Joe went into the kitchen, poured himself a cup of coffee, and ate a glazed donut while Angie made a last pass through Georgia's closet. The first time he'd been there had been soon after the murder, and there had been no sign the cottage had been searched. Or if it had been, the murderer had known what he was seeking, found it quickly, and left without leaving any trace behind.

When Angie left, Mary Margaret joined him in the kitchen. "Are there any donuts left?"

"Count them, I only took one. I'm thinking if Georgia used a diary merely to compile inspiring quotes, it would have been on her nightstand, or in a dresser drawer, not hidden where it wouldn't be found."

"I agree. What if she wasn't just copying something she'd read, but instead kept a record of her patients' treatment at the hospital? It would have held confidential information she wouldn't have left out for anyone to find and read."

The doorbell rang and she welcomed Carolina Saavedra, a nurse, and Bob Laine, a physical therapist. He shook Joe's hand with a near bone-crushing grip. "Are those donuts?" he asked.

"Help yourself," Mary Margaret offered. "I know you don't want any of Georgia's clothes, but is there something in particular you wanted of hers?"

"Maybe a book," he replied. He picked up a napkin and took a jelly donut. After a large bite, he murmured appreciatively, "These came from a great bakery."

Joe watched him eat two. He was a solid, muscular man, not overweight, but built like a tank. "If you and Georgia saw the same patients, did you know Curtis Mooney?"

"I did. Nice kid, but confused. He practiced the exercises I gave him, which is good, of course, but I don't know if he's continued with them."

"Do you think he was discharged too soon?"

Bob stepped close. "I wouldn't ask that too loud."

"Why not? Do you think it had something to do with Georgia's death?"

"The coffee smells good." Henry poured himself a cup. "I do my job and don't criticize others. Georgia was outspoken. Now I'm alive, and she isn't. One can't help but draw parallels."

"Would you be willing to talk with me privately?"

"I've already said too much." He carried his cup of coffee into the living room, set it on the coffee table, and began perusing the collection of books in the bookcase.

Two more nurses arrived, and with the kitchen getting crowded, Joe opened the backdoor and leaned against the porch railing. Soon after, Amy Hudson opened her rear door, and came out carrying a bag of trash. He stepped down onto the walk.

"Let me help you with that," he offered.

Amy twisted away. "I can handle it myself," she responded.

Joe didn't argue, but he followed her, and pulled the lid off the first trashcan. "Are you enjoying your summer?" he asked.

"Of course." She dropped the bag into the can with a bombardier's resolve. Her prim white blouse and black skirt didn't flatter her fair coloring or slim figure. She barely mumbled her thanks before heading back to her cottage.

Joe trailed right behind. "Georgia's friends are packing up her things. Is there anything you'd like to have to remember her by?"

Her expression grew fierce as she turned to face him. "What makes you think I'd want to remember her?"

"She was a lovely person," Joe countered. "Someone worth remembering."

Amy swung open her backdoor and entered her cottage without commenting. Joe thought the whole encounter odd. Clearly something had happened between Georgia and

Amy Hudson, or she was simply a mean-spirited woman who hated everyone in the world.

Bob found a copy of Greek mythology he wanted, and then stayed to help the nurses carry their choices to their cars. Joe hung back to stay out of the way, and resisted the temptation to eat the remainder of the donuts left in the pink box.

Thinking he ought to be doing something useful, he checked the cabinets above the kitchen counter and found a few cans of soup, and a couple of cookbooks, he thought Mary Margaret might want to see. He grabbed them, and when a red notebook slipped out of one, he looked over his shoulder to make certain no one was watching before he picked it up. He went outside to the rear path and opened it.

What he found were lists of initials and dates, and notes in some code Georgia must have devised herself. He tucked the book into his inside jacket pocket and hoped Mary Margaret would have some idea what the notations meant. It was nearly noon before everyone left, and he could speak to her alone.

"Help me gather the things for the charity truck," Mary Margaret called to him. She carried an armful of linens to a box on the coffee table, and checked her watch. "We don't have much time before Mike Torres comes back. Is there anywhere left to search?"

Joe pulled her into an enthusiastic hug. "I saved her cookbooks for you, and something else you might find interesting. I'll show it to you later."

"I want to see it now," she insisted.

Mike Torres came through the door. "I looked over your application, Miss McBride, and if you want the cottage, it's yours."

Mary Margaret responded with a delighted smile. "I do want it. I'll have to give my landlord two weeks notice, will that be a problem?"

"No, I like to have the cottages thoroughly cleaned between tenants."

"The locks should be changed," Joe urged. Even if he hadn't been able to talk her out of moving, he wanted her to be safe.

"The locksmith will be here Monday. You needn't worry someone else may have a key."

When Georgia's keys were found missing after her death, Joe wondered why Mike hadn't changed the locks immediately. It struck him as an oversight that might indicate what sort of a manager he'd be. They walked through the cottage with him, but everything had been taken by her friends, or left in boxes to donate.

Mary Margaret held the cookbooks and Joe carried the cans of soup to his car. "Now tell me what you found. I can't wait another minute."

"Let's go to the Jumpin' Plate for lunch and take in an early movie."

"Joe! You are a terrible tease. I'll only go to lunch if you promise to show me what you found, and before we eat, not after."

"All right, it's a deal."

The Jumpin' Plate was busy for lunch on Saturday, and they had to wait for a table. After they were seated and had ordered, Joe pulled the notebook from his pocket. "I found this inside one of the cookbooks. Maybe you can make sense of it."

Mary Margaret hid the book in her lap, and a quick pass through the pages left her both intrigued and bewildered. She slid the book into her purse and snapped the clasp. "Let's skip the movie and work on it this afternoon at my place. The initials have to refer to patients, and the dates begin when she was working in San Diego."

"Let's concentrate on the most recent entries," he suggested. "You'll know the physicians and patients, and I could never figure it out."

Their cheeseburgers tasted so good, neither offered anything more than appreciative murmurs for the next ten minutes. Joe swallowed and reached for a French fry. "Bob Laine wouldn't talk about the hospital. Is everyone afraid to say anything negative about the place or staff?"

"Many are," she replied. "Clearly I'm not, but Georgia didn't hesitate to criticize people she called incompetent fools. It would have been a lot easier to fire her rather than murder her though. I won't call Detective Lynch again, but I wonder how he is doing?"

"Poorly," he surmised.

When they arrived at Mary Margaret's home, they sat at the dining table, and Joe copied one of the notebook's last pages onto plain paper. "I'm assuming the dates are correct."

"Right. Without accurate dates, her notes wouldn't have had any value."

"She died July 14, let's go back a week to July 7. We have GJ, Guns, robin's egg. Do you remember her criticizing any man's care that day?"

Mary Margaret sat back. "I'm sorry, but one day blurs into another, and I don't know."

Joe leaned over to kiss her. "Forget the day then, who do you recall her mentioning?"

"Maybe I should make some coffee."

"In a minute. If Georgia loved to flirt, did she have any favorites?"

She signed unhappily. "Yes, and some of the men are still so depressed over her death they have to be coaxed to eat or exercise." She got up to go into the kitchen, and then turned around and came back. "There was a man named John Gilliam, a boy really, and Dr. Felberg discharged him before Georgia thought he could safely return home."

He read the line again, "GJ, Guns, robin's egg. Maybe she reversed John's initials, to GJ. What could Guns mean?"

"Gunter is Dr. Felberg's first name, so he could be Guns. Robins are some of the first birds seen in spring, so maybe that's leaving early."

"Makes sense," Joe assured her. "Who could Spider be, no wait, don't tell me, Gabriel Webb?"

She laughed. "He has to be spider." She sat down and ran her finger down the copied notes. "There's a Dr. Borowick, I'll bet he's Candle and Dr. Alford has to be Model T. I can almost hear Georgia laughing while she made these notes."

"Does LTF mean anything to you? How about someone with the initials GP, or PG?"

"There was a Patrick Garvey who died during surgery." She closed her eyes to concentrate. "Georgia told me he'd lost the fight, that's LTF. Is there another recent notation with LTF?"

"Yes, for a CH. If his initials were reversed, did you lose a Henry or Harry?"

"There was a Harry Clark who died soon after he'd been admitted. If Georgia was tracking patients whom she believed had received inferior care, she must have intended to do something with the results."

Joe sat back. "Blackmail is my first thought."

"No, she would never have stooped that low. It's more likely she wanted examples to cite when she went to the board."

"And someone stopped her."

She went into the kitchen to make coffee and laced her own with sugar and cream. She carried Joe's cup into him. "Spider, or Gabriel Webb, is on the list. They may have been lovers, but she was following his results too."

Her coffee was always better than his, and he savored a long swallow. "And if he discovered this notebook?"

"Then he'd have it, and we wouldn't." She copied the next page onto another sheet of paper. "Here's a new name, Wolf. I'll bet that's Gertrude Howland. There are no patient initials, just Wolf, CRZ."

"Crazy?" he guessed.

"Yes! That works. I'm sorry I haven't kept a work diary. It would make deciphering the notebook so much easier."

"None of you knew Georgia kept a record?"

"No, if I wasn't aware of it, then none of Georgia's other friends would have been. Patrick Wood only knew about a diary with uplifting sayings."

"Where could that be? Maybe the killer grabbed Georgia's keys, ran down the back stairs of my building, discarded whatever disguise he'd worn, and drove to Chrysanthemum Court. He could have entered through the rear door without being seen, found a diary on Georgia's nightstand, taken it along with her jewelry box, and left as quickly as he'd come."

"Only to discover it wasn't the book he'd been seeking. But how did he know there was a record of some sort?" she asked. "She must have mentioned it to someone she trusted, and it was a huge mistake."

"Gabriel Webb jumps to mind," he offered.

"Maybe he came across the book when he visited Georgia. She could have added to her list, and inadvertently left the book out."

"Why wouldn't he have taken it then?" he asked.

She gave it a moment's thought. "He wouldn't have wanted her to know he'd seen it. But when he came back after he'd killed her, it had disappeared."

"When we went to her cottage, nothing was out of place."

"He's a surgeon, he'd be careful."

"Maybe Gunter Felsberg heard about her list, or one of the other doctors you mentioned. I've only seen Gertrude Howland once, but she looked capable of murder."

She closed the notebook. "I don't want to keep this here. Will you take it to your office?"

"I've got a better idea, but first we'll make a copy. You take the left pages, and I'll take the right." He reached for a piece of paper and used his own pen. "Let's work backwards. The notes from San Diego won't mean anything to you, so we can stop there if we run out of time."

She glanced at her watch. "Won't we have all the time we'll need?"

"I want the notebook in Detective Lynch's hands before five o'clock. Otherwise, I might be accused of withholding evidence, or impeding his investigation."

"Well, then, let's get busy." She placed the notebook between them and began copying her page. "Here's a new notation, someone she called Nellie. I've no idea who that might be."

"A nurse, perhaps? Did she ever describe one as a Nervous Nellie?"

"No, but the name fits several we work with."

"Just keep copying, and we'll figure it out later."

She took a sip of her coffee, and focused on the notebook.

Mary Margaret waited in the car while Joe carried the red notebook into Detective Lynch's station. He returned before five minutes had gone by. "What did he say?"

"He's not in today, but I didn't think he would be on the weekend. The sergeant at the desk gave me a receipt for the notebook, and Lynch should have it first thing Monday morning. He won't be able to decipher the code without help from someone at the hospital, but that's his problem, not ours. Now let's go to the movies."

"That's fine with me. It will give me an excuse to put off packing for the move."

Joe wanted to avoid that subject as long as possible, and hummed to himself on the way to their favorite theater.

Monday morning, Joe met with Gilbert Werner, who was dressed in a navy blue suit and sadly, looked even more crestfallen than he had at their first meeting.

Joe had his folder ready, but hated to open it. "Did you see Miss Hethe Saturday night?"

Gilbert smiled with the memory. "Yes, we went to dinner and a movie, and both of us had a good time, or at least I hope Christine did."

"I'm sure she must have, or she wouldn't keep seeing you." Joe drew in a deep breath and strove to get the whole regrettable report over with quickly. "I didn't see her with another man. I followed her Friday night, and she met a woman for dinner." He showed him the photograph of the pair taken outside the restaurant. "Do you recognize her?"

Gilbert picked up the photo and studied it closely before handing it back to Joe. "No, but Christine has lots of friends."

Joe handed him the next photo. "After dinner they went to a motel." It was what he'd seen, a fact, and he didn't expand on it.

After studying the photo, Gilbert asked, "What were they doing at a motel? Could they have been meeting men there?"

That his client didn't understand what the motel photo clearly showed amazed Joe, but only momentarily. "None arrived while I was observing them."

"How long did you stay?" he asked.

"A couple of hours."

"Do you think that was long enough?"

"Yes, I do. What would you like to do? I can continue to follow Miss Hethe, or we can stop here. It's your choice."

Clearly torn, Gilbert shifted in his seat. "Let's stop now. May I take these photographs?"

"Yes, you may, but if you show them to Miss Hethe, you'll have to explain how you came to have them."

"Oh no, I'll just keep them. I won't tell her."

Joe had his bill ready and Gilbert paid him in cash. He gave him a receipt and an empty folder for the photos, but he hated to see him go without having gained a particle of insight into his relationship with Christine Hethe. "Do you by any chance play golf, Mr. Werner?"

He sat up straighter. "I played on my college team, and we did quite well. I haven't had much chance to play lately."

"I'm putting together a foursome to play Saturday mornings, would you care to join us?"

A wide smile made him far better looking. "Yes, I've missed playing."

Joe could count on Hal to understand why he wanted to befriend Gilbert. Now all he had to do was find a fourth man to join them. Standing at his door, he watched Detective Lynch pass Gilbert on the stairs, and the morning took another unexpected tilt.

Lynch entered Joe's office, and waved the red notebook in the air. "What did you expect me to do with this? Georgia Dixon's name isn't on it or in it, so it could have belonged to anyone. It's either gibberish, or a personal code only the writer could understand. Is this some sort of joke?"

Remaining calm, Joe leaned against his desk and crossed his arms over his chest. He rather enjoyed Lynch's fuming tirade, but didn't respond in kind. "I found it in a cookbook while Georgia's friends were cleaning out her cottage on Saturday. You met Mary Margaret McBride there, and she believes Georgia was tracking patients who might not have received optimum care."

"How many of Georgia's friends witnessed your 'discovery' of the notebook?"

Joe straightened up. "I was alone in the kitchen."

"Wonderful. Did you call someone, Miss McBride, or one of the others to come see what you'd found?"

"No, I waited until after we'd left to show her. She's the only one who saw it before I dropped it off for you at the police station."

"So no one can back up your story, Mr. Ezell. You could have written the notebook yourself and presented it to Miss McBride as being Georgia's."

"You've lost me. Why would I do that?"

"To insinuate yourself into the investigation of Miss Dixon's death. Are you too dim to see the obvious?"

"I doubt I'm the dim one here," Joe countered. "The notebook provides valuable clues as to who might have killed Georgia and why. Miss McBride and I can decipher much of it for you, if you'd like." *If Lynch asked nicely.*

The detective's expression darkened. "I'd rather eat nails." He walked out carrying the notebook and went thudding down the stairs with fierce, angry steps.

Joe went to the restroom to fill his coffee pot and took care when measuring the coffee in hopes it would improve the taste. It didn't. He'd always thought coffee was coffee, but maybe Mary Margaret used a more expensive brand.

CC came to his office door. "Good morning. It looks like you've been busy."

"That was Detective Lynch who's working on Georgia Dixon's case, or at least he claims he is, rather than a client."

"I thought I recognized him. Is he close to solving the crime?"

"No closer than we are, CC." His telephone rang, and the custodian left before he answered. "Discreet Investigations."

"This is Crystal, Mr. Ezell. I went to see Curtis last Friday morning. Can you meet me for lunch at Annette's at 1:00 o'clock today?"

"I'll be there." Joe again arrived first. He nodded and smiled at the women seated in the café as though he joined them every day and recognized them as friends. He waited until Crystal arrived to order a bacon, lettuce and tomato sandwich. She had the chicken salad.

"How did your visit go?" he asked.

"Edwin sat with us on the patio, and Curtis looked to him before he spoke. It's clear he's been coached, although as poor as his memory is, I don't see the point."

She was dressed in a lime green summer dress, and a ribbon-trimmed straw hat covered her upswept hair. Her manicure looked freshly done, and her make-up provided a subtle accent to her natural beauty. He felt like a frog seated opposite her, and her kiss wouldn't turn him into a prince.

"Other than that, how did the conversation go?" he asked.

"It's disheartening that Curtis doesn't remember me, but Edwin certainly does. If anything, he was overly friendly. At one time, Curtis had a lot of friends, and I asked if he had many callers. He frowned and looked to his brother for the answer. Apparently very few of his old friends have stopped by. I offered to visit again if he'd like, and Curtis answered for himself with a wide grin."

"Thank you for going to see him."

"Don't thank me before I get to the best part. As I was leaving, Edwin walked me to my car, and asked if I'd like to come back Monday night and bring a pretty friend. I said I'd love to if I could have Curtis, and his manner instantly turned icy cold. He told me to forget it because he'd not allow any woman to take advantage of his brother, as he knew I surely would. I left without arguing, but I feel sorry for Curtis being stuck with that ogre for a brother and will go back on a day when Edwin isn't home."

"You've provided a clear picture of what's happening with Curtis, so you needn't go back unless you really want to."

"I do. He was a one-time favorite of mine, and he enjoyed my visit even if Edwin didn't."

Joe drew in a deep breath. "It's been three weeks since Curtis's Saturday nurse was murdered. Edwin is still a suspect in my mind, and if he got away with one murder, he might press his luck with two. I don't want to see that happen to you."

"Neither do I," she agreed. "The apple tarts are especially good here. Do you want to split one?"

"Sure." Joe finished his sandwich, the whole time wondering how he could possibly tell Mary Margaret that he had brought an expensive call girl into his investigation.

Mary Margaret prepared spaghetti for their dinner, and Joe carried the heavy pot of water to the stove. Keeping the conversation low-key as they worked, he described Crystal as someone Hal had met while searching for his wife, and a friend of Curtis and Edwin. "Not only did Edwin seem overly-protective when she visited, he accused her of wanting to take advantage of his brother."

"Did he threaten her?"

"I'd say it was implied." He stepped out of her way as she gathered the ingredients for the sauce. "Madeline Price, the housekeeper, thought Georgia and Edwin could have been arguing about the female 'entertainers' he invited over on Monday night. We've also considered Edwin may have complained Georgia was growing too close Curtis."

"But if he fired her, she didn't tell anyone."

He was relieved she was focused on the case rather than Crystal. "Maybe she intended to tell me."

"Do you want to go back to the Mooney's tonight and see who appears?"

"We can't pretend we're lost if the same cop drives by, and that we saw the girls once is enough."

"Okay. Did you hear from Detective Lynch?"

"I did." Joe condensed their already brief conversation. "He doesn't know what he has, and we made a copy."

"It was a very wise move, Joe. The hospital keeps records of deaths, and I looked through the files and made some notes before anyone noticed what I was doing. Let's see if we can match initials with dates in Georgia's notes."

"I brought the copy with me, but let's talk about something else while we eat."

She slid the chopped onion and bell pepper into a pan with a little olive oil. "How are your other cases going? Have you had anything interesting?"

"More odd than anything, but I'm going to be discreet and keep the details to myself."

"How mysterious," she exclaimed. "Now I'm really curious."

"Save it for Georgia's case, please."

She laughed. "Yes, sir. Will do."

CHAPTER 11

◆

Marty Streech came by Joe's office Tuesday afternoon. He pulled a notebook stuffed with loose pages from his jacket pocket. "It's been three weeks since Georgia Dixon died. I still think the Black Dahlia killer is a surgeon Georgia knew, but I'm no closer to proving it than when I saw you last. How is your investigation going?"

The reporter had gotten a haircut, or at least a good trim, and looked far more professional than when they'd first met. "You're out checking your sources? What's the latest from Detective Lynch?" Joe asked.

"He hasn't arrested anyone, so he's no help. Don't dodge my question. What have you learned?"

Joe leaned back in his chair. "All sorts of amazing things, Mr. Streech, but nothing concrete as yet."

"Call me Marty. Why don't we share what we know? It will make work far easier for us both."

"You are a persistent fellow, aren't you?"

"Aren't you, Mr. Ezell?"

"Naturally, or I wouldn't call myself a detective." He checked his watch and stood. "I have a client scheduled, and can't give you more time today."

Marty swore under his breath, rose, and shoved his notebook into his pocket. "I'll stop by again soon."

"I'll look forward to it." Joe kept his face straight as Marty went out the door, but then he had to laugh.

Wednesday morning, Joe received a call from Gus Kershaw, a man with a soft Southern accent who described himself as the owner of Gus's Barbecue restaurant. "How may I help you, Mr. Kershaw?"

"A young man who used to work in my kitchen is selling my barbecue sauce by the bottle. He claims he developed his own recipe after working here, but that's a lie. It's my sauce he's selling as his own, and it has to stop."

While studying for his private investigator's license, Joe had come across a case involving recipes and had a knowledgeable answer. "You cannot copyright a list of ingredients, only recipes that are part of a cookbook. Is that the case here?"

"No, I'm not giving away my recipes for the price of a cookbook. They're too good to share with anyone who can read."

Joe inhaled a deep breath and tried again. "Is it possible the young man could have begun with your sauce and added some extra element, spices, perhaps, of his own to the mix?"

"Anyone could add an extra tablespoon of vinegar and call it his own recipe, but that don't make it so."

"I realize how disturbing this is, but I don't believe I can help you. If there's been a negative effect on your business, an attorney would be a better person to call."

"More people are coming in to eat my barbecue than ever; but no one should be selling my sauce but me."

"Are you selling bottles of your sauce?"

"Well, no, I run a restaurant, not a grocery store."

Joe leaned back in his chair and closed his eyes. "If you were to bottle your sauce and sell it in your restaurant, you'd undoubtedly put the young man out of business. People would want your authentic sauce, not his substitute."

"Authentic? I like that word. I'll need bottles and labels, but I've already got the sauce, and that has to be the hardest part. Come by the restaurant and have dinner on me any night you like. Just give your waiter your name and tell him you're my guest."

"Thank you, I'd like that." Joe hung up and checked the time. He'd solved Gus Kershaw's problem for the price of a dinner, but he'd never be able to buy a nice ring for Mary Margaret making deals like that. He would be able to take her someplace new though, and for now he'd be happy with that.

Mary Margaret nearly drooled over the menu at Gus's Barbecue. "Are ribs too messy to eat? Maybe I should order the chicken."

"I'll order ribs too, and we can help each other keep our faces clean," Joe offered. "Although with sawdust on the floor and paper placemats, they can't worry over a spilled drop of sauce or two."

"That's what I love about you, Joe. You're always so much fun, and after the day I've had, it's precisely what I need."

"Want to tell me what happened?"

"We lost a patient, and the family went nuts. It was no one's fault, but they needed a place to lay the blame."

Joe felt like smacking himself in the forehead. "We haven't even considered that a bereft family member might have thought Georgia was at fault for their loved one's death."

She caught herself before she gaped at him in wide-eyed wonder. "I should have thought of it, because we see our share of hysterical relatives. They expect us to work miracles, and are furious when we fail."

Gus came to their table to welcome them. He was a tall man in a spotless white apron over a chambray shirt and dark trousers. "Mr. Ezell, welcome to you and your lady. The ribs are especially tasty tonight. We season them the night before, smoke them over hickory logs, and my sauce gives them the smackin' good flavor of North Carolina. May I order some for you?"

"I'd love ribs," Mary Margaret answered first.

"Make it two," Joe added. "This is a great place, Gus. You ought to be able to sell gallons of your sauce."

"Better wait until you taste it before you make any predictions." He laughed and moved on to another table to chat with other diners.

"I'm so hungry I'm ready to chew on the edge of the table," Mary Margaret whispered. She took a drink of water, and reached for Joe's hand. "From what we've deciphered of Georgia's notebook, she wasn't tracking families, only patients and medical personnel."

"Could any families have written complaints to the hospital board?"

"Some may have, but most don't want anything more to do with the hospital. I'll make some discreet inquiries, and Angie, or Carolina, might recall a particularly bitter family."

"Gabriel Webb was in Georgia's notebook. Would he talk about the case she listed?"

"He might, speaking of Gabriel, I checked on the scholarship fund this afternoon, and would you care to make a guess at how much Edwin Mooney donated?"

"It probably depends on how guilty he felt."

"Very guilty apparently. He donated ten thousand dollars in his brother's name."

The waiter brought lemonade for Mary Margaret and a beer for Joe. A long drink kept him from fainting where he sat. "You could buy a nice house for that."

"He already has one, and apparently plenty of money to donate to worthwhile causes. Or, as we suspect, guilt prompted his generosity."

Their waiter brought a plate of warm cornbread, with butter and honey. Mary Margaret reached for a square. "I haven't baked cornbread in ages. Remind me to make some soon." She halved hers, drizzled honey over it, and the first bite lit her expression with a dreamy glow.

"We'll have to come here again," Joe responded. With cornbread bringing her to a near swoon, he couldn't wait to taste the ribs. Their plates arrived with ribs as delicious as promised, coleslaw, and French fries. "We won't have to eat again for a whole week."

"You needn't stuff yourself," she warned. "We can take home half for tomorrow night's dinner."

Joe was too busy gnawing on a rib to answer and nodded. He watched her begin with a French fry, and a bite of coleslaw before she picked up a rib. He did his best to hang onto his manners, but it was difficult when it was one of the best meals he'd ever eaten.

They thanked Gus profusely, and went home with a bulging bag of leftovers that lent his car a banquet's aroma. Mary Margaret put the food in her refrigerator, and washed her hands. "I want coffee even if you don't."

Joe slid his arms around her waist and gave her a playful hug. "Sure, I'd like coffee." He'd also like to spend some time reviewing Georgia's notebook, but not just yet.

Gabriel Webb had time to see Joe in his hospital office on Thursday afternoon. "Georgia never mentioned a diary, and it would be too sad to read her personal thoughts now."

Joe had brought his copy of the notebook in a folder. "Rather than writing romantic poetry, she was tracking patients with poor outcomes."

Gabriel sat up in his chair. "What?"

"You heard me. She made a list of patients who had died, or in her opinion had been discharged too early. Dr. Felsberg has the majority of entries, but you're in there too." He opened the folder. "Do you recall a patient with the initials DR from last month? He died on the second of July."

The surgeon kept his own record of patients on his desk calendar. He turned back to find the date. "David

Robinson. He suffered a ruptured appendix, developed peritonitis, and we lost him. Did she blame me?"

"I've no idea what her motivation was to include him, or you. Was there any argument about the cause of David's death?"

"No, had he entered the hospital sooner, we would have had a better chance of saving him. When I told his family, his mother shrieked like a banshee. She would have ripped out my eyes with her fingernails had her husband not caught her and taken her outside. He apologized to me as they left, but I understood the depth of her grief."

"Maybe their anger is what impressed Georgia. But who could have been so furious they'd be moved to kill her?"

Gabriel looked down at his hands. "We're treated as gods when we save someone, but Lord help us when we can't. I'd rather believe a crazy stranger killed Georgia than someone who hated her for failing to save a life that couldn't be saved. That's just too difficult to bear."

His sincerity touched Joe. "We may never know, but if you recall someone who might have been a threat, call Detective Lynch first, and then me."

"Do her notes include anyone in San Diego? We saw such severely injured men during the war, and many succumbed to their wounds despite our efforts to provide the best of care. Most didn't have families nearby, but a few did. I don't recall any specific cases though, and I'd rather not remember those years."

"I understand." Whenever Joe climbed the stairs to his office, he had to suppress the thoughts of Georgia's death. He couldn't imagine being a surgeon with all the bloody memories that must fill his head. "Thank you for your time."

"I wish I could have been more help." He rose and shook hands with Joe before he left.

Henry Hilburn called Joe late that afternoon. "Come on by tomorrow. I've heard something from my contacts at the LAPD that should interest you."

Joe appreciated the former detective's call and met with him on Friday. They again sat outside on the patio and this time, Joe had brought the beer. Rather than rush him, he waited for Henry to settle into his story.

"It seems Detective Lynch came across a notebook. He isn't sure if it's of any value in Georgia Dixon's case, but he has several men working to decode it. If they can't in the next couple of days, he'll toss her file into the bottom drawer of his desk and forget it."

Hilburn had just provided information Joe already knew, which proved he remained in touch with those working Georgia's case. Even if this wasn't news, Henry's sources in the LAPD might turn up some valuable insights soon.

"I gave him the notebook and offered to decode it for him," Joe replied. "He isn't the kind to tolerate outside help though, is he?"

"No, he's too impressed with himself to admit he can't solve a murder on his own, and he leaves a lot of cases open. Someone ought to bring it to the chief's attention." His smile spread into a sly smirk.

"I won't," Joe responded. "I don't want the chief to even know my name."

"I'm hoping for someone on the inside," Henry confided.

Inside information was what Joe wanted, but he refused to become involved in whatever grudge Henry had against Detective Lynch. He promptly changed the subject. "What's happening with the Black Dahlia case?"

Henry shrugged. "There's been no break yet. With no clear link found between the killer and victim, like a man who murders a cheating business partner, it's difficult, if not impossible, to catch the culprit. Someone has to know the killer's name, could even have been present when Elizabeth Short died. Her death might be weighing heavily on his conscience, and he could come forward. Or he might fear the killer will permanently silence him to remove the only witness to the crime. That worry ought to inspire him to talk real soon."

"Let's hope so." Joe stayed a while longer, and Henry's comments made him wonder if there weren't someone who could identify Georgia's killer. Someone, who might be getting real nervous and fear for his own life.

When Joe returned to his office, he telephoned Marty Streech, and the reporter came right over. "Have you considered that someone must know who killed Elisabeth Short?" Joe asked. "Either an accomplice who could have lured her to the murderer, or was present when she died? There's a reward for information leading to an arrest, but maybe you ought to play on the accomplice's fears for his own life."

Marty took notes as fast as he could write them. "I like that angle. If I write one person couldn't have worked alone on such a grisly crime, the accomplice could fear the police will come looking for him. I'll play up that angle, and urge him strongly to come to me with his story while he's still alive to tell it. I'll offer to accompany him when he turns himself in." He closed his notebook and grinned widely. "Now what can I do for you."

"The same approach should work on Georgia Dixon's case. With such a brutal killing, someone has to know a person capable of that level of violence, or saw bloody evidence of it. They might save their own life by giving his name to the police."

Marty scribbled more notes. "I knew we could work together. I'll get the Black Dahlia story in the paper tomorrow, and wait until next week to write about Miss Dixon."

Joe wasn't even tempted to ask him if he played golf.

Early Saturday morning, Gilbert Werner met Joe and Hal Marten for nine holes of golf. He carried a bag with the same expensive clubs the pros used, and Joe was glad he'd invited him. Hal welcomed him without attempting to sell him insurance, and the morning went well. Gilbert might lack for confidence in other settings, but with a golf club in his hands, he was a different man. He beat Joe by several strokes, but the detective didn't even care.

"Let's play again next week," Joe said.

"Yeah, this was fun," Gilbert replied, shook their hands, and walked to his car with an actual strut.

Hal waited until they were alone to speak. "He's awfully good, isn't he?"

"Yes, would you rather take lessons from him?" Joe asked with a good-natured chuckle.

"No, I didn't embarrass myself today, thanks to already having a great teacher. Let's continue with all the lessons we can work in before our next game."

"Will do." Joe agreed. They would concentrate on golf, and wait for Gilbert to ask for advice on his romance.

Joe rushed up the stairs later Saturday morning to answer a ringing telephone. He quickly caught his breath. "Discreet Investigations."

"Are you really discreet?" a man whispered.

There was a slight echo to the man's deep voice, as though the poor fellow was hiding in his bathroom to make the call. "Yes, I most definitely am. How may I help you?"

"I want you to investigate a former fiancée."

Rather than offer any suggestions that might solve the man's problem before earning himself a dime, Joe asked for a name, suggested an office visit, and provided directions. While he waited for the man to appear, he made coffee, with the more expensive brand he'd bought, and it did taste better. He was on his second cup when the prospective client arrived.

"I'm Bruce Corbett." He extended his hand.

Despite his hushed tone on the telephone, Bruce was a big, burly man. At six feet tall, he had an erect military posture, and a firm handshake. His hair was dark and thick, his skin deeply tanned, and his brown eyes held a world of sorrow. He politely refused an offered cup of coffee.

Joe opened a folder and raised a pencil to take notes. "Tell me about your former fiancée, Mr. Corbett. Did you part on good terms?"

He had entered the office with a forceful confidence, but now slumped in his chair as though the air had been sucked out of him. "We wouldn't have parted had we been on good terms, would we?"

Attitude was something Joe didn't need, but he did need a new client who could pay for his services. "Sometimes people realize that despite their best hopes and intentions, they simply aren't right for each other, and they part amicably. I take that wasn't the case?"

"No, there was nothing amicable about it. To put it frankly, she left me for another man. I need to know if she's happy with him. I haven't heard from her since last year, so I'm assuming that she is, but I'd like to know for sure."

"Of course. You're not dating anyone new?"

He sighed unhappily. "I've not even wanted to, but if Kathy is now happily married, maybe I'll be better able to get over her."

"What is Kathy's last name?"

"Her name is Katherine Sims. She teaches ballet at a dance studio she owns in the San Fernando Valley." He handed Joe one of her pink business cards. "She met an artist who has a studio in the same building, and suddenly, I became too dull to be tolerated. An artist!" he fumed.

"What sort of work do you do, Mr. Corbett?"

"I'm an accountant, and work primarily on internal business audits."

Joe tried not to grimace, but math had never been one of his favorite subjects. "That's a fine, steady occupation, one that allows you to invest wisely, I assume."

"Yes, it's that, but no one ever describes accountants as being exciting men. I took over my father's firm when he retired, but it looks as though I'll not have a son of my own to leave it to."

"You're still a young man."

"None of us who fought in the war can be described as young, Mr. Ezell. Did you serve?"

"I was in the Coast Guard off Greenland. We supplied weather reports to aid the Allies in planning their attacks."

"Weather," he whispered under his breath. "Well, the war's over, and we need to concentrate on the here and now."

"That's a good plan. Do you know the artist's name?"

"Roy Russell. He paints big pieces people describe as modern, but to me they look like a kid left his crayons out in the sun. Not that I'd ever be tempted to hurl paint against a canvas and call it art, but I'll bet I could do better than Roy Russell any day."

"Modern art doesn't appeal to everyone, Mr. Corbett, but I don't need to buy one of Mr. Russell's works to discover how he and Miss Sims are doing. She probably gives ballet lessons Saturday afternoons, so I'll stop by and ask about lessons for a niece. She needn't know I don't actually have one. If Mr. Russell's studio is still in the same building, I'll ask him about his art. An artist will discuss his work forever, so I should be able to learn a lot this afternoon."

"Will you call me later?" he asked.

"I'll call with a preliminary report if you'd like." Joe asked for and received his standard advance. He walked Corbett to the door, and checked the time. He'd leave for the San Fernando Valley now, find a place for lunch, and then tackle what looked like a case that would be almost too easy for a man of his talents.

The Sims' ballet studio had a beautiful hard wood floor and a mirrored wall. Little girls dressed in blue leotards with attached skirts, white tights, and pink ballet slippers were at the *barre* practicing a *plie,* bending their knees with a varying degree of grace. Joe joined the row of seated parents at the end of the studio.

The woman beside him smiled, and whispered, "Which girl is yours?"

"I came to ask about lessons for my niece. Are you pleased with Miss Sims' instruction?"

"Delighted. My daughter is the one with red hair. Isn't she precious?"

The little redhead had a firm grip on the *barre*, and rather than make a graceful gesture, she flailed her free arm as she though she were attempting to fly. Joe nodded and smiled. He was more interested in the teacher than her students.

Miss Sims, Kathy, wore a black leotard with a short jersey wrap skirt, and tights, an outfit that showed off her slender figure to every advantage. Her dark hair was drawn up into a bun atop her head, a style her students, or their parents, had copied with varying degrees of success.

She spoke to them sweetly, as though they were all her own dear children. If Joe had actually had a niece, he would definitely have sent her to Miss Sims for ballet. When she dismissed her students, he waited for her to speak with a parent who had a question before introducing himself, and inquiring about lessons.

She was perhaps five feet four, with dark eyes that held a hint of mischief. "Here is a brochure; a new round of classes begins in three weeks. How old is your niece?"

"She's seven. I'll see her mother gets this."

"Don't wait too long. My classes fill quickly." She brushed a stray curl back into her bun, and Joe noted her fingers were bare.

"While I'm in the building, I thought I'd go upstairs and look at Roy Russell's work. His name is familiar, so I've seen his art somewhere." He frowned, as though struggling to place him.

"I'm afraid you've missed him. He declared he'd outgrown Los Angeles, and moved to New York two months ago. He's determined to succeed in the art scene there. Are you fond of modern art?"

"Not really, but I recognized Roy's name." Students for the next class began trickling in, and Joe backed away. "Thank you for the information about classes, Miss Sims."

"My pleasure," she responded, and turned to greet her students.

Thinking Roy Russell might have left a forwarding address on his studio door, Joe climbed the stairs to the third floor. Roy had had the studio in back, and he'd painted good-bye in a colorful splash across the door. If he'd had a New York address, he hadn't left it there. The name of the management company was posted by the front door, and Joe jotted down the name and number. He'd call them later, and see if they knew Roy's new address.

He stopped for coffee and a piece of apple pie at a café down the street before driving home. Warm from the oven, the flakey pastry was superb. Mary Margaret seldom baked a dessert, which was probably a good thing for their waistlines. He took his notebook from his pocket and made a few notes about Miss Sims. She struck him as too elegant a woman to call herself Kathy. She would go by Katherine, or Miss Sims. He had some answers for Bruce Corbett, but they might not be enough for a man with an accountant's strict sensibilities.

He could report Miss Sims hadn't married Roy Russell, but he'd save the rest for an office visit next week. If she'd left Bruce for another man, she'd probably do so again, but he'd been paid for information, not advice.

CHAPTER 12

Joe and Mary Margaret ended their Saturday night movie date at Aunt Lucy's Ice Cream Parlor. They shared a banana split and in a relaxed mood, he couldn't resist the temptation to tell her about his latest case. "A man whose girlfriend left him for an artist came to me. He misses her and wanted to know if they'd married.

"They haven't, and the artist has moved to New York. I told the client his girlfriend was still single, and that I'd have more to tell him on Monday. He should be relieved to learn the artist is out of the picture, please forgive the awful pun, but that doesn't mean his former girlfriend will want to go back to him."

"That isn't really your concern, is it, Joe? Isn't it enough to answer his initial question?"

He swallowed a bite of banana. "It should be, but I have a feeling this case is going to drag on and on."

"Can you charge for giving sympathy to the lovelorn?" She giggled between bites.

She was the only girl he'd ever really cared about, and he told her so often. "I only know how to love you, Mary Margaret." He watched her blush the prettiest shade of rose, and loved her all the more.

"After Hal Marten's case, I have to look for unexpected consequences. Maybe I'm just a sucker for the underdog, but the man and his former girlfriend appear to be the classic mismatch. I'd rather steer his interest in another direction than have him pursue her when there's no hope of success."

"Have you considered she may remember him fondly?"

In his view, it would be a complete waste of time. "It seems unlikely."

"While it might be kind to warn the man his affections won't be returned, he might take out his anger on you."

Joe finished the last of the strawberry ice cream. "True, which might be the case with Georgia, if she'd been blamed for a patient's death. She would have recognized the relative coming up the stairs, and been apprehensive she'd seen them again, but she wouldn't have run screaming down the back stairs."

Mary Margaret shivered at the thought. "Why wouldn't the murderer have gone after the doctor rather than the nurse?"

"He might still intend to," Joe offered. They'd finished the banana split, but he didn't want to end the evening on such a sad note. "I need to leave my cases behind when I lock my office door rather than spoil our time together with such depressing thoughts."

"Georgia isn't merely a case, Joe. She means a whole lot more to both of us, and I'll be happy to listen to whatever thoughts you have about her. Let's get out of here and go to my place."

That was an invitation he never refused.

They spent Sunday afternoon packing Mary Margaret's things and cleaning her apartment. "I'd no idea I'd accumulated such a mountain of extraneous stuff," she complained. "Let's use this box for things I'll donate to charity."

"Is it big enough?" Joe asked.

"Yes, silly, of course it is. There's no reason to keep books I've read and will never read again. They'll go to the library for their yearly sale and can clutter up someone else's bookshelf." She began a stack of books by the door.

Joe's favorite books were mysteries, and nothing she was discarding appealed to him. He still didn't understand why she wanted to leave such a nice apartment, but he couldn't criticize her actions when he had no alternative ready to present.

Rather than admit it, he continued with yesterday's conversation about his work. "Maybe I could charge people for romantic advice. It might pay better than detective work, and there would be no guarantees."

"You'd have to listen to sad stories all day," she pointed out. "Is that how you want to spend your time?"

"Good point, although I'd like to have business cards made with Discreet Investigations plus Romantic Insights. They flow together almost as nicely as we do."

She laughed. "Concentrate on helping me with my move, will you please?"

"Yes, ma'am. I sure will." He gave her a quick hug and carried another armful of books to the door.

Monday, Bruce Corbett came into Discreet Investigations on his lunch hour. His dark gray suit matched his mood. "I'm glad to learn Kathy is still single, but I have an awful feeling it still won't be good news for me."

Joe laid the ballet studio brochure on his desk as proof he'd been there. "Maybe it's time to let go of the past and concentrate on your future."

Bruce squared his shoulders. "You told me there was more, let's hear it."

The detective chose his words with care. "Miss Sims told me Roy Russell had closed his studio and moved to New York. She was matter-of-fact about it, not sobbing because she'd been left behind. I checked with the management company, and Russell left no forwarding address."

Hope lit Bruce's eyes. "Do you suppose Kathy might be too embarrassed to call me and admit their romance fizzled?"

"I don't know, but it's also likely she is dating someone new."

"Would you speak with her again, Mr. Ezell? I'll be happy to pay for your time, but I don't want to approach Kathy without knowing whether or not I'd be welcomed."

Joe leaned back in his chair. "Why not write her a heartfelt letter? You could say you'd heard Roy Russell had moved away, and you're wondering if she's missed you as much as you've missed her. She'll respond if she wants to see you again."

"Isn't a letter rather cold? Kathy could just toss it into the trash, and I'd never know whether or not she'd read it."

"What if you included the letter in a delivery of a dozen roses? She'd be charmed, and want to read your message."

Unconvinced, Bruce frowned unhappily. "As you'll recall, we didn't part amicably. Other couples have fights and reconcile, but I don't want to get into another shouting match with her. I just want things to be as they were at first, when she liked me."

A glance at the office ceiling failed to offer useable insights, and Joe feared he had no choice in how to proceed. "If I visit Miss Sims one more time, and ask her directly if she'd like to see you, will you accept her answer whether it's yes or no?"

"I could try."

"That's not good enough," Joe cautioned. "I need your word now or I won't go."

Bruce responded with a deep sigh. "Yes, I'll accept whatever she says as final."

Joe picked up the brochure and checked the class times. "Miss Sims gives lessons this afternoon. I'll stop by after the last one and introduce myself a second time as a detective. She might be impressed that you cared enough to follow-up on your romance, but the chances are equally good that she'll be infuriated I tricked her into talking to me last Saturday."

"I'll take my chances." He handed Joe cash. "You'll call me again with your report?"

"I will," Joe promised. He'd give him a complete summary so he wouldn't need to see him in his office ever again.

Joe waited outside the ballet studio until the last of girls taking lessons had left with their mothers. He rapped lightly at the door as he entered. "Miss Sims, I hate to bother you again."

She greeted him with a friendly smile. "It's no bother at all. Is your niece interested in signing up for lessons?"

"I apologize, but I don't actually have a niece." He introduced himself as a detective working for Bruce Corbett. "He hasn't forgotten you, and he hopes you'd like to see him again."

"You're not serious." She returned the record she'd been playing for musical accompaniment to its cardboard sleeve and closed the lid on the record player. "Of course, you are. I'm going to be straight with you, and I want you to make my lack of interest in Bruce abundantly clear. Is it a deal?"

"Yes, Miss Sims." She wasn't screaming insults at him, which he took as a good sign.

"Bruce appeared to be a gentleman, and I enjoyed his company until he began telling me what I could and could not do. He went from adoring to controlling in a heartbeat, and I used Roy Russell as a convenient excuse to stop seeing him. Roy and I were merely friends, nothing more, but the idea I'd prefer an artist to him made him so angry he scared me. Please tell him I'm engaged to an attorney with a large practice in Beverly Hills. That sounds believable, doesn't it?"

"Is it true?"

"No, but what difference does it make? I don't want to crush Bruce's feelings, but I don't want to be in the same room with him ever again."

Bruce came through the door, and clearly he'd overheard every word of their conversation. "You didn't think I deserved honesty?" he shouted.

Joe stepped between them. "Mr. Corbett, we don't need an ugly scene." Bruce swung and punched Joe in the face before he could duck. Dazed, Joe swayed on his feet, and Katherine Sims caught hold of him around the waist.

She nearly spit out her anger, "Here's the truth, I don't like you. Now go away or I'll call the police and have you arrested for assaulting the detective you hired yourself. You're a bully, and I won't be bullied. Get out."

"But I love you," he responded, his features softening into a beguiling half-smile.

Outweighed by a good fifty pounds, Joe couldn't beat Bruce in a fight, but he was still badly embarrassed he hadn't seen the punch coming. Wobbly, he straightened up, grabbed a chair for support, and echoed her order.

"Leave now or I'll call the police myself. When a woman says she's not interested in you, believe her."

"I'll go when I'm ready!" He reached for Katherine, but she spun away from his grasp.

Joe threw himself at Bruce, tripping him, and they fell with a force that shook the hardwood floor. "Call the police!" Joe yelled to Katherine, and she did a flying leap over them and raced out the door.

All Joe could do was keep a clumsy grip on Bruce's jacket and dodge the powerful blows raining down on him. They rolled on the floor, and the furious man's greater weight pressed the wind out of him. Gasping for air, he fought to keep a frantic hold on Bruce's tie, and the distant sound of sirens offered a glimmer of hope he'd survive such a brutal pummeling.

The police officers raced up the stairs to the ballet studio, broke up the fight, and took Bruce Corbett away in handcuffs. Their sergeant helped Joe to his feet. "You need an ambulance?"

Joe felt as though he could use two. His left eye was swollen shut, and a bloody nose had made a gory mess of his shirt. He shook his head and a jolt of pain made him instantly sorry. "Just let me catch my breath, and I'll be all right." He sank into the closest chair.

Now certain her studio was safe, Katherine Sims rushed to his side. "Oh, Mr. Ezell, I'm so sorry." She brought a damp towel from the restroom and blotted the blood from his face.

"Thank God you were here. What if Bruce had come after me while I was alone?" She began to cry and her tears fell on Joe's bruised cheek. He remembered the boxer he'd met at the bus stop and wondered if he'd recommend his gym.

The sergeant opened his notebook. "Tell me your side of it."

Joe ran his tongue over his teeth and was grateful they were all still firmly planted in his gums. He gave the shortest account possible, and Katherine Sims vouched for every word.

"Don't try and drive home," the sergeant advised. "Do you have a friend you can call to come and get you?"

"I'll drive you home," Kathy offered. "You can come back for your car tomorrow. It will be safe in the building lot."

The sergeant observed Joe with a sympathetic gaze. "You should stop by an emergency room on the way home to be sure this isn't worse than it looks. Broken ribs can pierce a lung, and you'd drown in your own blood."

It wasn't a pleasant thought, but Joe had held onto Bruce too tightly for the man to get a solid punch to his ribs. "My ribs are the only part of me that doesn't hurt," he whispered.

"What's going to happen to Bruce?" Katherine asked.

"He's been arrested for assault, and he'll spend the night in jail. He'll appear in court tomorrow to answer to the charges, and probably make bail. You can provide testimony if the case comes to a trial. Don't worry about him bothering you again, miss. We'll make it real plain that

he won't enjoy spending more than a single night in jail."
He left to see to it.

Joe held his handkerchief to his nose and concentrated on breathing in and out. He thought about calling Hal for a ride, but it would be a long drive for him, and he wanted to go home now.

"Are you sure you want to give me a ride home?" he asked.

"Of course, it's the least I can do. Give me the directions, and you can ride in the back seat and rest the whole way."

She drove a 1940 Buick with a wide back seat Joe made the most of. He took care not to bleed on the upholstery, and when they reached his apartment, he thanked her profusely for the ride. "I had no idea Bruce would show up at your studio tonight and turn violent. If I had, I wouldn't have taken his case in the first place."

"I understand. I was also taken in when I first met him. Is your place on the first floor?"

"The second."

"I'll see you to your door." She helped him out of her car and slipped her arm around his waist to guide him toward the stairs. "Go ahead, lean on me. I dance all day, and I'm all muscle."

To need a ballet dancer's help to reach his door was thoroughly humiliating, and he grit his teeth and climbed the stairs slowly. "It's number six facing the street." His hands were so swollen he couldn't hold his keys, and she unlocked the door for him. He stumbled in, and made it to his easy chair.

"Let me get some ice for your eye before I go." She found the kitchen and wrapped what ice he had in a dishtowel, and brought it in to him. "I filled the ice cube trays, so you'll have more in the morning should you need it. I hate to leave you alone here. Is there someone I could call?"

The telephone rang before he could reply, and she answered. "Mr. Ezell's residence. I'm so sorry, but he's unable to come to the phone. May I take a message?" She put her hand over the speaker so she wouldn't be heard and whispered, "It's Mary Margaret McBride. Do you want to speak with her?"

He gestured weakly, and she brought him the phone. "Hello, dearest."

"Don't you dearest me. Who answered your phone?"

"I'm interviewing secretaries."

Katherine Sims took the phone out of his hand. "He's too embarrassed to tell you he's been in a fight. I'm leaving now, and if I were you, I'd come over right away. Good-bye." She hung up the telephone and moved toward the door. "Is there anything else you need before I go?"

Joe wondered if he'd be able to unzip his pants, but he kept that worry to himself. "No, thank you for the ride. If you want me to investigate a man before you date him, I'll do it for free."

"I may take you up on it." She closed the door quietly as she went out.

Mary Margaret found Joe's door unlocked and came in. She took one look at him and shook her head. "Let me guess, you spoke to the client who'd lost his girlfriend to the artist?"

"Unfortunately, yes." He gave her a brief description of their encounter. "The dancer brought me home."

"Is she cute?"

"I didn't notice."

"I'll take that for a yes. I brought some Epsom salts. Let's get you in a hot bath, and then into bed. You'll feel better in the morning."

Joe struggled to stand and sat back down. "I'll need you to help me out of my clothes."

She rested her hands on her hips. "Why doesn't that surprise me?"

The best he could do for a laugh resulted in only a dry chuckle. "Let's have some pity here. I really don't think I can stand."

"Sure you can." She untied his oxfords and eased them off his feet.

He was relieved his socks were new. He tossed them when they showed the first sign of wear rather than walk around with a toe sticking out. It was a very small point of pride tonight.

He felt sick to his stomach, but he wouldn't throw up in front of her. He swallowed hard. "Would you bring me a glass of water, please?"

When she went into the kitchen, he shoved himself to his feet. He'd take a bath and let her baby him tonight, but tomorrow, he'd pull himself together, and go out to the valley to get his car. He'd make it into the office if it killed him.

The enticing aroma of freshly brewed coffee and frying bacon woke Joe at 8:00 o'clock the next morning. He was surprised to be hungry, which was a good sign, but he downscaled his expectations for the day. He had no appointments for the morning so he could go by the office later, but he didn't want to leave his car in the ballet studio parking lot any longer than he had to.

Mary Margaret came to the door. "I see you're conscious, how about some breakfast?"

He sat up and swung his legs over the side of the bed. He'd slept in his boxer shorts and couldn't overlook the dark purple bruises on his knees. He'd hit the floor awfully hard when he'd made the flying leap for Corbett, and the result sure wasn't pretty.

"I'll come into the kitchen," he vowed. "I need the exercise."

"You needn't rush." She came on into the bedroom and smoothed his tousled hair. "I called in sick so I can help you, and have another day to work on my apartment."

It was nice having her around in the morning. "Thanks, but I'll pep up here in a minute." At least he thought he would.

* * *

Two hours later, they took the bus out to the valley, and while it required a couple of transfers, they spent their time observing their fellow passengers and making up stories of who they might be. Joe worked on sharpening his powers of observation, but wearing sunglasses to hide a truly hideous black eye limited what he could see.

He'd planned to introduce Mary Margaret and Katherine Sims, but the dancer's car wasn't in the lot. He walked around his Chevrolet to make certain it still had all four tires and looked none the worse for the wear. His hands weren't nearly so swollen today, and he unlocked the passenger door for Mary Margaret.

She took his keys. "You can't see well enough to drive, so I will. I do know how even if I don't own a car. Do you want to see my driver's license?"

"No, I'm a sucker for anything a pretty girl says." He got into the car slowly, and pulled his door closed. She had to adjust the seat position for her height, and then drove out of the lot and onto the street with a confidence that impressed him.

"Do you mind if I take a nap on the way back?" he asked.

"Not at all. I'll wake you when we get to your office. I'll drop you off there, and pick you up at 5 o'clock."

"Slave-driver," he mumbled. He closed his eyes and in what seemed like only a moment, Mary Margaret pulled to the curb by his building. He sat up, took a deep breath, and while he was still sore all over, he refused to take any further advantage of her loving sympathy. "I'll meet you right here."

CC stood at the top of the stairs, and Joe made the mistake of removing his sunglasses when he said hello.

"Oh, my goodness, Mr. Ezell, have you been in a car accident?"

"It was more of a two man brawl," he replied. "My nose wasn't broken, so I'll not be permanently disfigured. What's new with you?"

"My brother and his wife had a baby girl last weekend. Named her Lenora. She's a real pretty little girl."

"Congratulations. You'll make a wonderful uncle."

"I hope so." He walked ahead of Joe and unlocked his office door for him. "If you need anything at all, just let me know."

Joe pulled out his wallet and handed him a bill. "Would you get me a Coca-Cola from the fountain downstairs? Get one for yourself too, if you like."

"Thank you, Mr. Ezell, I believe I will."

The cold soda served to relieve Joe's aches, and soothed, his thoughts went straight to his file for Georgia Dixon. Edwin Mooney might be overly protective of his brother, but Joe moved him down his list of suspects. The VA hospital provided a wealth of possibilities, both from former patients, their grieved relatives, and the staff, but with a paucity of clues, it might well prove impossible to identify the killer. Which was no excuse not to try.

When the telephone rang, he debated whether or not to answer. His need to pay the rent prompted him to respond. "Discreet Investigations."

"I need you to follow someone," a woman stated in a hoarse rasp. "Are you up for it?"

He wasn't that day, but wouldn't admit it. "Of course. May I have your name?"

"Ophelia Rose."

She nearly hissed her name, not a good sign. "Mrs. Rose, I need you to come to my office to discuss the particulars of the job. Is ten o'clock tomorrow good for you?"

"I'll be there." She made it sound like a threat.

A dial tone greeted him before he could say good-bye. He put his head in his hands, and wondered how ridiculous Mrs. Rose's job might be. Perhaps Mr. Rose was involved in something interesting, maybe even dangerous, so it wouldn't be yet another follow and photograph afternoon.

A call from Gabriel Webb surprised him. "Dr. Webb, how are you?"

"I'm fine health-wise, but I keep thinking of the possibility a former patient, or relative of one we lost, might have killed Georgia. The problem is how to sift through the files for a person so angry they'd take their fury out on her. The patients ought to be in her notebook, but their relatives could have scattered in a hundred different directions."

"My thoughts exactly. What do you want to do?"

"I'd like to see the notebook. Maybe someone's initials will spark a memory. Are you free for dinner tonight?"

"Could we postpone it until tomorrow?" Joe doubted his looks would be much improved, but he had to feel better in twenty-four hours.

"Fine, I'll see you when you come to pick-up Mary Margaret, and she can help us."

"See you then."

Joe leaned back and closed his eyes. Anyone who had been so furiously angry they'd resort to murder, had probably written to the hospital to denounce the doctor or nurse they deemed responsible. He called Gabriel Webb and found him still in his office.

"Does the administration there keep threatening letters on file?"

"I'll find out," he promised. "See you tomorrow."

Joe called Hal to call off their golf lesson. "I ran into some trouble that was about six feet two and two hundred fifty pounds."

"Should you be in the hospital?" Hal asked.

"No, I have my own private nurse. I'm going to help her move this weekend, so we'll have to postpone our next game."

"That's fine. I'll get in some practice at the driving range. Take care now, and give me a call if I can do anything for you."

"Will do." Joe called Gilbert Werner to let him know he needed to postpone their next game a week.

"I understand if you'd rather not play with me," Gilbert responded.

"Nonsense. You're so good I have to play with you to sharpen my own game. I'll see you in two weeks." He hung up before Gilbert could make another pitiful comment. Putting some starch in the man's spine might take far more effort than he'd anticipated.

CC came in to empty the wastebasket. "How are you doing, Mr. Ezell?"

"I'm enjoying a peaceful afternoon, thank you."

"Glad to hear it. You're one of my favorite tenants."

"Do you say that to all of us?" Joe thought the friendly custodian might flatter everyone in the building, but CC instantly argued.

He drew the door closed and whispered. "Don't believe it for a minute, Mr. Ezell. I won't name names, but there are some here who are way down low on my favorites list."

Joe managed a low chuckle without causing himself too much anguish. "Well, thank you, CC. I can use all the good news I can get today."

"How are you doing on Miss Dixon's case?"

"I'm making inroads," Joe responded, hoping it was true. When Mary Margaret picked him up, he told her Dr. Webb had called.

"Let's get Georgia's other friends to help us," she responded. "She might have mentioned an irate relative or patient to one that she didn't say to us all. I'll make spaghetti for dinner. It should slide down your throat without too much effort."

"I love your spaghetti."

She laughed. "You love everything I make."

"True, but I do have favorites. Wait a minute, what if a wife or girlfriend of a patient became jealous of Georgia? It could be a man having a lengthy stay at the hospital."

"He could still be a patient now," she thought aloud. "Do you suppose we have a murderer visiting a loved one at the VA every day?"

"It could be, although I doubt a woman did it. Keep your eyes open tomorrow and if anyone looks in the least bit suspicious, make a note of their name, and we'll discuss them with the others tomorrow night."

She reached over to pat his knee and he winced. "Sorry. I'd rather think about you tonight."

Joe hadn't eaten since breakfast, and he was thinking about her delicious spaghetti, but he wisely kept it to himself.

Wednesday morning, Ophelia Rose arrived five minutes early for her appointment with Joe. She was tall and slender, with graying blonde hair pulled back in a tight bun. While her make-up was tastefully applied, and her navy blue dress modest, he gathered the impression she might once have been a showgirl who danced in reviews. She certainly had the height for it, and an innate elegance that would have taken her far. It was an intriguing thought.

"Good morning, Mrs. Rose. Please describe your problem, and we'll work to solve it."

"It looks as though you might have problems of your own, Mr. Ezell."

He'd not deny it. "Yes, it's true, but I did save the damsel in distress, so a black eye is a small price to pay."

"A hero, how adorably quaint. To return to why I'm here, I have a problem with my son, Matthew." She laid his photo on the desk. "I bought him a car to drive to UCLA. I've discovered he loans the car to his girlfriend while he's attending classes. I saw her behind the wheel with my own eyes, but he swears he's the only one driving the car."

Joe muffled a deep sigh of disappointment. "Would you like me to follow your son tomorrow and take some photos he can't dispute?"

"Yes, I would. It's a De Soto coupe, and I'll sell it and make him ride the bus rather than allow her to drive it."

"You don't care for her?" That took no powers of observation to reach.

She straightened her already stiff posture. "I do not use the type of language necessary to describe her accurately, but she's definitely not someone he needs to know."

He made a note of the Rose's address, and the time Matthew would leave for UCLA. He asked for his usual advance, and she opened her purse to remove the cash without quibbling over the price. He provided a receipt, walked her to his door, and returned to his desk to make additional notes in the case folder.

It was possible Ophelia Rose might never accept anyone her son dated, but that was the son's problem, and all he had been paid to do was check on who was driving his car. Hardly challenging, but it would get him out of the office in the morning. He leaned back in his chair, thinking a brief nap would be good, but before he closed his eyes, Marty Streech knocked on his door.

"Did you read my article?" he asked. He laid the latest copy of the *Los Angeles Examiner* on Joe's desk with it folded to his column. "I used the same logic I did with the Black Dahlia column last week: someone knows who killed Georgia, and if they know what's good for them, they'll come forward with information that will lead to an arrest and conviction."

The column was well-written, leaving Joe very pleasantly surprised. "Good work. Let's hope someone takes the bait."

Marty sat in one of the office chairs. "Speaking of bait, you look as though you were on the wrong end of a wild animal hunt."

"You could say that," he agreed, "but it won't make for a good story."

The reporter leaned forward. "Tell me what happened, and I'll shape it so it does."

"A detective who wants to stay in business, doesn't call attention to himself."

"No kidding? Is that in a rule book somewhere?" He looked decidedly skeptical.

"I'm sure it is, or it should be," Joe argued. "What was the response to your Black Dahlia column?"

"Many of Los Angeles's most peculiar people called to chat, and Detective Lynch got even more calls than the paper did. As you can imagine, he wasn't pleased."

There were several truly apt ways to describe the obnoxious detective, but Joe lacked the energy to express them with the proper vigor. "I'll give you a call if I think of anything else you might use."

Marty rose with a lop-sided lunge. "Do that. I think we're right. Someone has to know the killer or killers. A woman perhaps, who's afraid he'll kill her next."

Joe nodded. "If such a person exists, she'd have to be terrified."

"That's what we're hoping so she rats out her boyfriend or husband before he can murder another girl." He closed the door softly as he left.

The paper still lay on Joe's desk, and he read Marty's article a second time. There were some quotes he must have gotten at the memorial service, but they presented Georgia as a well-liked, thoughtful nurse. Clearly someone had held an opposite opinion.

CHAPTER 13

Mary Margaret stood alone in front of the VA hospital. "We're meeting Dr. Webb in a conference room," she told Joe. "Bob Laine went to get hamburgers for dinner, and I gave him money for ours. We can settle up later."

"Fine. I love a good burger." He gave her cheek a quick kiss. "How many of your friends will be there?"

"Angie, Carolina, Bob, and Dr. Webb. If there were more, we wouldn't get anything done."

"Good thinking." He had no idea how many people would be too many if they could come up with some valuable leads. They met Gabriel Webb in the hallway outside the conference room. He was dressed in street clothes and carried a thick folder.

"I inquired about complaint letters and a secretary said I shouldn't concern myself with them. I waited until she'd left for the day, and found the file with the latest entries. I'll return them in the morning before she comes in."

Joe had not expected Webb to have a talent for intrigue, but he restrained himself rather than slap him on the back. He removed his sunglasses as he pulled open the conference room door.

Angie laid yellow legal tablets and pencils on the long table. "Oh dear, Joe, what happened to you?"

"An occupational hazard," he answered, "and I failed to duck soon enough. Let's see if we can sort the letters into categories before Bob brings dinner. Some people might be merely perturbed, and others outraged."

"We ought to keep track of who receives the most complaints," Mary Margaret suggested.

"Who wins the unpopularity contest?" Angie asked. "We can probably sort the letters in multiple ways."

"How's this one?" Webb asked. "'Your nurses are so slow, they would come in last in a snail race.'"

"Tepid." Carolina wrote the word on one of the legal pads. "Let's stack those here."

"Here's a single sentence, 'May you be cursed into eternity'!"

"Without any details, we don't know whom they wish to curse," Mary Margaret offered.

"All of us probably," Carolina posed. "Is there a name?"

"Just a scrawled signature I can't read, and no address," Webb answered. "Here's the next one, 'My husband can't eat the wretched slop you serve for meals. Hire a chef before the dear man and all the rest of your patients starve to death.'"

Angie pointed to the tepid pile. "The food is a frequent complain I'm sorry to say, but it's not a threat."

Webb handed Joe half the letters in the folder. "Let's divide the work."

"Fine." At the top of the stack, Joe found a former patient had written to complain about a night nurse whose squeaky shoes woke him each time he fell asleep. "Tepid." He laid it on the pile.

The doctor laughed at the next one in his stack. "Here's a man who's asking for a nurse's telephone number. He isn't sure of her name, but writes she's a real cute redhead. That must be meant for you, Mary Margaret."

"How flattering. Give me some of the letters, and I'll make quick work of this."

Joe handed her some of his. "Someone thought his bed was deliberately made uncomfortable."

"The princess and the pea syndrome," the nurses replied in unison. "Tepid pile."

A savory aroma enveloped them as Bob Laine pushed open the door. Joe read the name on the bag. "The Flippin' Plate is one of my favorite places."

"Mine too, I got a variety so everyone can choose and lots of French fries." He'd also brought paper plates and plenty of napkins. They ate at one end of the conference table so they'd not drip grease on any of the letters.

"Is the food really terrible here?" Joe asked. He'd taken the bacon burger, and it tasted so good he chewed every bite a dozen times.

"Not truly terrible," Bob replied, "just not inspired, and if someone is on a salt-free diet, it's pretty tasteless."

"No one takes a date to a hospital cafeteria," Carolina pointed out.

"How's the lime Jello?" Joe asked.

"It's not bad," Mary Margaret answered, "but the whipped cream on top turns into a solid glob if it isn't fresh."

"I scrape it off and put it in my coffee," Angie added.

"Helpful hint," Bob murmured between bites.

The burgers were so good, they ate in a companionable silence and left the remainder of the letters unsorted until they finished.

"Other than the letter cursing us all, there doesn't seem to be much we can use," Webb summarized. He used a clean napkin to wipe his place at the table and tossed it with his paper plate into the trashcan in the corner. He turned around and found everyone staring at him.

"What?" he asked.

Angie laughed before the other nurses could. "We usually don't see a doctor clean up after himself."

Bob leaped to his feet to clean up his place too. "We all need to keep the room neat or someone will ask who used it and wonder why."

Joe finished the last French fry and tossed his trash. "Maybe we need to go back further in the complaint file."

"The business office will be locked now." Mary Margaret pointed out. "Let's concentrate on the letters we haven't read."

"Could the office have turned over any truly threatening letters to the police?" Joe asked. No one knew the answer. It had occurred to him that Gabriel Webb might have removed any letters pertaining to him before he showed them the file. He'd not confront him on the issue in front of the others, however.

Mary Margaret dropped the next letter and bent over to pick it up. "This is just awful. It describes Gertrude Howland as looking so much like a goat she makes anyone ill who wasn't already."

Bob shook his head. "She wouldn't win any beauty contests, but that was uncalled for. It's no wonder the secretary didn't want to show you the file, Dr. Webb."

Gabriel unfolded the next letter in his stack. "This is more promising. A Mrs. Fitz accuses the entire hospital of murder in her son's death. Do you bring the notebook Georgia kept, Joe?"

"The police have the original. Mary Margaret and I made a copy." He pulled it from his inside pocket. "What's the date on the letter?"

"Last May." He looked over Joe's shoulder. "Did she make any notes around May 12th?"

Joe ran his finger down the page. "She thought Dr. Felberg released someone with the initials JAI early on May 1st. There is a note MFO died on May 4, when he was in Felberg's care. There are no other initials listed until after May 12th."

"I'll check the records tomorrow for what we can learn about MFO, who may or may not be related to Mrs. Fitz.

Are there any other threatening letters in what's left?" Webb asked.

Joe scanned the few he had remaining. "No, another on food, a complaint patients are awakened too often for needless tests of vital signs, another asks for a nurse's telephone number. Nothing useful at all."

Webb also found nothing worth pursuing. "If threatening letters are sent to the police, then Mrs. Fitz's letter wouldn't be among these. Let's study Georgia's notebook and see if we have better luck."

"Let's concentrate on the deaths she noted," Mary Margaret urged.

Joe started three months back and read those dates and initials. Angie copied them and so did Bob. They could provide names for a few, but not many. "We really need access to the hospital records to match names and initials," he added.

Webb volunteered. "Doctors can check files without anyone suspecting their motives."

Discouraged, Mary Margaret leaned back in her chair. "I refuse to believe Georgia died because some violent man happened by in the mood to kill. She had to know him, and she spent most of her time here."

"We see too many patients to remember them all," Angie posed. "No one is on their best behavior when they're ill. Someone may have been discharged still feeling poorly and focused his hatred on Georgia. We could read files for years and not find him."

Mary Margaret tapped their copy of the notebook. "His initials are here, I'm sure of it. We're just not seeing them yet, but we will."

Joe feared she was being overly optimistic. He rose from his chair. "Let's call it a night."

Angie gave the copy of initials and dates she'd made to Gabriel Webb, and they all parted in front of the hospital to walk to their cars. Once they were alone, Joe took Mary Margaret's hand and drew her to a stop. "Gabriel Webb saw the letters first. What are the odds he removed any complaints pertaining to him?"

"I'd rather not guess. You still don't trust him, do you?"

"He sounds sincere, and I want to believe him, but he picked up the letters this afternoon and said he'd check on the initials Georgia noted tomorrow. That means he's controlling what we see and learn. He may be innocent of any wrong doing, but he's had the opportunity to do whatever puts him in the best light."

"I'll check the files too, and if Gabriel fails to report something we ought to know, we'll have him."

"Can you get into the records as easily as he can?"

"We'll see. There's a quart of Aunt Lucy's ice cream in my freezer, and we really ought to eat it, or it might melt when I move."

Joe licked his lips. "What flavor?"

"Chocolate chip."

"One of my favorites," Joe swore, and he laced his fingers in hers as they walked to his car.

Thursday morning, Joe parked down the street from Ophelia Rose's two-story Spanish style home. It had the requisite red tile roof and gracefully arched windows. Colorful pots of red geraniums were clustered near the front door.

If there had been a Mr. Rose in the picture, Ophelia would surely have told him to handle who drove the car. That meant she was either widowed or divorced, and divorced was the more likely.

Joe took his first photograph when Matthew came bounding out the front door. He hopped onto the De Soto coupe parked in the driveway, backed out and turned the car toward UCLA in Westwood. He drove with remarkable caution and slowed to a stop at every yellow light rather than gun the engine to race through it. Joe followed him into a huge outdoor lot designated for students and parked opposite him two spaces away.

Matthew got out, slammed the car door and walked off carrying an armful of books without pausing to lock his car. Joe waited until Matthew was out of sight before he checked the De Soto and found the keys hidden behind the sun visor. That meant he was either careless, or leaving the keys where his girlfriend would find them. Joe went back to his own car and made himself comfortable in the backseat to watch.

Within the hour, an attractive brunette appeared. She wore a slim skirt with a sweater, as a typical co-ed would. He photographed her as she opened the door of the De Soto, got in and reached for the keys. She drove out of the lot and Joe followed her to the Sunset Strip where she pulled into the parking next to Sherry's Restaurant. Mobsters were fond of the place, and Joe took care not to be seen photographing the girl there.

It was time for the lunch crowd, and the place had to attract a better class of patron at noon than late at night when striptease would be the entertainment. The stage would belong to some comely girl with a name like Candy Bar or Tempest Storm, two of the most popular stripers in Los Angeles.

What Joe needed was a drink. He went into Sherry's and sat down at the bar. The girl he'd been following soon came his way in a tight white blouse and black satin shorts. She was even prettier up close.

"You look like a martini man," she told him, her smile wide. "I'm Mae, what can I get you?"

"Beer, whatever you have on tap. I'm not particular." He planned to keep wearing his sunglasses rather than show off a black eye that had developed an artistic rush of purplish green.

"I would have guessed you're very particular," she teased.

She had a co-ed's fresh prettiness, combined with an accomplished bartender's easy patter. It was a powerful combination. Joe paid for his beer and told her to keep the change. She looked inordinately pleased. "Have you been bartending here long?" he asked.

"Nearly a year. I'm working my way through UCLA, and this part-time job pays a whole lot better than most."

"Are you studying nursing by any chance?"

"No, English. I like little kids, and plan to teach kindergarten or first grade."

The thought of being cooped up with a classroom of five-year-olds nearly brought a groan from Joe's lips, but he caught it just in time. He checked his watch. "I need to go. Good luck with your studies."

"Come in again," she offered with a wave.

Joe walked up the street to the corner and back again. Mae had impressed him as a sweet girl, and he doubted she and Ophelia had ever met. Of course, bartending at Sherry's wasn't an ideal job for a co-ed, but he didn't believe it ought to disqualify her as a nice girl to date. The issue was the car, however.

He checked his watch. The lunch hour shift probably ended around two, and he had a book to read while he waited for Mae to leave Sherry's. He never went out on a job without a book or two for company. He'd learned to glance up often enough to conduct a serious surveillance and did so today.

As expected, Mae left the restaurant at two-thirty and returned the car to the exact spot where it had been parked in the UCLA lot. He got a photo of her slamming the car door with her free hand before carrying her books to class. She'd struck him as a nice girl who'd be a serious student. He didn't blame Matthew for lying to his mother about Mae's use of the car either.

Now he was the one with the problem. If he returned Ophelia Rose's money and told her he couldn't take the job after all, she'd just hire another private eye to follow her son. It would also be a cowardly way out. He'd sided with Katherine Sims when Bruce Corbett had shown his true colors, and the Rose case presented the same option.

When Matthew Rose returned to his car later that afternoon, Joe hailed him. He flashed his private investigator license to impress him of the seriousness of their conversation. "Your mother asked me to get proof your girlfriend is driving your car, something she clearly forbids. I met Mae today, and I'm leaning toward your side of the argument."

Matthew paled and rested against his car for some much needed support. "Mae will be late for class if she has to take the bus to her job and back. I didn't expect my witch of a mother to ever find out, but apparently she saw Mae driving my car last week."

"So you denied it," Joe responded.

"Of course, what else could I do?"

"How old are you?"

"Nineteen. What's that got to do with it?" Matthew asked.

Joe looked toward the campus. "Even if you were too young to serve during WWII, a lot of nineteen-year-old men died in uniform. They were thought of as men, not boys who were afraid to face their mothers. It's time to grow up, Matthew. Tell your mother you'll get a job and save up to buy a car if she won't allow you to share this fine De Soto coupe with Mae."

"You don't know her," Matthew claimed.

"We've met, and I've seen enough to know she insists upon getting her way. Where's your father?"

"My parents divorced when I was four, and my dad lives in Seattle. I haven't seen him in years."

"That's a shame. Maybe it's time to transfer to the University of Washington, or make your mother believe you will."

He appeared horrified by the idea. "The term just began. I can't leave now."

"I'm attempting to give you some valuable advice," Joe insisted. "You need to get out from under your mother's beautifully manicured thumb. Tell her she can sell the blasted car, and you'll earn the money to buy one on your own. If that doesn't show enough independence to convince her you've grown up, tell her you'd like to transfer to the University of Washington to be closer to your dad."

"What if that doesn't work?" Matthew asked.

He was a handsome kid, but Joe couldn't understand how he could master college classes if he couldn't make a leap from one obvious idea to the next. "What's your major?"

"Mathematics. It's great field with many applications."

"Wonderful. If moving to Seattle doesn't faze your mother, tell her you want to move to Boston to attend M.I.T."

"You mean I should build the consequences?"

The light had finally begun to dawn. "Yes. That's the plan. Or would you rather not see Mae? But that's a poor way to solve the problem because your mother will undoubtedly disapprove of the next girl you date. What did she think of your high school girlfriends?"

Matthew looked down at the toes of his loafers. "I only had one girlfriend, and my mother complained she wasn't good enough for me."

"I see a pattern here, do you?"

"Yes, I'm good with patterns. I should have stood up to my mother a long time ago. What are you going to tell her?"

"I'll give her the photos she'd paid me to take. I'll put in a good word for Mae while I do. I doubt it will make much difference to her though. She'll confront you with the photos, and you can tell her you're glad she's found out you share your car with Mae. You know how to continue from there."

"Do you really think it will work?"

Joe handed him his card. "Absolutely. Impress her that you've become your own man. She'll respect you for it."

"And if she doesn't?"

"Call me, and we'll think of something else."

"I could tell her I want to marry Mae. That would terrify her."

Joe slapped his arm. "It would, but don't make idle threats when they could backfire. I'll ask your mother to come into my office tomorrow morning for my report. You should be safe until tomorrow afternoon."

Matthew straightened up and squared his shoulders. "Thanks. You didn't have to help me."

"I've met your mother, son, so yes, I did."

Joe and Mary Margaret ate dinner at a small Chinese restaurant near her apartment. She stared at him wide-eyed as he explained his latest case. "Isn't there some rule of ethics concerning a change in sides when you take on a client?" she asked.

"I doubt it, but it can't be seen as good form. Still, when I find someone is clearly in the wrong, like the jerk who gave me this beautiful black eye, I can't walk away. That would be a worse breach of ethics."

"Maybe you should ask the retired detective when you next see him. He's eager to give advice, isn't he?"

"Henry Hilburn? Sure, but the job of the police is to make arrests based on the evidence they have. They aren't known for doing their work with an abundance of sympathy, but I'll ask Henry the next time I see him. I should call him to see what Detective Lynch has made of the notebook." He laughed at the thought.

"You offered your help."

"Yes, I did, so Lynch has brought any trouble he has down upon himself." He reached for another spring roll.

Ophelia Rose wore a black linen sheath with black patent-leather pumps to Joe's office. Eager to hear his report, she perched on the edge of her chair and clutched her purse tightly.

Joe opened the folder. "I followed your son from your home to UCLA." He handed her those photos. "A young woman picked up the car after he'd left it. She drove to her part-time job, and returned the De Soto by three o'clock to attend her own classes at the university. She didn't realize I'd followed her, but we spoke briefly, and she seemed like a very nice girl."

"I assure you she isn't," Ophelia insisted. She studied the photos Joe had taken of Mae. "Why are there no photos of where she works?"

He was afraid she'd notice that. "She works the luncheon business at a restaurant, and it wasn't possible to photograph her entering without being seen. She's working her way through college, which is usually seen as a plus."

Ophelia drew in a deep breath, but her expression remained as pinched and disagreeable as her mood. "Must I pay you more to take these photographs with me?"

He smiled simply to annoy her. "No, they're yours." He usually invited clients to call should they have need of him in the future, but he extended no such invitation to Mrs. Rose. He stood to walk her to the door, and wished her a good afternoon, but he was counting on Matthew to make it truly miserable.

Henry Hilburn hadn't heard anything useful about Detective Lynch's investigation into Georgia Dixon's murder, but he invited Joe to come to his house anyway. Joe arrived with the beer he knew would be expected, and carried his bottle out to the patio.

"Gorgeous day," Joe remarked between sips.

"It is. When I first retired, I didn't know what to do with myself. Now I can spend an afternoon sitting out here reading a good book and feel it's worthwhile. I've also been making notes of some unsolved cases that are impossible to forget. I should just let them go, but they keep gnawing at me, like some tiny rodent chewing on my brain."

"That's quite an image. Will you be able to solve any now?"

"No, too much time has passed, witnesses are dead, and probably those who committed the crimes as well. It's like working a 1000 piece jigsaw puzzle and trying to find where all the pieces fit. You could dump the whole mess back into the box, but you just can't give up without finishing."

"I know the feeling." Joe waited until he was certain Henry would not add more. "I've a question for you. Have you ever had your sympathies shift during an investigation?"

"A time or two. New evidence went to the DA, and usually things ended the way they should."

"But not always?"

Henry shook his head. "Mistakes can be made all up and down the line, from the original arrest to the jury's vote for conviction. Those cases have stuck with me too. It doesn't make for sound sleeping."

Joe seized upon Henry's mention of new evidence. He hadn't worked against a client until they had shown themselves to be in the wrong. His conscience soothed, he considered it a productive afternoon. Relaxed, he listened to the former detective describe a spree of robberies that still remained open.

"It had to have been a series of inside jobs, but we just couldn't find the link. What annoys me most is that someone somewhere must still be laughing at us."

"They could have gone to prison for another job."

"You're an optimist," Henry grumbled. "Police work knocked that out of me a long time ago."

CHAPTER 14

Saturday morning, Joe loaded the first boxes of Mary Margaret's belongings into his car. Angie was working with Curtis Mooney, and wasn't available, but Carolina Saavedra and Bob Laine came ready to help. Mary Margaret had everything so well-organized by mid-morning they had transferred it all to her cottage in Chrysanthemum Court.

Joe parked his car in the alley behind the cottages to have the shortest distance to carry things. On his third trip, Amy Hudson came out her back door and stood on her porch frowning, as she usually did. She was dressed in beige slacks and a white blouse, which he considered an improvement over her usual drab gray or black.

"Good morning," he called to her. "I'm Joe Ezell, we've talked a couple of times. I'm helping Mary Margaret McBride move into Georgia's cottage. We'll probably see each other often."

"I hope not," she murmured under her breath, and quickly passed through her back door.

"Lovely woman," Joe muttered as he entered Mary Margaret's new kitchen.

"What woman is that?" she asked. Seated on the floor, she'd arranged her pots and pans in neat order.

"Your neighbor, Amy Hudson, who is not in the least bit neighborly."

"Perhaps she's had a very difficult life, or suffered some terrible tragedy," Mary Margaret surmised. "We shouldn't be too critical when we know so little about her."

"You're a very generous woman."

"Which works to your advantage, Joe, so don't make fun of me."

He bent down to kiss her. "It was simply a comment, not a criticism."

Bob and Carolina were hanging the pictures in the living room. Joe went in to help, but they were doing fine on their own. He stood back to appreciate the bright floral artwork he'd admired in her apartment, and thought it equally pretty here. Mary Margaret came up behind him and rubbed her hand over his back.

"It's beginning to look like home, isn't it?" she said.

"Yes, it is. I should invest in some art for my place, and get something to class up the office too. Maybe a California desert scene with eucalyptus and a couple of wild horses grazing in the distance."

"Sounds good. Are you getting hungry?" She turned to Carolina and Bob. "I need to go to the store for milk and eggs, and I thought I'd get lunchmeat for sandwiches. Will that be enough for you?"

"What about adding some baked beans and potato salad?" Bob asked. "This is hard work here and we need to keep up our strength."

"I'd love some potato chips," Carolina added. She stepped back to even up a frame.

Mary Margaret looked up at Joe. "We could stop by Aunt Lucy's for ice cream."

"Let's go before the list gets any longer," Joe replied. He'd taken her to the market a couple of times. She was a methodical shopper who read labels and compared prices and weights before putting something in her cart. He could breeze through a grocery store in ten minutes or less, but he was ready for a break in the unpacking and happy to go with her.

As they walked out to his car, he glanced over his shoulder, half-expecting Amy Hudson to be out on her porch watching them, but she wasn't there.

They sat crowded around the small dining table at the end of the living room closest to the kitchen. Bob Laine took up more space than most, and he also had a prodigious appetite. Mary Margaret had shopped accordingly.

"Thank you all so much for your help. I can handle things on my own from here," she said.

"We still have to do a final clean-up in your old apartment," Carolina said. "Do you want to give Bob and me the keys, and we'll handle it."

"I'll help her tomorrow," Joe offered. Mary Margaret kept such a clean apartment, he doubted there would be much to do other than turn in her keys.

Phyllis Cameron, who lived in the first cottage, knocked on the front door. "I brought you some lemon scones. I remembered how much you liked them."

"Aren't you sweet," Mary Margaret exclaimed. "I'll make something for you just as soon as I'm all moved in."

"We're planning a welcome party for next weekend, and you can share something with us all then." She turned away, waved, and walked the short distance to her home.

"I'll look forward to it," Mary Margaret called, and carried the plate of scones to the dining table. "I'm stuffed. Do you want to take a couple of scones with you?"

Bob had one wrapped in a napkin before Carolina could respond. She laughed, took a scone, and ushered him out of the cottage with her.

Mary Margaret sank into an easy chair and blew a curl out of her eyes. "Sit down with me a minute, Joe. I don't feel any spirits lurking here. Do you?"

"Did you expect Georgia's ghost would haunt the place?" He settled into the matching chair, and while tempted to rest his feet on the coffee table, he discounted the notion.

"No, not really, but I thought some of her essence might linger a while. Let's rest for the remainder of the afternoon, and strike out for the old place fresh tomorrow morning."

Joe didn't ask her to specify how she intended to rest, but he knew they'd both enjoy it.

Monday morning, an exuberant Matthew Rose called Joe from UCLA. "I followed your suggestions and it worked! My mother was so worried I'd actually move to Seattle, she backed down about who drives my car. I'd called my father to tell him I intended to threaten to move there, so he'd know if she called him."

Joe hadn't thought of warning the father, which was an important point he'd completely overlooked. "Good thinking. What did your father have to say?"

"He was surprised I'd called, but was happy to help me strike out on my own. He said he'd really missed me and asked me to come visit over the holidays. I'll save the money to go. It's good to have a family, even if ours is scattered."

"I'm glad everything worked out for you, Matthew. Good luck with your studies, and with Mae."

Matthew laughed. "She likes the fact I'm so smart. She's the only girl I've ever stunned with my brains, and I'm going to keep her."

"Good luck to you both."

Joe added some notes to Ophelia Rose's file on a separate sheet, so he could quickly remove it if need be. He considered the case a success, something he needed right now.

CC peeked in the door. "Good morning! I hope you had a nice weekend."

"I helped my girlfriend move, which was more fun than it sounds."

"That's good. Does she have a nice place?"

Joe chose not to reveal she'd moved into Georgia Dixon's cottage. The fewer reminders he had of the murder, the better. "Very nice except for one odd neighbor."

"He's not going to bother her, is he?"

"It's a she, and she's the reclusive type, so there's no danger she'll make a pest of herself."

"That's good. Have a nice day now."

"Thank you." Joe checked his calendar, and found all the days blank. He needed to reschedule a golf lesson with Hal, and plan a weekend game that included Gilbert Werner. What he needed was a case that would stretch out for weeks and earn him enough to buy Mary Margaret a diamond ring. Unfortunately, the telephone remained frustratingly silent.

Max Broderick, the dentist in the building stopped by Joe's office late that morning. "Do you have a minute?" he asked.

"I'll make one for you, come on in," Joe responded.

Max had removed his white coat and worn his suit jacket with his slacks to go out to lunch. "I've noticed a problem with my bank deposits. There has to be a reason for the discrepancies in payments made during the day and what goes into the bank at night. For all I know, this could have gone on for years, but I hope it was only last month."

"Who makes the deposits?"

"My receptionist, Patricia Gretz. She's been with me for years, so I hate to accuse her of siphoning money from the deposits, but I cannot think of any other reason for the shortage. It isn't every day, you understand, but at least once a week."

"Maybe you need an accountant. Is Stephen Bennett in his office today?" Joe asked.

"He's an excellent CPA, but I already know the earnings don't match the deposits. I usually pay little attention to my bank statements, which is careless, I know, but this month, something about the amounts deposited caught my eye. They were several that were smaller than usual, but I've been seeing as many patients. My earnings should have increased, or at least remained the same, but a dip just doesn't add up."

Joe nodded thoughtfully. "Have you considered making the deposits during your lunch hour, rather than have Mrs. Gertz do it in the afternoon?"

He shifted on his chair. "She'd ask why I suddenly wished to handle the banking myself."

"Are you afraid to tell her the truth? Money is disappearing between your office and the bank. Either the bank is making careless errors with your deposits, or she is keeping cash for herself."

Max looked down at his hands. "She's the best receptionist I've ever had, and my patients love her. I don't want to upset things, but theft is theft."

"It is. Do you want me to talk with her? I could say you're concerned about the deposits, and ask if she has an answer. She might owe someone money, and be desperate to pay it back. I'll make it very low key rather than accusatory."

"Would you, please?"

He looked so hopeful, Joe was happy to help. "I've seen Mrs. Gertz in the hallway occasionally, so she should know me. When is your last patient scheduled today?"

"I have a three o'clock, and then I'll be through. I always stay until five o'clock to catch up on reading in professional journals, and Mrs. Gertz is here to book appointments should anyone call."

"I'll come over at four."

"I'll be glad to pay you," Broderick replied.

"There's no need, but I wouldn't refuse a free check-up and cleaning."

The dentist laughed. "It's a deal."

Joe went for a long walk after he'd eaten a sandwich at the counter in the drug store downstairs. They made an especially good grilled cheese, and he hadn't had one in ages.

He tried to get out of the office every day, even if he had no place to go. He walked around several blocks, varying his usual route, while he thought how to approach Mrs. Gertz. It was doubtful a bookie had threatened her over gambling debts, but he liked that angle and eased his way into it when he saw her that afternoon.

"Mr. Ezell? Did you have an appointment?" Mrs. Gretz asked. She was an attractive brunette in her early forties and had an inviting smile. "I don't see anything in the book."

Joe pulled a visitor's chair close to her desk, and whispered, "Dr. Broderick is very worried about you. He's noticed discrepancies in payments made here at the office, and what you're depositing in the bank later in the day. Are you in some kind of trouble? Is someone pressuring you for money?"

Patricia Gretz burst into tears, reached into her pocket for a handkerchief, and sobbed into the crumpled linen. "I'm so sorry, but I couldn't think of anything else to do."

"Start at the beginning," Joe encouraged, astonished his wild story might have held a particle of the truth.

She blotted her eyes. "I have three sisters. One is very happily married to a wonderful man, and two are single and struggling to make ends meet. They've neglected their teeth, and I've worked them in as patients to see Dr. Broderick, but they don't have the money to pay."

"Go on."

"When they come in, I mark their account as paid, but it isn't. Dr. Broderick has never given the slightest bit of attention to the deposit slips, and it never occurred to me that he'd discover what I've done. When my sisters are working at better jobs, they'll have the money to pay Dr. Broderick and make everything right. It was always our intention that he'll be paid in full, we were just putting it off for a while. Now I'll have to look for another job, won't I?" She began to sob all over again, and then looked up, her eyes wide with fright. "Will he call the police to arrest me?"

Joe could see why Max Broderick was so fond of her. She was a genuinely sweet woman who had wanted to help her sisters. "No, of course not. I'll speak to Dr. Broderick, and straighten everything out. Perhaps your sisters could pay something each week."

She squared her shoulders and summoned an admirable resolve. "I should handle this myself rather than ask you to speak to him on my behalf." She stood, straightened her skirt, and knocked lightly on Max's office door. "Dr. Broderick, may I speak with you please?"

Impressed by her courage, Joe stood and replaced his chair along the waiting room wall. He was too curious to leave while she was in the dentist's office and waited to see how things would work out. From what he'd seen of Max Broderick, he expected a happy outcome.

Max followed his receptionist from his office. "I wish you'd come to me about your sisters' money problems in the first place, Patricia, and I'd have arranged for them to make small payments over time. Go home and relax this evening. Tomorrow we'll figure out how much is owed."

"I know exactly, and you won't lose a penny you're owed," she insisted. She plucked her purse from the bottom drawer of her desk and left before the dentist could change his mind.

Joe opened the door for her and waited until she'd reached the end of the hall to speak. "It sounds like everything worked out well."

"It did, but I'm grateful she doesn't have a larger family!"

A couple of new cases, the usual follow and photograph, filled the rest of the week, and he played golf Saturday morning with Hal and Gilbert. Gilbert made no mention of his girlfriend, and provided no opening for advice, but Joe was sure it was a disaster waiting to happen. In the meanwhile, Gilbert had inspired him to hone his technique, and he'd improved his game.

Saturday night, he took Mary Margaret to the movies and to Aunt Lucy's to buy ice cream for the Sunday welcome party. "Rather than bake a cake, I'll make little sundaes in paper cups. It should be something different from what the others will serve."

"Sounds good. Do you suppose Amy Hudson will offer everyone a deviled egg in her fancy egg plate?"

"Probably, I haven't seen much of her. We leave for work about the same time, but she owns a car, and I rely on the bus. Maybe we'll have a chance to get to know her better tomorrow."

Joe doubted it, but he smiled as though he couldn't wait.

Sunday afternoon, Phyllis and John Cameron set up two card tables near the fountain in the center of Chrysanthemum Court. They pushed them together and covered them with a white tablecloth and added a vase of colorful flowers to provide a setting for the shared welcome meal. Phyllis placed a freshly baked angel food cake on the end of the long table.

Daniel and Polly Hill came out with baby Catherine. They brought a green salad, and Patrick Wood carried a platter of fried chicken.

"I order it from my favorite cafe," he explained. "It's far better than anything I could prepare on my own."

Tim and Barbara offered a big bowl of potato salad, and as expected, Amy Hudson had prepared deviled eggs. Joe had brought carrot sticks and celery to have something to share. Each provided his own plate and silverware.

"This is wonderful!" Mary Margaret exclaimed. "You've all made me feel so welcome. I have ice cream I'll bring out when we're ready for the cake."

The Camerons, and Patrick Wood brought out chairs. Joe and Mary Margaret joined the Hills and Garcias seated on the thick grass lawn and chatted easily with her new neighbors. Amy placed a chair on the fringe of the group.

When spoken to, she replied in a few words, or with a nod or shrug. She was the first to leave.

No one appeared to consider Amy's less than festive mood odd, but Mary Margaret certainly did. "I was hoping to have a chance to talk with Amy, but she seemed to have been in a hurry to go."

"She stayed longer than usual," Patrick Wood observed. "Sometimes she just circles the table and runs right back inside her cottage with her plate."

"Her deviled eggs were quite good," Joe offered. "This whole meal has been delicious. Thank you for including me."

"We couldn't have left out Mary Margaret's sweetheart," Phyllis Cameron replied, her eyes twinkling.

"Thank you." Joe glanced toward Amy's cottage and saw the curtains move in the front window. She had been part of the party, so why would she go inside and watch them? It made no sense at all.

"How long has Amy been living here?" he asked.

John Cameron turned to Patrick Wood. "We've been here the longest, but I don't recall exactly when she moved in. Do you?"

"A couple of years ago, I think," Patrick answered. "A young couple had her cottage before her."

"The Stewarts," Phyllis recalled. "They were so cute and moved to Santa Barbara. Amy was the next to move into cottage five."

The others weren't nearly as interested in Amy Hudson as Joe, and he let the conversation follow its natural course rather than make further inquiries about her. When the party ended, he carried the Cameron's card tables inside for them. It had been a wonderful party, and he told them so again.

Mary Margaret kissed him as he followed her into her cottage. "Thank you for coming and being so helpful. Now if anyone sees you on the walk, they'll know who you are."

"Unlike Gabriel Webb, who snuck in under the cover of darkness," Joe whispered in her ear.

"Exactly."

Monday morning, Joe opened a folder for Amy Hudson. Mike Torres should have kept the application she submitted before moving into Chrysanthemum Court. The problem would be in inspiring him to share her information. He stood up and paced his office while he shuffled through persuasive ideas. When he finally had a believable story, he found Mike's number in the small notebook he carried on cases and called him.

Joe first reminded him how they had met. "There was a nice welcome party for Mary Margaret yesterday at the cottages. I kept thinking I knew Amy Hudson from somewhere, but I just can't place her. Do you have her previous address?" He held his breath, but Mike appeared to be in a talkative mood.

"Sure, I have it in my files. Give me a minute." He returned to the telephone after a lengthy pause. "She'd been living in San Diego."

"Of course, that's where I knew her. Did you call her previous landlord for a reference?"

"Yeah, a Mrs. Tabor. She was so fond of Amy, I could barely get her off the phone."

"I remember her well," Joe exclaimed. "Would you mind giving me her number? I'd meant to keep in touch, and I'd like to call her."

"Are you sure you really want to?"

"I don't have much scheduled for the day," Joe explained. He wrote down the landlady's name and number and thanked Mike for his help.

Mike laughed. "Look, I'm so glad to have cottage five rented, I'm in the mood to grant favors. If there's ever anything Miss McBride needs, have her call me. I'll take care of it right away."

"I'll tell her. Thanks again." While he was disappointed to learn how easily he could get information from Mike for Mary Margaret's sake, he was eager to follow up on the lead.

He waited until eleven o'clock to call, but Mrs. Tabor didn't answer. Disappointed, he went out for a walk, and the telephone was ringing when he returned to his office. "Discreet Investigations."

"It's Gilbert Werner. I have another question about Christine."

Joe could feel a chill torrent coming. "Do you want to come in to discuss it?"

"I probably should. Will half an hour work for you?"

"Yes, come on over." Joe made coffee and sipped a cup as he reviewed Gilbert's folder. He'd given Gilbert photos that showed Christine Hethe being cozy with a female friend, but the young man had been too naïve to recognize what they showed.

CC knocked on the door before he came in to empty the trash. "No clients this morning?" he asked.

"One is on his way. Tell me something, CC. If you knew something about a friend's girlfriend, but he didn't react the way you'd thought he would, would you tell him in a different way, or let the matter go."

"That would depend on the friend," CC answered. "If it was someone who was likely to punch me in the nose, I'd let him find out on his own."

Joe nodded thoughtfully. He doubted Gilbert had ever punched anyone in the nose, and that criteria didn't fit this case. "Good advice, thanks."

Gilbert arrived carrying the folder with the photos. He took a chair and handed a photo to Joe. "I wanted to keep these because Christine is so pretty, but the more I look at them, the more confused get. There's nothing unusual about friends going out to dinner, but checking into a motel together is odd, isn't it?"

Joe took a deep breath but what he saw as the truth was no easier to share. "It depends on the friends, Gilbert. I may have recommended that you not show these photos to Christine, but maybe it's time that you did."

He sat back. "I didn't want to admit that I had her followed."

"Where are you from, Gilbert?"

"A little town in Northern California where we didn't have more than a hundred students in the high school. I couldn't wait to leave for college. After I graduated, I stayed here, but that I'm from the sticks hasn't washed off."

"Many women find it charming," Joe assured him. "Were there any women who lived together in your town?"

"There were a couple of sisters, widows I think, who shared a home. What's that got to do with anything?"

Joe had danced around the subject all he could. It was time to dive in. "There are some women who prefer to be with women rather than men, just as there are men who like other men rather than women."

Gilbert stared at him, and then at the photos of Christine and her friend. "You mean they might be girlfriends, not just friends?"

"It's possible."

A deep blush flooded Gilbert's cheeks. "I've heard of homosexuals. We just didn't have any back home. If Christine is in love with a woman, what's she doing with me?"

"She must like you, but she's the one you need to ask."

"But the question would spoil everything, although I don't want her laughing at me behind my back. I couldn't bear it. I knew she was too good to be true. That's why I came to you."

Joe felt sorry for him, and he didn't want the poor guy to suffer over any woman, especially Christine. "Men have intuition as well as women, and it was wise of you to trust yours. You felt something wasn't right with Christine, and the photos provide clear evidence that it isn't. Life is filled with difficult dilemmas, but it's often better to confront them head on rather than let them play out over time. In this case, it could save you eventual heartache."

"A broken heart now is better than one a few months from now?" Skeptical, he sagged back in his chair.

"Yes. It's like ripping off a bandage. It hurts like hell, but it's over with quickly." He waited for Gilbert to absorb at least a particle of his advice and took a quick glance at his watch.

Gilbert looked up at him. "What would you do?"

"I'd show her the photos and ask her to explain. You can say if she's meeting other men or women at motels, you'll wish her luck, but not see her again."

"Suppose she cries."

"Carry a clean handkerchief to give her. Pull yourself together so you can go back to work this afternoon and decide what you want to do when you get home."

"It is my decision, isn't it?" He returned the photos to the manila folder and stood.

"Yes, it is. I'll see you on Saturday for our golf game."

Gilbert paused at the door. "Does Hal know about Christine?"

Joe had confided in Hal because Gilbert was in such a desperate need of help with women. A white lie wouldn't hurt now, and he had an easy answer. "Of course not, this is Discreet Investigations."

Reassured, Gilbert left and Joe soon followed to go out on a walk. He had not become a private investigator to offer advice, but he'd had a run of clients who seemed little able to cope on their own. Maybe he should raise his fees.

CHAPTER 15

Wednesday morning, Harriet Whitley came into Joe's office with the type of complaint he heard often. She was petite, blonde and gestured as she spoke, flashing her bright red fingernails.

"Was it difficult for you to arrange time off work?" he asked.

"No, I'm a manicurist and have Wednesday mornings off. As I told you on the telephone, I've been dating a fireman, and with his irregular hours, we usual meet for early morning dates rather than evenings. When I asked if he didn't have some days off so we could go out on a proper dinner date, he told me they were shorthanded at the fire station, and he had to work every day. Jake's a lot of fun, but I'm beginning to feel something isn't right."

Joe had a yellow legal pad ready to take notes. "What's Jake's last name?"

"Nichols, like five cents, but it's spelled differently."

"Got it. Do you know at which fire station he works?"

She pursed her lips thoughtfully. "He told me Station 27 on Cahuenga, but he warned me never to call him there because they need the phone lines to take emergency calls reporting fires. Chatting with girlfriends simply isn't allowed. He always calls me when he has time for us to get together."

"What time does he usually call?"

"Early morning, maybe 7:00 o'clock, and then he'll come to my apartment at eight."

Joe tapped his pencil against his desk. "So Jake is free only in the mornings, and he's never available to take your calls?"

"Sounds fishy, doesn't it?" she asked. "We met in the produce section of the market. He was buying groceries for the firehouse."

"Was he dressed in a uniform that identified him as a fireman?"

"No, he wore his usual dark blue pants with a white shirt, and a navy blue jacket. I thought they were his off-duty clothes."

"Perhaps they are. What is it you'd like me to do, Miss Whitley?"

"I thought maybe you could go by the firehouse and check on what his hours actually are. If he's not telling the truth and juggling half-a-dozen girlfriends, I'm done with him."

"That would be a wise decision. I'll check the fire station today. I'll give you my home telephone number, and if he calls to ask you for a date tomorrow morning or Friday, give me a call." He wrote the number on the back of his business card and handed it to her.

"He often calls me on Thursdays. Do you plan to speak to him?"

"No, I'll just follow him, see where he goes, and give you a full report. You can trust me to answer your questions in a few days time." He asked for a retainer, and she had cash ready.

"I figure this is a wise investment," she responded when he handed her a receipt.

When she left, he called Mrs. Tabor in San Diego again, but there was still no answer. Maybe she went out in the morning, or had a job. He'd keep calling her until he found her home.

Joe walked into the office at Fire Station 27 and used the story he had found most effective. He handed the man at the desk his business card. "I'm trying to locate Jake Nichols with news of a substantial inheritance. I'd heard he worked here."

The man read Joe's card and handed it back. "You heard wrong. We've no one on the roster with that name."

Harriet Whitley hadn't given him a photo, so the man she knew as Jake Nichols could work there, but under another name. "Thank you, perhaps he's at another fire house."

"Maybe."

"Thank you for your time." Joe frequently met people who were less than helpful, but he smiled and walked out as though he didn't mind at all.

He took Mary Margaret to dinner at Clifton's Cafeteria that night. "What would you think of a man who told you he was a fireman, but never wore clothing with the fire department's insignia, and claimed with his schedule, he could only see you in the mornings a couple of times a week. To top it off, what if he told you not to call him at the station and tie up lines needed for emergencies?"

She had a chicken potpie, and had to swallow a bite before answering. "There are several possibilities. He might be posing as a fireman because it's a more exciting career than the one he has. He could actually be a fireman, but want to avoid being teased by his friends at the firehouse, so he tells women not to call him there. The occasional morning date makes me think he's married, and wouldn't want anyone at the firehouse to know he cheated on his wife."

"Thank you, that's exactly my thinking as well. I don't understand why men lie to women about who they are, or why women are so easily misled."

She laughed. "Well, I wasn't, but if I'd asked another detective to check up on my sailor boyfriend, we'd never have met."

"That's a sad thought." His meatloaf was especially good, but it didn't compare to her cooking. "Are you all moved in?"

"I've lined the last drawer and put everything away. I love the little cottage. It's cozy and feels more like a real home than my apartment did."

"That's nice. Have you seen anything more of Amy Hudson?"

"We've met on the walkway a couple of times. She'll return my greeting, but either hurry away or duck into her cottage rather than linger to chat. Her lights are on in the evenings, but I assume she's home alone. I feel sorry for her."

"You're a nurse, and the sympathetic sort, but let her be the first to make any gesture of friendship. Otherwise, she might feel crowded."

"I will."

Joe got up early Thursday morning just in case Harriet Whitley called, and he wasn't disappointed. He drove to her apartment house, parked across the street, and she waved to him from a second story window. He didn't have long to wait before a young man arrived in a dark coupe. He was carrying a flower bouquet and entered the building with a brisk step.

Harriet waved to Joe again as Jake knocked on her door, and Joe opened his book to read while he waited. He checked his watch, and Jake reappeared two hours later, almost to the dot. He tucked in his shirt as he got into his car, revealing what their morning dates entailed.

Joe followed at a distance, and Jake drove to a plumbing supply store and parked in the rear. He entered through the back door and didn't come out, so he hadn't stopped for a sprinkler on the way to the firehouse. Joe entered A-One

Plumbing through the front door, and found Jake at the counter. He'd switched to a gray work shirt with the name Frank embroidered in red over the breast pocket.

"Good morning," he called to Joe. "How can we help you?"

"I'm thinking of remodeling my home, and wanted some prices on fixtures," Joe replied. Frank responded as Joe hoped he would and showed him a couple of floor displays before referring to a wholesale catalogue on the counter. He was friendly with the easy manner of a fine salesman. He was also a very handsome man with thick dark hair and blue eyes.

Joe jotted some prices in his notebook. "Your figures look good. Have you been working here long?"

"Forever," Frank responded with a good-natured laugh. "My dad owned the business, and I've taken over from him."

"Are you a licensed plumber?" Joe asked.

"Sure am, just like my father and uncle. We can install whatever you need and make sure it works beautifully."

Next to the cash register, there was a framed photograph of a young woman and two curly-haired little boys. "Is that your family?" Joe asked.

Frank's smile grew wide. "Yes, they're the joy of my life. Do you have kids?"

"Not yet, but someday soon I hope to have a family. Right now, I need to go home and take some measurements. I'll come back in to talk with you again, Frank."

Frank handed him a business card for A-One Plumbing Supply with his name, Frank Atkins. "Atkins? That's where you get the A-One?"

"Sure is. I'll look forward to seeing you again soon, Mr.?"

"Joe Ezell." Taking an almost fiendish delight, he handed him a card for Discreet Investigations. Frank noticeably paled, and if he'd wanted to speak, it stuck in his throat.

When Joe reached his office, he called the beauty salon where Harriet worked, and she arranged to come by on her way home after work. The case had been too easy, which warned him it could get messy real fast.

Harriet listened without interrupting as Joe described his meeting with Frank Atkins. "He's a married plumber who owns A-One Plumbing Supply. The next time he calls, tell him you're no longer available and let it go at that."

"Frank Atkins? The snake. I think I'll drop by A-One and tell him what I think of him in person."

"Believe me, nothing can be gained from such a sorry confrontation. He's the imaginative sort, and he might call the police and report you've threatened him."

"He wouldn't dare." Smoldering with anger, she sat very still. "I'll bet his address is in the telephone book. When he calls next week, and he will, I'll tell him I'm on my way to visit his wife. That scare ought to turn his hair white."

"It might, but even if it's only a threat, don't make it. The odds are you aren't the first pretty woman he's charmed with his fireman story. I doubt you'll be the last. His wife might suspect he's playing around, or maybe she doesn't care, but leave her out of it. I'd hate to see things turn violent, and you could be badly hurt."

"Jake, or Frank, is a real charmer, and he isn't violent at all."

"His wife could be the fiercest housewife on the block. Don't go near her, or Frank either. He knows where you live, and if you make trouble for him, he could make it right back. Tell him good-bye on the telephone and look for a man who likes to go dancing on Saturday night."

"How did you know I love to dance?" She smiled for the first time that afternoon.

"I'm a detective, remember? It's my job to know things." It had been a wild guess, but he kept talking until she assured him she wanted nothing more to do with Frank Atkins.

"Do I owe you more money?" she asked.

"No, your account is paid in full. Please come back to me if you think another man you're dating isn't telling the truth."

She stood and slipped her purse under her arm. "You can be sure I will, Mr. Ezell. Good-bye."

Joe walked her to the door, and after making a few last minute notes in her file, he started for home. He met CC in the hallway. "Staying late tonight, CC?"

"I'm leaving in a minute. You have yourself a good evening now."

"Thanks, you too."

Joe and Mary Margaret hadn't planned to get together that night, and he'd save the end of the fireman story to tell her over the weekend.

Friday morning he made another try at finding Amy Hudson's former landlady, Mrs. Tabor, at home. When she answered, he nearly dropped the phone. "Mrs. Tabor, my name is Joe Ezell, and I'm a friend of Amy Hudson."

"How is the darling girl?" the woman asked, her voice sugary as syrup. "She is such a sweetheart, and yet tragedy overtook her before she could even blink. Terrible shame it was. I doubted moving up to Los Angeles would heal such a deep wound, but she couldn't bear to stay here. How is she doing?"

"She's teaching math in high school."

"Good, I'm relieved to hear she's pursuing her career, but what about after work? Is she able to have fun or is she still lost in misery?"

"Lost in misery is a good way to put it. Of course, she doesn't wish to discuss what happened, but I thought if I contacted you, you might share something of her background, and her friends here would know better how to help her."

"You're such a dear, Mr. Ezell, I can tell that over the telephone. Does Amy have many friends there? She was such a popular girl at one time, but that was before she lost her fiancé."

Joe was taking notes as fast as he could write. "I'm unclear as to how that happened. What was his name?"

"Mark Birch, like the tree, and he was such a swell fellow, good looking, and soft spoken. Now the way it was written up in the *San Diego Union,* Mark and Amy were leaving a movie theater, and some sort of scuffle broke out on the sidewalk between a couple of young sailors and some army men. The sailors were getting the worse of it and Mark stepped in to break up the fight. Did I say he was a naval officer? Well, he was, and it served to enrage the soldiers even further, and the fight ended in the most horrible way possible."

"How did it end, Mrs. Tabor?"

"One of the soldiers pulled a knife, stabbed Mark, and the wound nicked his heart. He was rushed to the hospital, but couldn't be saved. It was the end of Amy's world, and I was afraid she might commit suicide to join her beloved Mark in heaven, but somehow she found the strength to go on. She wasn't the same though, but a mere shell of the carefree girl she'd once been. I didn't even try to convince her she'd find love again as it would have dismissed her pain, but I do hope she finds another man as fine as Mark Birch. Is she dating anyone there?"

"No, not yet, but I hope she soon will. Thank you for talking with me, Mrs. Tabor. You've been a great help. Was the man who stabbed Mark caught?"

"No, and I doubt anyone is still looking for him. Mark's loss was tragic in every way. Please tell Amy I said hello. Will you do that for me?"

"I'll be happy to," Joe told her good-bye, and sat for a long while visualizing the knife fight she'd described in such detail. As a naval officer, it was likely Mark Birch had been rushed to San Diego's VA hospital.

He opened the file with the copy of Georgia's notebook and turned the pages quickly to find her notes on San

Diego. If Amy had lived at the Chrysanthemum Court a couple of years, then Mark could have died in 1945, or late in 1944. He looked for the initials MB, or BM, but didn't find them. If Mark had expired in the emergency room, Georgia wouldn't have been his nurse, so she'd not have made a note of his death. He replaced the copied pages in the manila folder and returned them to his file cabinet.

Hal Marten's girlfriend, Gladys Swartz, had lost her husband in one of the fierce sea battles in the Pacific, but she was a warm, outgoing woman. Perhaps what Amy Hudson needed was a psychologist or psychiatrist to lift her spirits. His own efforts to speak with her had gone nowhere, and Mary Margaret had had no more success, but he hated to think of how unhappy she must be.

If he told Mary Margaret Amy's sad story, she'd make a point of befriending her, and it couldn't end well. She'd be better off simply ignoring her reclusive neighbor until, as he'd suggested, Amy took an interest in her. He didn't tell Mary Margaret about all his cases because some were too sensitive, or dull to repeat, but this time he felt justified in shielding his girl from another woman's tragic sorrow.

CHAPTER 16

Joe couldn't sleep, and rather than toss and turn all night, he got up, dressed, and went out for a walk. His neighborhood was as safe as most in Los Angeles, and while Bruce Corbett had gotten the better of him, the next man who swung a fist at him wouldn't. His colorful black eye had faded, and he didn't have a reminder of the sorry incident every morning when he shaved. That was something to celebrate right there. Otherwise, he had the itchy sensation he'd not done nearly enough to grow his business. That brought him to sad thoughts of Georgia Dixon and a succession of disappointing dead ends.

When he returned home, he went to sleep, and woke in the morning looking forward to playing golf with Hal and Gilbert. Hal was in an expansive mood and told jokes that were so funny Gilbert came out of his shell to laugh with them. The quiet young man again impressed them with his skill, and shot well under par. He left without mentioning Christine, and Joe was relieved he appeared to be doing so well.

"We need to add another man," Joe told Hal. "Do you know anyone who'd like to join us?"

"Do you suppose Lou King plays golf?"

"The bail bondsman? I doubt it. Go ahead and ask him if you like. It would make for an interesting foursome."

"Will do."

They made plans to resume Hal's lessons in the coming week, and Joe went on home. He wanted to take Mary Margaret someplace new, and recalled how Harriet Whitley had brightened at the mention of dancing. He knew how to dance, if not that well, but maybe it was something Mary Margaret would love to do.

"Go dancing?" she asked. "I'd love to. I've heard nurses mention a Polynesian club that sounds very nice, and not too expensive."

Joe knew she wasn't calling him cheap, but it did hurt that she knew how limited his resources were. When they got there, they found Carolina Saavedra and Bob Laine seated at a table meant for four. Bob gestured for them to join them, and Joe followed Mary Margaret to their table. He scanned the dance floor and didn't see anyone who looked as though they'd taken lessons from Fred Astaire, and relaxed into the fun.

The lighting held a seductive aqua tinge, and murals of island shores conveyed the club's South Seas theme from every angle. The waitresses wore colorful print tops and grass skirts that swayed provocatively as they moved between the tables serving fruit flavored rum drinks. The band played tunes that had been popular during the war, and Joe had a better time than he had anticipated. Mary Margaret didn't stop smiling until the band took a break, and Bob asked about Joe's investigation into Georgia's murder.

The question sucked the fun right out of the evening. Joe had nothing to report and said so. "I'll keep working on it," he promised. He was relieved when the band returned to the small stage, and led Mary Margaret out on the dance floor.

She raised up on her tiptoes to whisper in his ear, "Let's just dance and think of nothing except each other."

"Sounds good to me. Let's come here again."

She squeezed his hand, and he kissed her curls, but he kept thinking about Georgia Dixon with every single step. She deserved justice, but it remained maddeningly out of reach. He had to do more, but he was stymied as to what to do next.

Monday morning, Timothy Remson called to make an appointment with Joe. He was a husky man with red hair and pale blue eyes. "How well can you deal with ex-wives?" he asked.

Another goofy case, Joe thought to himself. "I've never been married, so I've no advice to give in that regard."

"I don't need advice, I need action."

"Could you explain in more detail?" Joe inquired.

Tim stood, walked around his chair, and then gripped the back to lean against it. "My ex-wife, Arlene, may she roast in hell forever, is mistreating our dog. Frankly, I was so eager to get away from her that I thought letting her have Flash during the week while I had him on the weekends would work out. A neighbor, his name's Fred, called to let me know Arlene is chaining Flash in the backyard when she goes to work. I don't mind him being in the backyard all day, but he shouldn't be kept on a short chain. That's cruel."

"I agree. What would you like me to do, Mr. Remson?"

"I told Arlene not to keep Flash on a chain, but she laughed, and said she'd do whatever she pleased when he was with her. I'd like you to take photographs of Flash chained in the yard so I can go to Animal Control and file a protest with evidence behind it. I'd do it myself, but I'm not supposed to be hanging around her house, you understand. With Animal Control on my side, I figure our lawyers can work out a deal so I get Flash permanently."

"What sort of dog is Flash?"

"He's a greyhound. He raced some in Florida before we got him. He's a fine pet, and I miss having him with me."

"Your wife works during the day?"

"Yes, she's a secretary and is gone from eight o'clock in the morning until six o'clock at night."

Joe handed him a sheet of paper and a pencil. "I'll need a drawing showing the street, which house is hers and the yard. Include Fred's house. I want to stop at his home first, so he won't think I'm a prowler and call the police."

"I'd not thought of that. How long do you think this will take?"

"Finish the drawing, and then I'll decide." He'd not expected Tim to go into such detail, but he produced a sketch that would have made an architect proud. The house was in the middle of the block, with Fred, the friendly neighbor, on the east.

"What about the people who live on the west? Are they friendly?"

"Both work so they'll be away from home. You could go now."

Clearly Tim hoped Joe would handle his complaint that promptly. With nothing else on his calendar, he agreed. "I will stop by there today. I'll have the photos for you tomorrow afternoon."

It had sounded like the usual observe and photograph job, but things went wrong right from the beginning. The helpful neighbor wasn't in the least bit friendly.

"I don't want anything to do with fights between Tim and Arlene. I told him about the dog because I thought he'd do something about it himself, not hire some private eye to handle it."

Fred swung his front door closed before Joe could state his case. He had notified Fred he'd be there, which was all that really mattered. He took his camera from his car and walked up the driveway of Tim's former home. He looked over the wooden backyard gate, and sure enough, there was Flash chained to a stake driven into the ground. The sleek dog stood, wagged his tail, and tried to come to him, but the short chain jerked him back to the pole.

"That's a good boy," Joe called to him softly. He took photos and had already turned to leave when the back door swung open. A woman stepped out on the small porch in her bathrobe, her bleached blonde hair a frazzled mop. He assumed she had to be Arlene, and she looked somewhat green, as though she'd just left her sickbed. Unfortunately, the backdoor opened onto the driveway, so he'd have to walk around her to reach his car.

He instantly grabbed for a believable excuse for being there. He pulled a business card from his pocket, but didn't hand it to her. "I got a call from Animal Control about a dog being chained up in your yard."

"So what? It's my dog." Her voice was hoarse, she choked, and coughed into a tissue.

Joe seized the opportunity to move past her so he'd have a straight shot to his car. "The city doesn't allow it, ma'am. Better take him off the chain, or the next man from Animal Control will charge you with disobeying municipal codes and assess a large fine."

"Oh yeah? We'll see about that!"

She erupted in another coughing fit and Joe hurried to his car. Before he could start the engine, Flash ran by him with the speed that must have won his previous owner a great deal of cash. Unable to catch the swift dog on foot, Joe pursued him in his car, hoping Flash would soon tire. The dog was a light gray, and a mere streak as he sped down the street.

A car approached the cross street corner, and Joe pounded on his horn rather than allow Flash to be hit and splattered on the pavement. Startled by the shrill blast, the driver glanced Joe's way, spotted Flash, and slammed on his breaks. The greyhound sprinted by showing no sign of tiring until a lawn sprinkler caught his eye. He ran up on the front yard to play in the water.

Joe parked at the curb. He had a rope in the trunk for emergencies, and this was surely one. He wound it up, knelt on the sidewalk, and called to Flash.

The dog looked toward him, and then down the street, apparently weighing his options. "Come on, boy," Joe coaxed, and at last the greyhound trotted toward him. Joe tied the rope to his collar and urged him into the car. Flash sat on the front seat with his wet paws on the dashboard, panting, and eager to go for a ride.

Joe looked up the street, but Arlene wasn't following. She must have deliberately let the dog out just to spite him, or her ex-husband. He saw no sign of Fred either, so apparently no one had seen the dog escape his yard, or cared. Joe drove back to his office. He dropped off the film at the camera shop and walked Flash around the block to make certain he'd had a chance to relieve himself before he took him upstairs.

CC looked in the door. "Did I see you with a dog just now?" he asked.

Flash looked out from behind Joe's desk. "Yes, this is a fine greyhound, as a matter of fact. His name is Flash."

"Are you finding lost dogs now, Mr. Ezell?"

"If it pays well, I sure will. I'm phoning the owner right now, so Flash won't be here long."

CC stepped into the office. "That dog sure is thin. Isn't anyone feeding him?"

"They must be born thin. I'm sure his owner feeds him well." He called Timothy Remson, and told him he had Flash in his office.

"What? I didn't ask you to steal him! Are you trying to get me into more trouble with my ex-wife than I already am?"

"No, not at all." Joe waved to CC as he went out the door. He described how he happened to have Flash. "As I see it, your ex-wife took Flash off the chain, opened the back gate, and abandoned the dog to whatever fate might befall him. Flash might have been hit by a car, and there was a terrifying near miss. If I hadn't picked him up, another dog might have attacked him. He'd run six blocks from your house, I might add. Do you want me to call him a lost dog and take him to the pound?"

"Good lord, no! I'll come get him as soon as I can."

"Great." Joe filled a cup with water for Flash. The dog slurped it up, and went to sleep under Joe's desk. Joe had had dogs growing up, but hadn't thought he'd have another until he owned his own home. That day was nowhere in sight, so he enjoyed Flash's quiet company until Tim Remson arrived carrying a leash.

Flash ran to him and danced around his legs. "Good boy! I didn't expect Arlene to be home. Do you suppose she's been fired?" He removed the rope from Flash's collar and clipped on the leather leash.

"No, she appeared to be home sick. The photos won't be ready until tomorrow, and you may still need them to prove how badly Flash was being treated."

"Right. I'll come by for them. I think I'll go by Arlene's on Saturday morning ready to pick up Flash and see what she says. I'll bet she cries and blames the dog for getting out on his own."

Joe understood completely. "You'll be devastated she lost your beloved pet."

"Of course, I will, but I'll react with a cold fury and leave. Do I owe you a reward for finding Flash after he got loose?"

"No, my retainer covered it all." Joe gave the dog a last pat on the head as they left, and figured the day had ended better than he'd hoped.

Mary Margaret invited Joe to her cottage for dinner and served crispy fried chicken with mashed potatoes and carrots. "It always takes a while to get comfortable in a new kitchen, but I think dinner came out pretty well."

Joe wiped his mouth on his napkin. "Everything is delicious as always. The fried chicken Patrick Wood brought to the welcome party wasn't nearly as good."

"It probably would have been if we'd eaten at the café rather than here."

"You always look on the bright side. I love that about you."

"Thank you, but I'd make a very poor detective, wouldn't I? I'd believe everything anyone told me and never solve a single crime."

"The secret is to believe no one until you're certain they're telling the truth."

"That's undoubtedly a wise strategy with everyone you meet." She rested her fork on her plate. "When Amy Hudson left for work this morning, she gave me a nearly imperceptible nod, or maybe she merely adjusted the fit of her coat. She always looks so unhappy. Do you suppose she lost someone she loved dearly during the war?"

Joe hesitated mid-bite. He hadn't planned to share what he'd learned about Amy from her former landlady, but now that Mary Margaret had asked, he couldn't withhold the sad tale. "I did some investigating into her past." He told her the story and as expected, her eyes filled with tears. She dried them on her napkin.

"That's so sad, Joe. That Amy's fiancé survived the war only to die in a street fight in San Diego is doubly tragic. It's no wonder she's so morose. We can't tell her we know her story though, can we?"

"No, she'd probably react very badly to my total disregard for her privacy. Wait until she warms to you and tells you on her own. You can be sympathetic then."

"She must not have told anyone living here in Chrysanthemum Court." Mary Margaret countered. "Unless she told Georgia." Her eyes widened. "Who was the VA doctor who couldn't save Amy's fiancé? Gabriel worked in the hospital there, and so did Georgia. Could they have treated him?"

"I don't know who the physician might have been, but I checked Georgia's notebook copy, and Mark Birch isn't there. Did Gabriel ever work in the emergency room in San Diego?"

"Let's call him and ask." She left her chair and returned with her personal address book. "I'm sorry, I don't have his home number. I'll have to ask him in the morning. Maybe he'll remember the case."

Joe drew in a deep breath. "Georgia and Amy were both living here, and as far as we know, Amy never confided in her nor accosted her verbally or otherwise."

She nodded thoughtfully. "Amy could have ignored Georgia until she saw Gabriel Webb coming to see her. She told us she'd seen a man coming by late at night. Suppose she recognized Gabriel as the doctor from San Diego who hadn't saved her fiancé?"

Sickened by the thought, he pushed his slicked clean plate away. "Are you thinking she may have killed Georgia to punish Gabriel? That borders on the diabolical, but let's follow that thread for a minute. Amy owns a car. She could have followed Georgia to my office, killed her with a single swipe of a knife, run down the backstairs, and returned home to dispose of her bloody clothing. It's plausible, but unlikely, and impossible to prove."

"Maybe not," she argued. "We couldn't find Georgia's jewelry box. It's missing, and so are her keys, and diary. If Amy has them, wouldn't it prove her guilt?"

"Of theft maybe, but not murder."

"Should we call Detective Lynch and let him pursue it?" she asked.

"It would be a waste of breath," he replied. "We'd need some hard evidence before he'd bother to investigate, not merely imaginative supposition."

"The man completely lacks imagination, or he'd solve many more crimes." She folded her arms over her bosom. "Amy could have dropped a bloodstained coat in any trashcan she passed, and it would be under a ton of garbage at the landfill by now. What about her car? Could she have killed Georgia and fled without getting any blood on her shoes?"

"There were no bloody footprints at the scene," he replied. "Blood might have splattered on her shoes and dripped onto the floor mat in her car. Do you know which car is hers?"

"No, but someone here must. I'll go ask Patrick Wood and be right back."

"Fine. I'll get the flashlight I keep in my glove compartment." Joe thought Amy had a murderer's belligerent toughness, but that didn't mean she'd committed any crime. He'd parked on the street in front of the Chrysanthemum Court and quickly returned with his flashlight. The lights were on in Amy Hudson's home, and he doubted she would be going out again that late.

Mary Margaret met him on her front porch, and whispered, "Amy drives a dark red Plymouth coupe. Do you think it might have been her fiancé's car?" She drew Joe inside her cottage.

"A red coupe does seem like an odd choice for her, so maybe it was. Have you seen the car? Do you know where Amy usually parks?"

"I haven't paid any attention to the cars parked near here, but it's a good night for a walk."

"Let's go." He took her hand, and they went out the back door to walk down the alley to the side street. The streetlights provided only a soft glow, but it was enough light to spot Amy's car, or one just like it.

Joe pulled out his handkerchief to cover his hand and tried the driver's side door. Unlocked, it swung open. He stopped to look around at the houses nearby, but no curious neighbors were on their front porches watching. A quick swipe from his flashlight showed the car mats were brand new.

He closed the car door and leaned back against it. "Car mats aren't replaced that often. Amy could have disposed of the old ones for many reasons, maybe her heel caught in a small tear whenever she climbed in."

"Or more likely, the driver's side mat was stained with blood."

"It might have been, or we're letting our imaginations run wild. I wish you hadn't moved to the cottages. If Amy Hudson killed one nurse, which we can't prove, she might be tempted to kill another."

"She has no reason to dislike me," Mary Margaret insisted.

"For all we know, she had no reason to dislike Georgia either, but that doesn't make Georgia any the less dead." He reached for her hand, and they walked back to her new home.

Mary Margaret made coffee. "Do you know how to pick a lock?" she asked.

"No, I don't, and breaking and entering is a crime. I don't know about you, but I have no interest whatsoever in spending any time in jail."

"Sorry. I was just thinking that if we went into Amy's cottage when she wasn't home, we might find Georgia's jewelry and diary."

"On the Saturday we cleaned the cottage, I asked Amy if she'd like to have something of Amy's. She didn't, but she could say she was invited to take whatever she liked."

"But she didn't come over and take them then."

"Difficult to prove." He'd brought chocolate marble ice cream from Aunt Lucy's and scooped it into glass dishes while she poured their coffee. "Let's have dessert and think of more enjoyable subjects than murder."

Once seated at the table, she raked her spoon through her ice cream. "At the hospital, we can't save every patient, but we try awfully hard to save lives."

"Are you calling me a quitter?"

"No, of course not. I just wish we had something more we could do. When you speak with Gabriel Webb in the morning, maybe you'll learn something new."

Joe bit the inside of his cheek rather than comment and reveal how jealous of Dr. Webb he truly was. "I've talked to him several times, but we've not covered San Diego. If he remembers Mark Birch, or Amy Hudson, it will be another intriguing bit of information, but not proof she's a murderer."

"No, but we'd already thought it could be a relative of a patient who had died. Maybe it's only conjecture, but what more can we do?"

The ice cream was so good, he savored a bite before replying. "I'll urge Webb to call Detective Lynch, and let him put two and two together. Lynch is more likely to give credence to what a physician says than a private investigator."

"Let's hope, but I don't trust him to follow up on it. This is a depressing mess."

"Which is why we were going to change the subject. Do you want another bowl of ice cream?" he asked. "This is especially good."

She reached for his hand and gave his fingers a loving squeeze. "I understand the subject is closed, but only for this evening."

They played cribbage, but neither felt in a competitive mood, and they soon called it a night. Mary Margaret walked Joe to her door and kissed him goodnight. He stood on the front porch and nodded toward Amy's cottage. "If she invites you to stop by for coffee, tea, or cupcakes, tell her you're busy."

"Right, I won't spend any time alone with her."

Joe gave her a last lingering kiss, and walked out to his car. He drove a block before pulling over to the curb. Something just wasn't right. He flipped through the suspects in Georgia's murder, their names, faces, and motives vivid in his mind. Detective Lynch believed the murderer had been a stranger she'd not met until her last fateful morning. Joe felt equally certain it had been someone she knew who had harbored a virulent hatred toward her.

Which made it likely that someone knew, and possibly hated, Mary Margaret as well. He didn't feel right leaving her alone in her cottage with a neighbor who might pose a lethal threat. He made a U-turn, and again parked on the street in front of Chrysanthemum Court. He moved quietly down the walk so he'd not disturb anyone who had already gone to bed, but when he saw Mary Margaret's door standing open, he ran.

Amy Hudson stood just inside the door with her right hand hidden in the folds of her skirt. When she heard Joe approaching, she looked over her shoulder. "Oh, it's the boyfriend. I told Mary Margaret if she's ever late for work, I'll give her a ride."

Before she could step by him, he grabbed for her right hand and a straight razor fell from her grasp. It was an expensive one with a fine ram horn handle, and he grabbed for it before she could wrench free.

She punched him in the jaw with her left hand. "Give that to me! You've no right to take my things!"

He ignored her and slipped the razor into his pocket. "Call the police, Mary Margaret. We need them here now."

Amy continued to squirm in an effort to break free, but Joe refused to release her and soon held both her hands behind her back. She began to scream, alarming all the residents of Chrysanthemum Court. "Help!" she yelled. "He's trying to kill me! There's a razor in his pocket. Search him, and you'll see."

Mary Margaret came out on the walk. "No one is searching anybody. We're waiting for the police."

Amy sobbed, her chin trembling. "He tried to kill me."

Patrick Wood kept several feet away. "That's a serious accusation, Amy." He looked toward his neighbors who were stunned by Amy's howling and offered no opinions of their own. "I can hear sirens, so the police are on their way. They'll settle everything I'm sure."

The gray-haired LAPD sergeant took the whole matter seriously. "Why would you be carrying a straight razor when you're visiting a neighbor?" he asked Amy.

"I wasn't. He had the razor in his pocket. It's his, not mine."

Joe took a good look at it before he handed it to the sergeant. "The initials MB are carved into the handle, and Mark Birch was her late fiancé. There's a good possibility she may have used it to cut Georgia Dixon's throat."

Polly Hill had come outside carrying baby Catherine, and horrified, she wheeled around and quickly returned home. Anxious to see what would happen next, her husband remained where he stood. Phyllis and John Cameron took a cautious backwards step, but then leaned forward to better hear what would happen next. Tim Garcia wrapped his wife in his arms.

Deeply perplexed, Patrick Wood stood by himself. "I heard you yell, 'You've no right to take my things!'"

"I did not," Amy insisted. Standing with her arms free, she rubbed her wrists.

"Yes, you did," Patrick argued. "I heard her clearly, Sergeant. That's why I came outside."

"Will you call Detective Jacob Lynch?" Joe asked. "He's investigating Miss Dixon's death, and we've found the murder weapon."

"Then you killed her!" Amy yelled.

The sergeant turned to the officer with him. "Radio the station and ask for Lynch. The rest of us will wait right here until he arrives."

Mary Margaret took Joe's hand, and he could feel her shaking. He refused to think what might have happened if he hadn't come back, and he was real glad that he had.

CHAPTER 17

Clearly having had other plans for the evening, Jacob Lynch arrived at the Chrysanthemum Court dressed in a well-tailored tuxedo. While his mood was never good, tonight, his gaze was darkly melancholy. He grimaced when he saw Joe. He nodded to the sergeant who'd summoned him. "I can't wait to hear why you required my presence this evening."

The sergeant read from his notebook in clear, simple sentences. Amy Hudson had gone to Mary Margaret McBride's cottage carrying a straight razor. Joe Ezell had taken it away from her.

Lynch turned the razor over in his hands. "Who is MB?"

Joe hesitated, but when Amy didn't speak, he did. "I believe those are Mark Birch's initials. He was Amy Hudson's fiancé. He was killed in a knife fight in San Diego."

Amy's eyes narrowed to menacing slits. "You aren't fit to speak his name. Had Mark had a physician worthy of the name, he'd still be alive, it's Gabriel Webb who killed him!" She collapsed on Mary Margaret's front porch step and wept with loud, gulping sobs.

Mary Margaret caught Joe's eye, and then sat down beside Amy and spoke softly, "Is that why you thought Georgia had to die?"

In an instant, Amy sprang to her feet and grabbed the razor from Detective Lynch's hand. She flipped the blade open from the handle and swung at Mary Margaret with a vicious downward slash, but caught only a flying red curl as Mary Margaret lunged away.

Joe heard Lynch yell to his officers, but went after Amy himself. He grabbed for her and missed, and she sliced the razor through his jacket sleeve and across his arm. Pain shot clear to his shoulder, but didn't stop him. He caught the back of Amy's sweater as she spun away, tripped her, and shoved her face down on the grass.

"Don't get up!" Lynch ordered. He stepped on Amy's wrist and reclaimed the straight razor before she could use it to cut her own throat. "Call for an ambulance."

Mary Margaret raced inside for a dishtowel and wrapped it tightly around Joe's forearm. "Amy should be hospitalized, but I'm driving Joe to the hospital myself. Keep this towel twisted tight, Joe. Can you walk to your car?"

Blood ran down his hand and dripped on the grass. He pressed harder on the towel. "Yes, let's go."

Patrick Wood trotted along beside them. "Amy killed Georgia? How could she have harbored such an evil hatred for another human being?"

They left him on the curb with his question unanswered. "We're going to the VA hospital where I'm sure you'll get excellent care."

Joe grit his teeth. "I wouldn't go anywhere else."

Dr. Nick Cochran was on duty in the emergency room and sewed up the cut in Joe's arm with neat, tiny stitches. "The wound isn't deep, and it shouldn't leave a bad scar," Cochran assured him.

"Don't worry, there's no danger a scar will spoil my looks," Joe replied.

Mary Margaret sat beside Joe and held his hand. "I'm still shaking. How can you make jokes?"

"That was no joke." He leaned over to kiss her cheek.

Gabriel Webb pushed back the curtain on their cubicle. "I just finished my last surgery for the day and heard you were here. What happened?"

"It's a long story, but I got into an argument with a woman waving a straight razor," Joe answered.

"We need to speak with you privately, Gabriel," Mary Margaret interjected. "May we come to your office when we're finished here?"

"I'll meet you there."

She waited until he had gone before speaking. "What can we possibly tell him?"

"The truth, because he'll hear it from Detective Lynch or read about in the *Los Angeles Times* tomorrow."

"He's not going to take it well," she mused.

"Want to practice the story on me?" Cochran asked. "I strive to be sympathetic."

"That's wonderful, but we've discovered who killed Georgia Dixon, and I don't believe we can go through it more than once," she said. "It's just so terribly senseless and sad."

"But if you've caught who did it, that's something good. Last knot," Cochran announced. "Mary Margaret can change the dressing for you. Come back in a week, and we'll remove the stitches."

"Thank you." Joe's jacket and shirt were torn and stained with blood. "Do you have a shirt I could borrow? I can't walk through the hospital in my undershirt."

"I keep a couple in my locker, and I'll get you one," he offered.

They were close to the same size, and Joe was relieved to have something presentable to wear. He stood, felt a bit woozy, and drew in a deep breath to gather himself.

"Are you all right?" Mary Margaret asked.

"No, but I need to speak to Dr. Webb and get this over with." He left the emergency room with his arm in a sling, and made every effort to walk in a straight line. Fortunately, Mary Margaret asked him to stop at a hall bench on the way to go over what they needed to say.

"He knows we've been searching for a former patient or relative of one who could have killed her," Joe reminded her.

"True, but he didn't realize Georgia's death would have anything to do with him, and it's going to be tough to take."

"Telling him won't be any easier later," Joe cautioned, and they made their way to Gabriel's office. He was seated behind his desk making notes.

Joe needed to sit down, and Mary Margaret took the chair beside him. "We've found who killed Georgia, but the story is almost too horrible to repeat," she said.

"Tell me anyway," Gabriel encouraged.

"Mark Birch, a naval officer, died in the San Diego VA hospital while you were there. He was stabbed as he attempted to break up a fight between some sailors and soldiers. Does that sound familiar in any way?" she asked.

Gabriel leaned back in his chair. "Knife fights weren't all that uncommon, Mary Margaret. Can you tell me anything more?"

Joe squeezed her hand. "His fiancée, Amy Hudson, would have been there, and she must have reacted very badly when you told her Mark had died," Joe added.

Gabriel shook his head. "Hysterical fiancées weren't unusual either. I'm sorry, but I can't place either of them."

Mary Margaret gave him a moment to recall his time in San Diego before she continued. "Amy Hudson was Georgia's neighbor, and she recognized you when you visited her. She killed Georgia because you'd failed to save Mark. It was an act of cold-blooded revenge."

"You don't mean it." Badly shaken, Gabriel leaned forward and rested his arms on his desk. "I'll send for a copy of Mark's records. Maybe when I read them, I'll remember him. How awful is this, for Georgia to die for a death I can't even recall? Where is the woman now?"

"She's probably in the psychiatric ward at the downtown jail," Mary Margaret answered.

"Let's hope she stays there." He stood. "Do you mind? It's been a long day, and I'd like to go home."

Joe rose slowly. "So would I. Detective Lynch should talk to you tomorrow, and the story might be in the *Los Angeles Times,* as well."

"Thanks for the warning, and for coming here to tell me yourselves. Georgia's death has been so hard to take, and now this tragic turn makes it even worse. Maybe I'll take a long vacation and keep going."

"You're a fine surgeon and needed too desperately here," Mary Margaret argued.

"Thank you. I like to believe I do some good." He walked with them out into the hallway. "Good-night."

Joe watched the surgeon walk away with his head bowed, and his step lacking its usual confident bounce. "I thought I'd feel better when we caught Georgia's killer, but I feel even worse."

"So do I. I'll drive you home. Do you mind if I stay over again? I don't feel like being alone tonight."

"Neither do I." Joe's arm ached, and a hospital corridor was no place to propose, but he really wanted to, and sometime soon.

When he woke the next morning, Joe heard Mary Margaret moving around in his kitchen. He rolled out of bed, and pulled up the bedspread as best he could with one arm. He'd been a firm believer in making his bed each morning even before the Coast Guard had insisted upon neatly made bunks. He'd readily admit it was to impress women, and it worked.

He could hold his razor well enough to shave and wash up. He dressed for the office and followed the tantalizing aroma of bacon into the kitchen. "Good morning."

"Yes, isn't it?" Mary Margaret greeted him warmly. "Do you feel as good as you look?"

"Is that a trick question?"

"No, silly. I've always thought you were a handsome man." She poured him a cup of coffee and waited for him to take a sip. "You know what else I think?"

"Surprise me."

"I think we should get married."

Joe caught himself before he blew hot coffee out through his nose. "I beg your pardon?"

"You heard me. We're terrific together, and love each other. What more do we need?"

Joe grabbed a kitchen chair and fell into it. "I've longed to propose to you, but I wanted the perfect time and place."

She sat in his lap and looped her arms around his neck. "This is the perfect time and place."

"I should have a ring for you."

"My grandmother left me her gorgeous diamond ring, and we don't need to buy another. I'd love to have a Christmas wedding because it's such a magical time. We can live at Chrysanthemum Court, unless you'd rather live elsewhere. When we combine our incomes, we should do fine. Want some bacon?"

Clearly she'd given a lot more thought to getting married than he had, and he didn't mind at all. "In a minute. How long have you been thinking about this?"

"A while, but I didn't want to broach the subject on an evening in Clifton's Cafeteria, although the Flippin' Plate was awfully tempting."

He laughed. "I've been thinking about it too. Mary Margaret McBride, will you do me the great honor of becoming my wife?"

"Yes!" She hugged and kissed him. "I love you, Joe."

The telephone rang, and she slid off his lap so he could step into the living room and answer. He returned to the kitchen in less than a minute.

"That was Detective Lynch. He wants us to meet him at Amy's cottage. I told him we'd be there as soon as we'd finished breakfast."

"What do you suppose he's found?" she asked.

"We'll soon see." He took her hand to pull her close. "I love having you here in the morning."

"See, I told you this was the perfect time and place."

Detective Lynch handed them a leather diary found in Amy Hudson's desk. "From the early entries, it's plain this belonged to Georgia Dixon. Look at the last pages."

Mary Margaret sat down at the dining table and opened the book. "I recognize Georgia's writing, but these hideous drawings can't be hers."

Joe studied the black ink drawings, flying creatures, swooping demons, perhaps, filled page after page. "No sane person could have drawn these."

"We'll leave that for Ms. Hudson's attorney to prove. Amy had this jewelry box and set of keys hidden in a rain boot. Do you recognize them as Georgia's?"

The small blue box contained the bracelets and pearl ring Mary Margaret had often seen Georgia wear. She also recognized the rabbit's foot on the key ring. "Yes, these are her things." She pushed them toward the detective. "Do you think I might have the jewelry once the trial is over?"

"They are evidence, but I'll do what I can. Miss Hudson hasn't spoken since we arrested her. She's sitting on the bed in her cell, facing the wall, and rocking slowly. I rely on our psychiatrists' opinions, but she doesn't look well."

"She couldn't be," Mary Margaret agreed. "Thank you for showing us the diary. Last night, Amy rang my bell soon after Joe had left. I thought he'd forgotten something and opened the door without looking to see who it was first."

"Promise you won't do it again," Joe asked.

"I won't. Amy asked me to call her if I ever needed a ride to work. Do you suppose she might have driven Georgia to your office, Joe?"

"It makes sense. No one who had ridden on the bus that stops there remembered Georgia. Amy might have come upstairs with her, or joined her shortly thereafter. Georgia wouldn't have been on guard, and Amy seized the advantage and killed her."

"Makes you sick, doesn't it?" Lynch said.

"It does. Thank you for talking with us this morning," Joe offered sincerely.

"I owed you that much, although I hope you'll stick to the cases people bring to you, Mr. Ezell, rather than continue horning in on mine."

"I'll do my best, sir." Joe managed to keep a straight face. "If you don't mind, I'd like to look at the last pages Georgia wrote in her diary. It might help me discover why she'd wanted to see me that morning."

Lynch handed it over, and Joe read the final pages in her writing. Her last entry described a heated argument with Edwin Mooney over his treatment of Curtis. "Curtis deserves so much better," he read aloud. "It looks as though this is what troubled her, and I would have helped her all I could."

"Of course you would have," Mary Margaret agreed.

Joe waited until after he and Mary Margaret had entered her cottage next door to say more. "This morning, Lynch actually seemed almost human, and I'd like nothing better than to stay out of his way. Do you think I can convince him to stay out of mine?"

"My hero," she murmured, "of course you can. I need to dress for work." She tossed him the morning copy of the *Los Angeles Times* she had delivered. "Amuse yourself with the crossword puzzle. I'll be ready in a minute."

"Sure." Joe sorted through the sections to find the puzzle, and as he folded back a page, a photograph caught his eye. It showed a handsome couple that had been married at city hall yesterday. Crystal Cavanaugh, identified as a fashion model, carried a bouquet of white roses, and beamed as widely as her new husband, Curtis Mooney, who was described as a former Marine captain. They looked overjoyed to be together, and after the brief ceremony, they'd sailed on a luxury liner for a honeymoon in Hawaii.

Joe threw back his head and laughed. Crystal had rescued Curtis from his overbearing brother, but he was sure this wouldn't be the end of their story. "Mary Margaret, wait until you see this," he called to her. "Life has become so exciting, I can't wait for tomorrow!"

*Turn the page for an
excerpt from*

Murder

On

Ice

A Detective Joe Ezell Mystery

Book Three

P.J. Conn

Joe Ezell had just pulled on his trousers when someone began a furious pounding on his apartment door. It was 8:00 o'clock in the morning, the first Tuesday in September, 1947, and as far as he knew the police weren't looking for him. His fiancée, the delightful Mary Margaret McBride, would use only a genteel tap to announce her presence, so the only person he cared to see hadn't come calling.

"Hold on, I'm coming," he yelled. When he swung open the door, he found the apartment manager, Leon Helms, a jovial man in his fifties who loved wearing Hawaiian shirts. "What's wrong, Leon? Is the building on fire?" He took a deep breath, but didn't smell smoke.

Leon Helms leaned against the doorjamb and struggled to catch his breath. "You've got to come with me, Joe. Something awful has happened in apartment three."

"Where the new couple moved in?"

"They've disappeared. Come look at what they left behind."

Joe grabbed his keys, closed his door, and buttoned his shirt as he followed Helms down the outdoor stairway to the central patio. There were six units in the building, and Joe's was number six on the second floor east corner overlooking the street. Number three was in the back on the ground floor. He'd only seen the new tenants a few times, coming and going to work. Now that he was in his thirties, the fair-haired pair had looked impossibly young, but they'd had to at least be in their twenties.

The door to number three was standing ajar, and Helms pushed it open. "I was watering the plants in the patio this morning, and noticed their door wasn't latched. I felt something was wrong right there, maybe they were ill, but they've gone, and taken everything they moved in with. The bed is stripped, there are no towels in the bathroom, and the medicine cabinet is empty."

"Do they owe you rent?"

"No, they're paid up until the end of the month. Go take a look at the refrigerator."

Expecting to find it empty, Joe walked into the kitchen to oblige. He noticed the refrigerator racks had been removed and placed on the counter. That would leave the Frigidaire as empty as a new freezer. He began to get a very bad feeling. Gathering his courage, he pulled open the door.

"Good God!" he gasped.

"That's exactly what I said," Helms responded.

A nude young woman had been folded in half with her chin on her knees and her arms looped around her ankles so she fit neatly inside the refrigerator. Her skin had a blue cast and felt as cold as ice.

"How long do you suppose she's been dead?" Helms asked.

"A while."

Her long black hair covered her face, and Joe gently tucked a strand behind her ear. She'd been a very pretty girl, but even without knowing her name, he recognized her as big trouble.

MURDER ON ICE

available in print and ebook

THE
DETECTIVE JOE EZELL MYSTERY
SERIES

MURDER ME TWICE
STAIRWAY TO MURDER
MURDER ON ICE

A native Californian, P.J. Conn attended the University of Arizona and California State University at Los Angeles where she earned a BA in Art History and an MA in Education. Her Historical Romance and Futuristic novels, written under Phoebe Conn, have won many awards.

Phoebe is the proud mother of two grown sons and two adorable grandchildren, who love to have her read to them.